“Ya killed my son,” Hillberry

Isabel looked at Patty, clearly

“Now there’re two of ya,” Hillberry said as he leaned

toward the girls, moving forward with uncontrolled, staggering mini-steps, and squinted at them. *Was he having hallucinations?*

“Stop!” Patty extended her arms, palms out. “Seriously! are you crazy, as well as drunk? Tommy Lee was arrested for taking me against my will and locking me in an old shed. As you well know he was murdered as he sat in his jail cell.”

“Ya led ’im on, an’ ya knowed it.”

“Seriously! Don’t kid yourself. I wouldn’t have been able to get to and from school safely if it weren’t for my brother, Joe. Tommy Lee stalked me day and night, and you know it.” Patty shook her finger in Andy’s face. “Your son was the one who kept me hostage for days and days. Now! Get out of my way!”

Andy Hillberry swayed back and forth until one foot lost its purchase and, making involuntarily, toddling steps, he staggered toward the car. He locked his arms at the elbows to try to stop his fall. When both hands found the hood of the car, the solid hit brought his forward momentum to a sudden end. But the heat coming from the hood of the car caused him to rear back suddenly. Without fanfare, he landed on his rear end. Too drunk to feel much pain, he sat staring, legs outstretched on the cobblestone road.

“Patty, so far I don’t find anything familiar about this town,” Isabel declared. She stood with her arms folded at her breasts, attempting to look unafraid, trying to ignore the drunken bum. In truth, she was frightened by the pitiful old man—and the things he had said. He looked like an overgrown child, refusing to go any further.

ISBN: 1451536453
EAN13: 9781451536454

C.J. HENDERSON

ABOUT THE AUTHOR

CJ towns of Farmington and Rivesville, West Virginia. High points in her early life were long trips to visit family who lived in remote areas of Appalachia. Over time, this environment became as familiar to her as her own modern home, and gradually she was introduced to many families whose homes in the outback were scattered miles apart.

A typical visit included hours of walking with a group of friends and cousins from house to house, looking for something to do. In those years, there were no televisions or telephones to keep the girls occupied, just like young people everywhere, the group invented games and told tales. Just as she had observed her father doing for many years, CJ kept her companions entertained for hours with her stories, in which she combined her own imagination with real-life events that played out in the isolated and poverty-stricken mountain culture.

CJ married just out of high school and lived on a farm, putting off her longing to write and attend college. She raised two sons, and as they matured, she attended night school at Fairmont State College, and later at Parkersburg Community College. Years later her position as a land agent for Equitable Gas Company took her to even more remote and isolated regions where she had spent time as a child. She found nothing had changed. The impoverished still had no higher education available to them. Also, they lived without electricity, inside plumbing, telephones, television, and other conveniences. This renewed knowledge of their extraordinary lifestyle fueled her desire to create stories about that parallel world of people who live alongside us but remain separate at the same time.

After she resigned from her job with the utility company, CJ moved to the West Coast and spent three years writing and setting the groundwork for the six novels in *The Cabin Series.* She then returned to West Virginia and, drawing on her experience as a realtor and as a land acquisition agent, she opened her own real estate company, which she continues to operate. She also continues to devote herself to writing and publishing her novels.

CJ's life and work led up to the creation of *The Cabin Series.*

For my loving parents, Mabel and Orval
whom I miss each and every day.

Acknowledgements

I could never have continued this series without
the encouragement of the many loyal readers, editors,
and my family.
Huge thanks to my editor Valerie Gittings.

1 Corinthians 13: 4-7

[4]Love is patient, love is kind. It does not envy, it does not boast, it is not proud. [5]It is not rude, it is not self-seeking, it is not easily angered, it keeps no record of wrongs. [6]Love does not delight in evil but rejoices with the truth. [7]It always protects, always trusts, always hopes, always perseveres.

Photo of author by Warner Photography, Fairmont, WV

CHAPTER 1

IT'S HARD TO BELIEVE HOW MANY YEARS HAVE gone by since the fateful attack on the World Trade Center. I was closely scrutinized by the law after that because I was last known to have been at the towers that very day, and thought to have been killed in the attack, but that's over for now, and I'm on my way home to bring my family back together. Other than my women, I have no use for those who have formed an unforgiving opinion about me. They've all judged me wrongly. The way I see it, no one sees the big picture so they simply don't understand me—maybe not even my one-and-only unwavering ally, Aunt Aggie, truly does.

The first thing I see, as I crest the hill, is the huge mansion I bought for Tuesday and my daughter, Winter Ann. That was back when I was blindly bent on having them under my wing. Now it's all just like I remember it. And as far as I can tell, the house and property are abandoned as they should be. The hum of my V-8 engine is the only sound save for crickets, birds, and other animal calls. Other than that it's quiet as hell. In case you haven't had the pleasure of visiting the Appalachian Mountains, I can tell you, the racket you have to deal with in the city is blessedly absent here in my homeland, and now my final retreat.

I can see right away that the grounds have suffered miserably from neglect, but my place, having stood for generations, has long been—and to this day—stands impressive on its broad front lawn, with the grove of trees standing in a semi-circle at the rear. Actually, it's like a smaller version of the White House. Of course, right now, you have to ignore the untamed tangle of weeds and vines to see that image. It makes a pretty picture, the way the long-neglected foliage sways as the breeze touches it, if only because its evidence that there's still some life there—wild as it may be.

But the closer I get it becomes more and more apparent that I've damn well stayed away far too long. I should have known I couldn't depend on Ike Harris to take care of the place. Hell, the man ran when things got tough, acting like the felon he really is. Not to worry—if I'm going to carry on with my plans, I need to keep cool.

Now, I'm here to tell you, this is the way it's going down. This is the place that I'm going to finally make my fortune. Not like my futile attempts in the past, putting myself in the sights of the law with only penny-ante payoffs. Compared to what I stand to make now, those were insulting compensations for taking big chances back then. Now I have a bona fide plan that will bring me the big bucks that will set me up for life.

Up to now, I haven't really considered the state of the property, virtually abandoned these past few years, nor have I dealt with the possibility of Ike Harris skipping out on me, leaving my place to the wild. I obviously need to rethink a few details. And giving the matter second thought, the way it looks now, no one's apt to nose around and find that I'm back till I'm ready for them. For now, it'll be better to allow the grounds to stay just the way they are. Hell yes, that's best, that's for sure. Anyway, that's what I need for my master plan: privacy. I'll just lay low a day or two while I set the stage for the most ingenious conspiracy of all time. If you're thinking that I'm getting in over my head, just keep reading.

By the way, I am Jacob. You know me, the notorious Jacob McCallister. My family calls me Pa or Jeb. Either way, it doesn't matter. You may think I'm an uncaring beast because of times past, but I can honestly tell you that I'm not the fiend everyone thinks me to be. Just look how the women have loved me no matter what, and still do.

Don't tell me that I'm evil. I know perfectly well what evil is—I've lived with it. Evil is my mother and father. Up until I was seven years old my father spent his days and nights raising roosters for cockfighting games. Of course, he had to keep one step ahead of the law—cockfighting is illegal—but from those ill-gotten gains, he did keep a home for me and my mother, although scarcely. Because of all of that, it's a blessing that my parents had no other children besides me. When my father didn't have winnings for us to live on, as a youngster not yet muscled out, I was forced to hunt and forage for our food while he tended to the raising of a seemingly endless line of cockfighting roosters. Also, as was my grandfather in his day, my father was the man running the pit at each and every fight.

Here's the clincher, though: when I was seven my parents planned to sell me to a man who owned the local coal mine, Gordon Maxwell. He's dead now, got killed in his attempt to break a wild stallion. The horse was not inclined to be broken, though, and bucked and reared single-mindedly until his burden fell to the ground. Then the stallion kicked the old man in the chest, a mighty blow. They say that that one great kick from the stallion stopped Maxwell's cold heart, and he died on the spot. When he was found, he lay with the reins still wrapped around his clasped fist. The stallion stood triumphantly next to him, occasionally pawing the ground, snorting, and tossing his head, waiting to be free of the dead man.

The black-hearted man wanted me because he needed someone to care for Banner, the pony that was destined to live out his life hauling coal. Maxwell needed someone to work along with Banner, keeping him fed and curried to make him as productive as possible. The way I understood it, I was to live in the mine along with the pony, work him, and take care of him between the running shifts.

The one good thing about Banner's plight was that his siblings were saved by the Michael boys, a family that had their roots in Rivesville. They bought the ponies from Maxwell's widow, and there is to this day a pony named for Banner from the same blood line.

When Gordon Maxwell came up with the job for me in the coal mine, my father accepted with no intention of consulting me; he considered the job as big money in his pocket. Before that, though, he was all for me getting an education. In all likelihood, the education was my father's idea of portraying himself as the big man among the townsmen. My father was well known as a dreamer, not a worker, but his talk of my schooling was no game in my mind. No. Education became a goal for me. Unknown to my father, he had instilled in me a desire to better myself, and had shown me a way to do it, education. I knew it was true by his own example, because he sure didn't have one, and therefore he had nothing. Over the years, his bragging around town about his desire for me to have an education became my own dream, my personal goal—one I carried through with long after he and my mother were dead.

Anyway, as a young boy I didn't know he was blowing smoke and had no real intentions of paying for my education. Therefore, I didn't understand why he was willing to sell me out for a nowhere job. I'd always known that my parents didn't have the love for me that you'd see in the movies, particularly the variety that fool women liked to watch at the town movie theater. But the day I learned about the job in the mine was the day I finally got it . . . My mother and father had absolutely no parental love in their black hearts at all.

Before my father could carry out his plans for me to take over Banner's care, though, I took steps to protect myself. I locked my parents in our cellar house and left them there until they died. I had to. After a few hard years of working the mine, the pony and the boy who ended up with the job went blind from being kept in total darkness day and night, but I never did . . . Go blind, I mean.

Aunt Aggie knows. But she won't tell. . .

She helped me get rid of the bodies—prone to declare that she was forever cleaning up after my messes, and in agreement that I move their bodies from the farmhouse where I was born and raised, and hide them in her cellar house where they have been decomposing for years now.

When the law was nosing around looking for Tuesday Summers, the year I hooked up with her and brought her to the mountain to live with me, I became more than a little worried about those hidden bodies. Anyway, I dodged the bullet because, to my knowledge, no one has ever found my black-hearted parents' remains.

Aggie and I have been of one heart and mind since.

I'd bet a shrink would say that that one act set the pattern of my life.

Enough said on that dead subject, haw, haw, but regardless of what folks think of me, I am the one who knows what's best for my family. If not for me, the women and all their children would have been sold off years ago to a poor farmer—to live on his barren land in a cold and primitive farmhouse, to do his thankless work, and the boys to end up working the coal mine. At least I allowed them to keep three of them. Besides each and every one of my women will tell you they live just to be with me. No matter what you believe or what the situation, that's just the way it is.

Why, at night, the women vied with one another to be the one in my bed. I can tell you that I miss those days, sleeping with one while the others slept on mats at the foot of the bed.

I am the master.

If not for the interference of that big-feeling Cliff Moran, my family and I would be living in wealth on this plantation right now. My fool women could be boasting that they live on the largest estate in the area. I know what you're thinking: *Has he forgotten the reality of their lives, the poverty they endured all those years in the cabin above Winding Ridge, a place with no electric and no inside plumbing?* The answer is no. I haven't forgotten. Like I was saying, I was coming up with the cash to buy and restore this estate when Cliff Moran interfered once again. And by the way, I haven't forgotten that I'm going to get even one day. That big-feeling jerk is responsible for me having to spend time keeping out of sight, and he is to blame for the time I spent in jail—while my place became this jungle I see before me right now. I'll not let him or anyone interfere this time, I can tell you that. I have friends in high places now, and this time I will carry out my plan.

The worst of it is that for the past two years, I've had no choice but to live off my emergency stash. Now, though, through my ingenuity, and because of new and wealthier connections that I've acquired over the past few years, my financial status will be changing in a few months. It will grow to an amount these ignorant mountain folks could never even dream of.

At long last, here I am, pulling in amongst the growth of weeds that's overtaking my driveway, and after seeing even from a distance the place was abandoned, I was worrying about the possibility of unwanted squatters in my absence! Not now though. There's not one trampled place to evidence the passage of a human or an animal.

You should see this place!

As I climb from my truck and my lower legs disappear into the brush, there's a mighty rustle of wings and a flock of wild turkeys take flight. Mr. Man! I jump back into the truck. My heart is pounding, like I'm having a heart attack. After I calm down, I stay in the cab and look around. I can see that the wild turkeys are gone and realize that the wild life has taken over the grounds. It's back to square one—at least for the outside. The work Ike Harris and Joe had done on the grounds is now lost in time and neglect. The front lawn, to the left and right, and the surrounding property I own, other than what nature's hand has done, hasn't been disturbed by any man that I can tell. The front gate's rusted shut. I'm of a mind that it's best left immobile. I'm not apt to have any visitors coming on foot. I'm not inclined to trample the heavy growth of weeds, possibly signaling my return to the locals, just yet.

Leastways, not the path to the gate where Paul Frank was found dead—back then. He was done with one shot, but I don't want to think about that today, or ever for that matter.

Anyhow, until after my visitor comes and goes, I won't bother to stop by Aunt Aggie's or take the time to check on Annabelle and Sara. First I need to be fully informed about what is expected of me in my new endeavor. As you know, seeing to their needs is Joe's job any time I'm otherwise occupied.

I've accounted for the need to fit the women into my plan—when I'm ready they are to take care of this place. It takes a lot of work to keep up a huge house, and I can tell you, they're the ones to do it.

Very soon after my visitor has come and gone and I've organized in my mind the duties for my son, Joe, and Buddy Dean Howerton, then—and only then—I'll be ready to visit my women and let them know that I'm going to bring them to the great house. Hell, I hadn't realized until the drive back to the mountain after all these years that I actually miss Aunt Aggie. Damn it, I miss Annabelle and the others too, although I'm never going to forget Tuesday, Patty, or Daisy's outright disobedience. *That* you can count on!

"What's that?" Now, I'm talking to myself! I drop the load that I'd been carrying on my shoulder—a box filled with candles and kerosene lamps. I'll need these items until I have the utilities turned on. I'll not have them turned on just now. I can't speak to anyone—whether they work for the utility companies or not. The word would get out because anything anyone does in these parts is fodder for gossip like twigs for a new fire, and everyone knows everyone else. This house being opened after two years would not go unnoticed. Man, the curious are the last people I need right now. My plans are too big for outside interference to muddy up the water.

I accidentally kick the box that I'd just set down out of my way. I look more closely and see what I hadn't recognized at first. It's the large brass doorknocker. I hadn't paid attention to the knocker in the past. It had been so tarnished it blended into the door itself. The five-pointed star must have been cleaned and shined. By Harris before he took off? I imagine. I have no idea why, but it looks like Joe or Harris put a lot of time and energy into the job. I can't imagine either one of them being vaguely interested in such a tedious job, but I have no idea who else would do it.

Humph, I would like to know. It sure is puzzling to me.

I enter the house, hefting the box to my shoulder, with my mind racing over my new line of business.

Enough of that right now, at the moment I need to prepare for my guest.

I'll keep the lamps and candles confined to my back bedroom after dark; even then, I guess I'll need to hang heavy blankets over the windows. Anyway, I must make sure my guest is never seen on my property and connected to me. I can't take a chance on anyone encountering him as he might come and go. I know it's going to feel like a blackout during wartime, but now while there's light filtering in from the windows, and because I have no idea when my visitor will show up, I take up the broom.

Intent on keeping the cobwebs and dirt under control, I move through the house, and fortunately for Joe and Ike Harris, I find that the valuable furnishings—bed, sofa, and side tables—are covered with dust covers which in turn are covered with layers of dust. Man, I tell you, I need to get Annabelle and Aunt Aggie here, and soon. No man should have to do housework. They could get this mess under control in no time. Hell, it wouldn't even matter that there are no utilities on. They've spent their lives without them. Aunt Aggie and Annabelle can make a home anywhere, and whip up a meal from a simple bag of flour.

As I'm working, quiet as a thief, my anticipated guest, my new employer, Abu-Musab, appears at the backdoor.

"Come in, Abu."

I'm spooked at his sudden appearance, but I don't show any sign that I am. I'm not giving him the satisfaction. Hell, I'm not supporting his belief that American men are soft and, as I've heard him say more than once, "scared of their own shadows."

You'll see. The bastard'll change his mind when I'm finished with him. I can now venture to say that my life has come to this. If I fail at the job he entrusts to me, I will be known around the world as a traitor. If I'm successful, I will be a very rich man and travel wherever I please, even around the world if I want.

"Let us talk," Abu says, breaking into my thoughts of wine and women.

I say, "Sit at the table and make yourself comfortable."

"Thank you," he nods, and takes a chair.

"As I've told you all along," I say, facing him and straddling my chair, "for the amount of money you're willing to pay, I'm up for the job. Let's get done with dancing around and playing fool games. Just tell me about the job. I'm more than ready."

Abu looks at me for a long minute and, Mr. Man, I'd like to grab him by his self-righteous . . . scruff of the neck, squeezing the breath from him, until he gets on with it. I checked him out, and I know he's a low level messenger, probably a plant just waiting over the years for his assignment, and I don't appreciate being talked down to by a lackey. I'm slowly losing the battle of holding myself back from jerking him into action, when he speaks up.

"My contact," Abu says, "needs to know more about you, on orders of Al Qaeda. Al Qaeda knows why our own countrymen are willing die for our cause. My contact Al-Zarquwi wants to know why you risk your own death for it."

"Not for anyone's cause but my own!" I'm holding my anger back. "Make no mistake, I'm not going to die, but I will take a great risk for wealth. I'm a man with luck on my side. I do what I want, and the law is useless when it comes to stopping me from what I choose to do. You must know, I'm a very gifted man or your so called Al-Zarquwi would not be so interested in me."

"You Americans talk too much," Abu says with a sweep of his hand, dismissing anything I have to say on the matter. He goes on, "Tell me, McCallister, what do you say, if I tell you that you will surely die if you think to deceive Al Qaeda?"

"I won't," I tell Abu. "The payoff's too huge, and I'm not one to run scared, anyway. I chose to play the game a long time ago. Don't worry! For me the money is everything. I'm up to the challenge. I'm your man."

"Tell your story," Abu says and sits back in his chair.

"My story?"

"You know, as they say, what makes you the man for this job? Your experience in crime so to speak."

I tell Abu the story of my life, leaving out the part about my parents; I'm not fool enough to give him something to hold against me, but I do tell how I helped my Aunt Aggie sell off her stepchildren, since I've already done time for that. How we started with small change, selling my great step-nephews and nieces. How I eventually met George Cunningham, the attorney, and Doctor Sam Johnson, a man George introduced me to later. These men were instrumental in the way I mapped out my life, taking on several women to bear my children and then selling my own children for profit. Like I said, crimes I've already done time for.

After sitting quietly and listening to my story, Abu-Musab says, "You pass my test. You are self-seeking, greedy man. Here's what we do."

On the hunt of his lists, he pats his chest down before digging several sheets of paper from his breast pocket. "This is listing of what you are to purchase. I have separated items into four pages. Do not keep the purchases together in same place. They will tell story if they are found together; otherwise, they will seem like innocent items.

"I understand you have access to underground tunnel above Winding Ridge," Abu raises his eyebrows, and I almost laugh. If only he knew---the expression made him look almost girlish.

"I do," I tell him, stifling my urge to laugh in his face.

"Al Qaeda has had the entrance watched for the past several years. Since the American terrorists have been arrested, it has not been used except for few teenage gangs, and even they have stayed away since the murder about two years back." Abu adopts the severe, unfeeling look once again. I lose my urge to laugh in his face, switching to an impulse to smash it in.

"They are referred to as militia," I correct.

"There is no difference," Abu spits, and all I can do is hide the fact that my temper is at the boiling-over point. "You think it makes a man more a man if he calls himself militia instead of terrorist? They have the same ends, not unlike the two of us. No?"

I want to smash his face and watch him bleed but, managing to keep an outward calm, I listen as he continues with his message, which had obviously sifted down from someone in Al Qaeda. I was sure he was a longtime plant in the United States, a man who stayed close to his own kind, one who did not allow himself to become too American. Nonetheless, the job they have for me is of importance.

"Your place of operation will be safe from the eyes of others. Followers of Al Qaeda will continue to have the entrance of the tunnel watched."

"If that's the case, your people are not as smart as I would have thought. Anyone, especially the teenage gangs, come and go in and out of the tunnel. We might as well operate on the streets. The tunnel runs across many states, with all sorts of unknown entrances. Why not operate from right here in my place?"

"You are the stupid one," Abu says with disgust, and I have to put my hands in my jeans pockets to keep from grabbing him by the neck and jerking a knot in it. I grit my teeth while he continues talking. All the while I can see his eyes darting around. Although he'd never admit it, I can tell he's impressed with the imposing mansion and its furnishings. I bet the pompous jerk has lived his boring life in a dump of a house waiting for this meeting today. Bringing his attention away from the grand house and back to me, he continues, "The great cavern leading off the new entrance, which was built by the militia, is what I speak of. It has been sealed off from the main tunnel. The portal cannot be an exit for those who seek to enter any other gateway on the great length of the tunnel. And whether you like it or not, you are being watched by law enforcement agent. His name, Cliff Moran. Take my word; use tunnel for your operation, we—not Americans—think of everything."

With everything I have, I continue fighting to keep my temper under control, not wanting Abu to read me. I fear my face is blood-red from the effort, so I busy myself with adjusting the oil lamp. I've never been called stupid, and in the end, I won't forget Abu and his fateful remark. After I have my full payment in my hands, I'll see to it he gets his due.

Still, on the other hand, I can go ahead and have the power turned on, and bring the women in right away since the mansion will not be the place of operations for Abu and me.

"Other questions?" Abu raises his eyebrows, giving his face that comic, girlish expression. I have to suppress a sneer lest he think I'm not serious.

"No," I cross my arms, and to my surprise Abu brings his fist from under the table and sets a briefcase in the center. Clicking it open, he lifts the lid, revealing stacks of money. Then Abu leans back in the chair and crosses his arms, watching me closely. I think he is expecting to see a gleeful look in my eyes at his attempt to impress me, so I remain expressionless, as I have trained myself to do over the years. As a matter of fact, I'd be willing to die rather than let this pompous ass know that he *has* impressed me—me, the infamous Jacob McCallister.

"This is money required to make necessary purchases, and the documentation and ID's needed for the men you hire. The flight schools on one of the lists I gave to you have participated in the past for cash payments. Above all you must not leave smallest thread of a trail. Also, you will find one third of the money you are to be paid for the job, including travel expenses. Finally, 'your orders,' as your American generals say," he concludes, handing me the final list, not bothering to hide his contemptuous look.

Scanning the list, I warn Abu, "I don't believe there's a chance in hell you'll get away with a second surprise attack, so what're you going to do with all this?" I wave the lists in his face.

Abu sits still for a long moment, looking at me as if I were a bug that was an annoyance to him. "You are more a fool than I thought if you truly think I freely give that information. I will tell you this: it will be a surprise for all."

"Suit yourself. I'll take care of everything." I do not tell him that I'm very intrigued at seeing this obscene amount of money, or that if they don't keep their word and pay the rest after I do my job, it's not going to hurt my feelings. I've already gotten more than I expected to. I do boast, "I'm sure you have no more idea than I do what's coming down." I don't enlighten him that whatever they're planning probably will be stopped by the government. Anyway, I don't care either way. I don't want to see anymore suffering at those ragheads' hands. but I have my payoff.

And to tell you the truth, I'm relieved as Abu—without another word—rises from his chair and leaves as unobtrusively as he showed up.

CHAPTER 2

THE MORNING SUN FILTERED THROUGH THE grimy kitchen window, picking up dancing particles of dust but allowing Annabelle sufficient light to attend to her chores. The warming rays washed away the coolness of the night, and the fire in the potbelly stove comforted her to her very bones, as she was wont to say. By noontime it would be wretchedly hot, though, if she did not douse the fires in the potbelly and also the old woodburning stove she used for cooking.

She commenced the first task of the day, which was mixing dough for the biscuits Sara and her daughter would be expecting with their eggs and bacon at breakfast. As she labored, Annabelle listened intently to the radio, which to this day had been her only source of entertainment. As anonymous voices reported the news, she occupied herself by attempting to envision other people's diverse lives, inspired by the stories she heard. Many were conditions and situations she did not have the experience to truly understand.

She pulled out and down on the spiral handle, opening the heavy metal door of the firebox below the oven, and tossed a few more pieces of kindling into the fire. From the flame that licked toward the exterior of the woodburner, light danced across her haggard features. She closed the door and the flames were effectively confined to the inside of the stove. She reached up to her bun, which was everlastingly untidy, and absently fingered a few wayward strands of her prematurely steel gray hair back into the knot.

Loneliness was Annabelle's constant companion now that her husband had gone off, thoughtlessly staying away for longer stretches of time and sending their son, Joe, in his stead to bring supplies. She also missed other family members—babies who had been sold and others who had moved on or died. Betty had died in childbirth, and Rose, the last and youngest of the women Jeb had taken to wife, had been too young for child bearing and had died shortly after the difficult birth of a son. Only a few days old, he was taken away to be sold.

Daisy and her twins were making new lives far from the mountain cabin. The last Annabelle had seen of them was the night that Jeb, too drunk to make it further than the living room sofa, had announced his discovery that Daisy was disobeying him by working at the town bar. Then he had passed out, and the others had gone to bed.

The next morning, to everyone's dismay, Daisy and her twins were gone.

With her money box tucked under her arm and with one twin clasping her left hand and the other holding the hem of her skirt, Daisy became not only the first of the mountain women to escape Jeb, but the first to truly want too. That night, she and her children had tiptoed quietly from the cabin, fearfully passing by Jeb as he lay slumbering, nearly unconscious from too much booze.

No one would have predicted it, because Annabelle's son, Joe, and his father had never had a father-son relationship, but Joe now lived in the city with Jeb, and he was the one coming back to the mountain to bring supplies when necessary. Other than Annabelle, the only ones still living in the small cabin were daughter, Sara, and her granddaughter, Kelly Sue. And Sara was away most of the time, working at The Company Store in the town at the foot of the mountain, leaving Annabelle to look after Kelly Sue.

Without the four women Annabelle had shared her husband with throughout her young adult life, and the coming and going of the children who were born to be sold, the cabin was now almost too quiet. Everything had changed without Jeb and the others, living crowded together in the small space. She was lonely without them, but the consolation was that they were free from anguish at the loss of the children they bore. Jeb had, with the exception of Joe, Patty, and Sara, sold them as fast as the women could have them—until about four years ago when he was imprisoned for the crime.

Freed from prison now, Jeb stayed away, leaving Joe to divide his time between his father's house in the city and short visits to the cabin. With the downsizing of the family over the past few years, there was little in the way of chores to be done. Annabelle had more time for the highlight of her day—the radio—a gift, several years back from Joe. *How had I ever got on all those years without it?* she wondered.

Hearing no activity coming from the room next to the kitchen, Annabelle went to the doorway, and pulling back the tattered curtain, she saw that Sara and Kelly Sue were still asleep, sprawled out on their new mattress—a purchase Sara was able to make from her first few paychecks. The mattress lay directly on the floor, as she had not saved the money for the box springs and frame.

"Time to eat," Annabelle called, and got only a muffled, "In a minute," in return, as Sara pulled the quilt over her head.

Unlike Daisy, who had hoarded most of her earnings from the town bar toward the goal of escaping the mountain life forever, Sara did not want to move away and leave her mother behind. So she was interested in replacing the threadbare mats she and the children of the family had slept on their entire lives. Since her pa and brother were gone so much of the time, they never noticed that she was working in town or the little extras she bought for the others. She used the money she earned working at The Company Store to buy, for her mother and her daughter, things that Jeb and Joe did not think the females needed.

Annabelle continued to sleep in the great four-poster bed in the only other bedroom alone—for the first time in her life.

Sleeping in the great bed without Daisy and the other women was difficult for Annabelle now—taking care of others and having to share the small rooms with them, over the years, had become her way of life. Although it had always been her wish to share the bed with her husband alone, early on he had taken Betty as a second woman, and she found herself sharing a bed with the first of a series of women she had to care for as if they were her sisters.

She had had no trouble getting used to the arrangement, because in her entire life, she had never slept alone. She had come from a poor mountain family overtaxed with too many children to care for. Her father sold them for just a few hundred dollars each, as he could not earn enough money to feed them.

I even miss th' other women sleepin' at th' foot of th' bed when I was sharin' th' bed with him, she thought. *Although I don't miss sleepin' on th' floor, tryin' to stuff th' space between th' floor planks with my mat to keep th' cold air out, when one of th' other's was sleepin' with Jeb.*

Thinking of the past and the sleeping arrangements brought back unwanted memories, and she pushed back her recollection of Jeb bringing Tuesday to live in the small four-room cabin. At first, Annabelle did not know that Jeb brought Tuesday to the cabin against her will. Annabelle could not imagine that any woman would actually not want to be with her Jeb.

Now, she turned her attention to the radio, which was the only thing these days, other than Aggie's visits, to brighten Annabelle's dreary environment. Her slippers flapped as she ducked under the clothesline that stretched across the kitchen. Pushing back a damp housedress, she crossed the floor to turn on the radio, thinking that just the day before Aggie had come calling.

As usual, she had traveled on foot from her isolated cabin located four miles higher on the mountain, and when she arrived, she and Annabelle had immediately begun dredging up every news story they had heard about Jeb in the past years. Based on the lack of interest by the news media in recent months, the women thought that Jeb had been dropped as a suspect in the murder of Tommy Lee Hillberry, because Hump and Fran Rudd's son Robbie had been charged and convicted of the murder of Paul Frank Ruble. Although, neither Jeb nor Robbie Rudd had been connected to Tommy Lee's death, the consensus was that even though it was known that Robbie killed Tommy Lee, Jeb's actions had started the chain of events that ultimately led to both Paul Frank's and Tommy Lee Hillberry's deaths. Some believed

Jeb was the one who killed Tommy Lee. He had been seen in town on that fateful September day, after one of his habitual, extended absences, but it also appeared that he had been in one of the World Trade Center Towers during the terrorist attack. Many people, including law officers, believed Jeb had been killed there, because his rental car was found near the Towers, and his secretary, Brandi Rose, had not heard from him.

Movement from the corner of her eye had pulled Annabelle from her pity party. A mere speck, moving down the nearby mountain, was growing larger and larger. As it drew nearer, the speck turned out to be Aunt Aggie, dressed as usual in her feedsack housedress, threadbare, quilted shawl, and ankle-high, laced boots. She was stepping gingerly down the path, tree root by stone by tree root, drawing closer and closer to the flat that led to Annabelle's back door. Annabelle pulled the towel from across her shoulder and wiped her hands as she headed to the door, welcoming Aggie. She was eager to talk with someone who was as interested in Jeb as she was. The only other person Annabelle had to talk to was Sara, and she was most definitely not interested in talking about her pa.

"I'm surprised to see ya again so soon. Ain't like ya to come callin' two days straight," Annabelle said, leaning forward to hold the screen door open as Aggie crossed the rutted-out, dirt parking area next to the cabin.

Aggie's demeanor made it obvious that she couldn't wait until she was in the kitchen to share her news. "Times ain't th' same no more. Ya'll never guess what just happened, so ya'll not."

"What is it?" Annabelle gave the older woman a hand to speed her progress up the single step to the porch and into the kitchen. Eager to hear the gossip Aggie was so excited about sharing, Annabelle hurriedly removed the feedsack housedresses, jeans, underwear, aprons, and ragged towels from the clothesline. Fashioned from baling twine and stretched across the kitchen, the clothesline was held taut by spike nails that were pounded into the logs that made up the cabin walls. The store-bought underwear and jeans were the first ever in the cabin, as Jeb held that there was no need for the women to have such things. They were the earliest personal items Sara had purchased with her first paycheck.

"Now we can have a nice talk without th' laundry slapping us in th' face every time we rock to an' fro," Annabelle said as she threw the laundry in the direction of the table, and it landed dead center of the crude piece of furniture fashioned from raw wood planks.

"Ya ain't goin' to believe it, so ya ain't," Aggie said, ignoring the pieces of clean laundry caught in splinters to hang from the edge of the table, as she settled herself in a rocking chair beside the potbelly stove, "not what I've got to say, so ya won't."

At the foot of the rocking chair, Annabelle's old tomcat sat quietly on its haunches, its muscles tensed, as if waiting for Aggie to get comfortable. As Aggie reached for the spittoon Annabelle kept there for her, the cat sprang onto her lap. "Joe came back by my cabin after he brought your supplies an' told me that Jeb's comin' back to th' mountain, so he did," Aggie patted the cat's head after it had pranced around and found a comfortable place to lie across her familiar lap.

"Why in tarnation didn't he tell me? I'm his mother," Annabelle grumbled.

"I knowed how to get information outa a body, so I do. Besides, ya don't need to knowed everythin', so ya don't"

While Aggie paused to spit in her spittoon, Sara and Kelly Sue appeared at the curtained doorway. Kelly Sue held back, but Sara, needing to hurry if she were to be on time for work, moved forward. She put one bare foot over the bench attached to the table and lowered herself. Bringing her other leg across, shoving the damp laundry aside, she asked, "What's for breakfast?"

"Ain't ya goin' to say nothin' to your Aunt Aggie?" Annabelle asked, "Where's your manners?"

"Hi, Aunt Aggie," Sara yawned. "Kelly Sue, go hug your aunt." Kelly Sue untangled herself from the curtain and ran to her great, great aunt, hugging and kissing her, unmindful of the dark spittle dripping down the woman's chin.

"Ma, we're hungry. Can I help?" Sara asked, watching Kelly Sue who was now on her knees in Aggie's lap, vying with the old tomcat for her own space.

"No, I don't need no help," Annabelle said. "Just sit where y'are an' I'll set your food on th' table."

"Thanks, Ma. Now that we have money to buy food, I really enjoy eatin' your cookin' 'cause we can have what we want to eat—not what somebody happened to shoot that day or th' meager vegetables we was able to grow an' can ourselves."

"Yeah, Daisy, was savin' her money to move to th' city so she didn't spend as much as ya do on th' food an' nicer clothes. I can tell ya it helps to have th' food to cook an' I appreciate it too," Annabelle said. "I love havin' eggs, milk, an' bacon an', sausage whenever we're wantin' it.

"Lip-smackin' good it is," Annabelle said, smacking her own lips to show her appreciation.

"Ya can fix me some of those eggs an' bacon too, so ya can," Aggie said, as she often did, seizing the opportunity to partake of the fresh food Sara provided. Truth be known, although Jeb was all she wanted to talk about, the food was a major reason, recently, for her more frequent, early morning visits. She, too, had had little opportunity to enjoy a variety of foods.

The women and child finished eating breakfast, leaving their tin plates clean after using biscuits to sop up every bit and morsel of the eggs they could. Leaving Annabelle to clean up and take care of Kelly Sue, Sara went off to work.

"Now we can get back to th' important matters, so we can." Aggie said, wiping her mouth with her apron, and handing her plate to Annabelle so as not to disturb the child or the cat. "We don't knowed when Jeb's comin' home, but we do knowed he is."

"As much as I'm wantin' to be with my man, I'm thinkin' there's goin' to be trouble. Ain't never fails when Jeb's around there's trouble brewin'."

"Ya can't make up your mind, so ya can't. Do ya want him here or don't ya? First ya say ya can't wait to see him, an' th' next thin' ya thinkin' he's goin' to be makin' trouble. Maybe ya goin' to get what ya expect, so ya will." It always irritated Aggie when anyone criticized her nephew.

"Mark my word, old woman, there's goin' to be trouble comin' our way with our man's return, an' he's goin' to bring grief back into our lives, like he always does."

CHAPTER 3

WIDE AWAKE AND KNOWING THAT SHE was doomed to endure another unsettling, dream-filled night, Isabel threw back the covers. As on other similar occasions when she was awakened by her vivid dreams, she rose from her cozy bed, found her moccasins and slipped her toes inside. Pulling on her robe, she went looking for a midnight snack. Quietly, she opened the door leading to the hallway, where a soft halo glowed around the nightlight at the top of the stairs. So as not to disturb those who would be sleeping at this time, she crept down the stairs, preceded eerily by her own shadowy form, and found her way into the kitchen. She stopped short when she saw her mother wearily standing at the pale yellow, ceramic counter unloading the dishwasher.

Having heard her daughter creeping down the stairs, Sherry wiped her hands on the tea towel she was holding. "You're having trouble sleeping again?"

"Oh! I didn't know anyone was up," Isabel cried out, a little startled, but she welcomed the sight of her mother puttering around the pleasant kitchen.

Sherry and her husband, Thomas, had always loved Isabel as if she had been born to them and never thought of her as being adopted. And now these many recurring and unwelcome dreams, which bespoke actual memories of a completely foreign childhood, had taken power over all their lives. Though, how could such a thing be? Isabel was only two and a half years old when she was brought to them, much too young to remember anything. So the idea of memories surfacing from her infant years was discarded.

The clinic Sherry had gone to fifteen years ago, in the hopes of being told of a new, scientific way for her to give birth to her own child, had found that she was unable to conceive even with the most recent in vitro methods. Thus, the couple was led to the solution of adoption.

They were considered too old to adopt through normal channels. Doctor Sam Johnson, who ran the clinic in Wheeling, a person she would never have come in contact with under a normal approach to adoption, had given her an alternative. The option was an attorney named George Cunningham; he arranged adoptions for a fee. Although both Sherry and her husband were apprehensive about the legality of the adoption, wanting a child so badly, they had never spoken of their concerns to each other, let alone to anyone else.

Because of the dubiousness of the adoption, and in light of the recurring dreams that Isabel perceived as long-ago memories, Sherry was uneasy about Isabel learning the truth of her origins. Like many adoptive parents, Sherry and Thomas were naturally anxious that the birth parents could come swooping back into the child's life, or that Isabel would make an attempt to find her roots, as adopted children were prone to do. Sherry's fear was that it would all end in the birth parents coming into their lives and taking the only child they ever had— or expected to have—away.

But, because of Isabel's desperate pleading to be taken to a psychiatrist where the young girl was sure to learn what triggered the memory-like dreams, Sherry decided she would take the chance. After all, having the child for fifteen of her seventeen and half years should count for something.

Shouldn't it?

CHAPTER

NOW THAT ABU HAD COME AND GONE, having insisting the operation be established inside the great cavern at the entrance to the tunnel, McCallister had not bothered to cover the windows to hide from the outside world the light coming from the oil lamps. After he thought about it, he rather liked not having his base of operations under the women's noses, which was the most important consideration. He could handle the mountain folk gossips wagging tongues that no one took serious, and asking if the notorious Jacob McCallister was up to something no good once again. Yes, keeping matters from the women was best—they would be the ones the law would listen to. Neither of them—most especially Aggie—would keep her nose out of his business if confronted with it. The women had inadvertently been responsible for providing the most crucial evidence to get McCallister convicted and sent to prison with a substantial sentence.

McCallister was headed toward the great hall leading to his bedroom when he heard a banging at the front door.

He stormed back to the front door and saw Buddy Dean Howerton through the the side pane, hanging the door-knocker soundly against the brass plate, as though he were stamping out a fire. "What the . . . ?" McCallister opened the door, jerking the doorknocker from Buddy Dean's fist.

"McCallister!" Buddy Dean held out his hand, his engaging and ever-present smile painted across his face, "I'm here to see how you liked the artwork I picked out for you."

"Come in," McCallister said, stepping out of Howerton's way, "It's perfect, but what the hell are you doing here this time of night?"

Buddy Dean sauntered down the entry hall with his hands in the pockets of his trench coat, stopping in front of each piece of art. "Very nice," Buddy Dean murmured, nodding in appreciation. He tilted his head and looked down at his feet as he strolled back toward where McCallister was standing.

"Thanks, Howerton, but I can't imagine why on earth you would come all the way from Wheeling just to admire artwork you've all ready seen!"

"Don't sweat it." Buddy Dean looked up then to face McCallister, appearing as if he had made a decision unknown to anyone but himself. He extended his hands, palms up, to prove he was no threat to McCallister. "I want to work with you, and that's all. I needed to make sure you liked my choices."

"I've already told you I have a job for you," McCallister said, noting Buddy Dean's arrogant demeanor.

"That's why it's important to me that you were pleased with what I've all ready done for you. I want to continue."

"You could've used the phone."

"I'm not that kind of guy." Buddy Dean grinned, once again pushing his hands out in a gesture of openness. "I like the personal touch."

"I don't like your timing," McCallister told him in his most threatening voice, "and I'm in no mood for company."

McCallister, in a nasty mood, was especially suspicious of Howerton's showing up on the heels of Abu's meeting, and he meant to remember the intrusion.

CHAPTER

5

ONCE AGAIN, THE MORNING WAS COOL and bright. Aggie, having finished her chores earlier than usual, set off down the old, rocky mountain path, eager to visit with Annabelle for the third straight day. She was upset at Annabelle's prediction of doom; the day before, because of Jeb's pending return. She was bent on her mission—her nephew—and on talking to her only confidante, Annabelle, over and over again in anticipation of Jeb's return to the mountain.

Impatient to see Annabelle and discuss what was in store for them when Jeb returned, and hurrying along, bubbling at the prospect of bantering with someone who shared a long history with her, Aggie almost took a bad fall. She was so absorbed in her musing that she carelessly stepped on a loose rock. Before her feet flew out from under her, though, she was able to grab onto a branch.

"I'm goin' to break my neck if'n I don't watch where I'm goin', so I am," Aggie admonished herself as her heart skipped a frightening beat or two. To distract herself, she began considering a less absorbing subject: her great nieces and great nephew.

The days were long gone when Jeb sent his children to help Aggie with the chores. Secretly, she had always been able to keep up on her own, but she enjoyed the company of her great nieces and great nephew, so, in keeping with her habit of contriving to manipulate others, she had always allowed Jeb to believe she needed the help.

Aggie believed—and it was true—that the children got something from the visits as well. They loved for her to tell them her bizarre, colorful stories. They thought of the tales as entertainment and never realized that most of them were true.

As Aggie trudged down the well-worn path, reminiscing about the children and the stories she had told them, a determination filled her mind to one day tell Winter Ann the true story of her beginnings. The particulars of where the girl really came from—in regard to her true relationship with herself and Jeb—were at times all-consuming for Aggie.

Aggie kept a steady pace, although she was more careful now that she had almost taken a fall a piece back up the mountain. As she picked her way closer to the cabin, she was aware that Annabelle was watching from her favorite spot at the window above the woodburning stove, eager—as she herself was—to share every iota of news there was about Jeb.

When Aggie finally reached the back door of the cabin, the tail of her skirt was streaked with mud stains, and—thanks to the branch that she'd grabbed to keep her footing back up on the mountain—two long scratches marked her arm from elbow to wrist, Annabelle was waiting impatiently, with the screen door held open in welcome. She too wanted to continue their conversation about Jeb's return to the mountain after these years of being away.

During the first years of his absence from the mountain, he had been doing time in prison. After that, Annabelle and Aggie really didn't know what had kept him away, sending Joe in his place to do the things he had always done. Although Jeb was suspected of the murder of Tommy Lee Hillberry, there was no real evidence as to whether he had done it or not. His being gone had cast some suspicion on his possible part in the crime, but the women had no idea of what had actually happened. The two of them could remember a time when Jeb was not consumed with any matter other than the prospect of one or more of his women carrying his child. During that time in their lives, his women and Aunt Aggie could count on Jeb being around for weeks at a time every few months, bringing them supplies. He paid attention to Annabelle and the others as women, like he never did these days.

"Oh, I'm glad to see ya," Annabelle said, practically pulling Aggie bodily inside, hoping Aggie had remembered something new to tell her. Annabelle was aware that Aggie had already most likely reported everything Joe had told her. She knew, as well, that she would be content just to savor the thought of his impending return and rehash it all over again.

Ignoring Annabelle's greeting, Aggie admonished, "I knowed ya seen me fall, so ya did. Y'are always lookin' outta th' window 'bove th' sink. Ain't ya goin' to ask if I hurt myself? Or is Jeb th' only subject y'are wantin' to talk 'bout?"

"I knowed ya didn't hurt your self, an' I saw th' mud an' scratches. I knowed if ya hurt yourself, Aggie," Annabelle scoffed, "ya'd be howlin' like a baby. Anyway, y'are one to be getting' on to a body about thinkin' an' talkin' of nothin' but Jeb, I ain't ever heard ya talkin' about anythin' else."

"When do ya think he's comin' back?" Aggie had chosen to ignore Annabelle's ill-mannered reaction to her taking a fall and headed for her favorite rocking chair. She carefully scooped the sleeping tomcat from the rocking chair's cushion, a homemade feedsack pillowcase filled with feathers. She held the cat in her arms while she settled into the chair. She had her own cats and she was quick to fault Annabelle, who paid no attention to the big tomcat, except to throw him outside when she could catch him. Apparently Jeb did not hold with animals sharing the small cabin. With the cat cozy in her lap, Aggie unconsciously began the rocking motion, in anticipation of the social pleasure of having someone to discuss her nephew with.

"You're th' one with th' news," Annabelle said, taking the rocking chair alongside Aggie. "Why're ya askin' me? Is there somethin' ya didn't tell me?"

"No, so there ain't, I just needed someone to talk to, so I do. But there's one thing we ain't talked about, so there is."

Annabelle brightened, "What is it?"

"Remember, Jeb'd said he's movin' us off th' mountain, so he did."

"You mentioned that, Aggie. So what of it/"

"I'm not of a mind to move, so I'm not."

"Forevermore, Aggie, ya just got your bloomers in a bunch just thinkin' of movin', an' ya come fallin' down th' mountain tryin' to break yer neck."

"I don't have not one pair of bloomers, so I don't," Aggie huffed. "Ya ain't got no underclothes neither."

"Ya knowed Sara does, but I'm not talkin' 'bout bloomers, Aggie. Don't ya knowed a joke when ya hear one?"

"Ya don't knowed anythin' 'bout what I got, so ya don't. I didn't come here to talk 'bout bloomers or hear your jokes, so I didn't. I came to talk 'bout Jeb an' 'bout him takin' us outta our cabin's to live somewhere we ain't never seen."

"I knowed how ya feel, I don't want to leave neither," Annabelle fretted, losing her halfhearted mood to joke. "Sara'll never hear of it, ya knowed that."

"She'll have to do what he says, so she will."

"Yeah, I knowed."

"Yeah, an' I'll go along too, so I will, but even if my place wasn't fixed so nice, I'd' want to stay. But ya knowed, I'd do anythin' to have my Jeb back, so I would."

"Ya don't have to tell me that! If I don't knowed anythin' else, I knowed how ya feel about Jeb."

"Speakin' 'bout Sara. Where is she?" Aggie asked.

"She's ate breakfast an' gone to work," Annabelle answered. Ya didn't get here as early as ya did yesterday, but I have plenty left over."

Annabelle opened the oven door and brought out a few iron skillets.

"That sure smells good, so it does," Aggie said, her mouth watering just watching Annabelle heap eggs, sausage, and biscuits from the skillets onto a plate.

"Where's Kelly Sue? Aggie asked, missing the attention the child gave her.

"She's nappin'," Annabelle said. "She had breakfast with her mother an' when I peeked in on her, she was sleepin' on th' mattress with her toys next to her."

"She's a good child, so she is."

"Where do ya think he's takin' us?" Annabelle asked holding out the tin plate and a fork for Aggie.

"Hold on a minute. I need to get rid of my snuff. An' I told ya yesterday that I don't knowed where he's takin' us, so

I did. An' if I don't knowed it yesterday, I sure don't knowed it today."

Aggie set the cat on his feet beside the rocking chair. He scurried across the room and sat on his haunches—flicking his pink tongue in and out, busily washing himself from neck to toe—as he waited for the chance to jump back into the warm comfort of Aggie's lap.

With her forefinger, Aggie swiped the snuff from between her lip and gum at the right side of her jaw. Picking up the spittoon, she flipped the glob into the cracked, clay pot with a soft splat and set it back on the floor by her side. "Set th' plate here in my lap," Aggie said.

Annabelle did so and returned to her rocking chair.

Aggie wiped her finger on her homemade housedress and picked up the fork.

"I remember all that, Aggie. Yesterday weren't that long ago. Ya knowed I'm only wantin' to talk, th' same as ya do," Annabelle said, picking up the conversation again, impatient to hear more. "So go on an' tell me."

"That's all I knowed. He's goin' to take us away from here, so he is. I just wanted somebody to talk to an' help me figure it all out." Aggie talked around a mouth full of food.

"Looks like ya was more interested in havin' a plate of eggs an' sausage. Surprised ya wasn't here earlier."

"Hogwash," Aggie said. "It ain't just th' food. Ya knowed I like to have someone to talk to about Jeb, so ya do. I sorely miss 'im."

"Yeah, I do too, but I just don't understand why Joe didn't tell me about Jeb comin' home, Aggie. After all, I'm his mother."

"Ya done told me that, so ya did," Aggie said, between mouthfuls of food.

"I knowed."

"Ya knowed how ya an' Daisy an' 'em woman of his are. Ya all act like y'are th' ones in charge, so ya do." Aggie greedily sopped up the remaining egg yellow with her biscuit. Stuffing the soggy bit of food into her mouth, she handed the plate and fork to Annabelle.

"Nobody has to be in charge," Annabelle said, taking the plate and setting it on the edge of the table where she could reach without getting out of her chair. "Jeb an' Joe think we've been put on this earth for their own convenience, an' they're thinkin' we don't have no needs."

"Can'cha see that's just why Jeb always did, an' now Joe, come to me when they want to discuss business, so it is." Aggie opened her snuff can and pulled out her bottom lip at the lower left corner. With her free hand, using her forefinger, she scooped out a digit of snuff and placed it between her lip and gum. Smacking her lips, she said, "Ya don't have no respect."

"Forevermore, Aggie, are ya ever goin' to see your own stubbornness an' shortsightedness when it comes to Jeb? Daisy an' Patty showed us that women can make a life without a man tellin' 'em what to do."

"Oh, what big words y'are learnin', so ya are."

"Well, I'm right."

"Yeah, but ya love every minute Jeb pays attention to ya, so ya do."

Annabelle flushed. "He's my man. That's why."

"Th' other ones always claimed him as their man, too, so they did, but ya knowed he's his own man. He ain't goin' to let no one tell him how to live, or what to do, so he ain't."

"I just don't understand why he's thinkin' 'bout movin' us."

"Don't knowed, so I don't."

"I don't like it when I'm not told what's goin' to affect me."

"Hogwash, since when? Ya an' th' others've always done what he says, an' ya knowed if'n you're goin' to be with my Jeb, you're goin' to have to do it his way, so y'are."

"'My' Jeb? Ain't ya th' one! Always thinkin' he's all for ya. I'm th' mother of his youngins. Y'are just his aunt."

"Ya an, all th' other ones can say th' same thing. They mothered youngins from his loins too, but I raised him, so I did. Ya have no idea what we've gone through together. No idea at all, for it made us tight, so it did,"

Aggie found the spittoon at her feet, picked it up, spit a long stream, and wiped her chin as she set it back on the plank floor, ready to hold her own in the ongoing quarrel with Annabelle.

Later, Annabelle watched as Aggie made her way back to her cabin, noting that when Jeb came around more often, Aggie came around less often. Jealously, Annabelle knew it was because Jeb always made his first stop at his Aunt Aggie's cabin.

CHAPTER 6

MCCALLISTER'S SECOND DAY AT THE mansion was a busy one, and he put aside the nagging thought of Howerton's visit so close on the heels of his meeting with Abu-Musab. He had begun the assignment by organizing the purchases on the list Abu had given him into three groups, one he himself would take care of, and the other two groups to be assigned to Howerton and his son, Joe.

Later, McCallister planned to visit their new place of operation, which was built about five years ago, and check it out for himself. Back then, Benjamin Booker had gathered the militiamen together to build the cavern for use as their headquarters while they commenced their takeover. The gathering at Winding Ridge was to be the kick-off for taking back their country, as the militiamen saw it. The militia used the cavern for storing food and supplies, plenty enough to sustain them for years if they had to go underground. Most important, they used it for their secret comings and goings, a place to conduct business without detection—a connection to most any state on the East Coast they wanted to go.

For years McCallister had known that the tunnel entrance was located two miles below his cabin. He had found it within a year of building the cabin when he had bought Annabelle for two hundred dollars from her father. He had, in fact, never had much interest in the tunnel but felt secure knowing it was there and how to gain entry and set off underground if needed. He had never mentioned the tunnel to his aunt, his women, or his children.

McCallister had no intention or relying upon Abu-Musab's word that the cavern was indeed sealed off from the tunnel. He had learned from Joe that the cavern was constructed by the militia, and they did take care of camouflaging the opening that led from tunnel to the cavern in both directions. The militiamen and even Booker himself had been confident that only those who knew that the connection was there could find it.

The cavern was compartmented for various secret uses: militiamen's offices, grand storage areas, and quarters for the militiamen. The outdoor entrance led to the section where the general population of militia worked, and that entrance into the cavern was skillfully camouflaged from the outside. The section toward the rear was designated for storage of ammunition, protective clothing, first-aid supplies, medicine, and enough food to carry them for years if and when it became necessary. The mid section was set aside for offices for the Supreme Commander and militia lords. In the days of the militia, the opening leading from the tunnel into the huge, man-made cavern had been so well disguised that people exploring the tunnel without already knowing about the addition would never suspect its existence. The cavernous room was expertly and totally hidden from the view of anyone traveling along the seemingly endless tunnel, which snaked on and on until it was lost in total darkness.

Back then, the whole reason for the building of the cavern in proximity to the tunnel was that, in the event of a standoff with law enforcement agencies, the militiamen could come and go—to and from the outside world—using the underground tunnel. By entering and exiting at the many portals along the length of the tunnel, the militiamen would leave the law unaware that they were, at all times, fully equipped and fed.

Having decided that he would give Joe and Buddy Dean each a dozen items to seek out and buy, he had made a separate list for each of them, leaving two thirds of the items for later. As for the flight schools, he was not going to trust those arrangements to anyone else, and a plan was forming in his head. McCallister could not take a chance on any of this pointing back to himself—especially the flight schools. He had an idea.

With a watchful eye on each of the passengers occupying the few cars he passed, McCallister headed out on Route Seven, toward the road leading up into Winding Ridge. After he drove through the edge of Winding Ridge, McCallister headed for the cavern, about one mile above the town and three miles below his cabin, dodging the ruts in the road as he maneuvered the truck up the mountain. It had been a couple of years since he had been anywhere near the tunnels. Jacob McCallister had no use for the militia and refused to be involved with it, believing that it was made up of bigoted, self–important men whose aim was to govern through force and intimidation, He thought of them as a form of cancer, targeting groups of people they did not know or understand. If nothing else, McCallister knew that skin color or place of birth did not make an individual good or bad. His motto was "live and let live," unless of course someone got in his way.

The tunnel was located off an old dirt lane, the leavings of a logging company that had timbered the area a decade ago. The acreage had been owned by Gordon Maxwell, the former owner of the coalmine. That road had been the deciding factor in Benjamin Booker's decision to build his shelter at the tunnel's Winding Ridge entrance.

There were several entrances to the tunnel in the state; one of them was the one above Winding Ridge and the other located on Broad Run. At Broad Run the entrance was on private property—an old farmhouse owned by Paul Frank Ruble's late father. A weathered, horizontal door located at the side of the house led into the basement, which in turn led into the tunnel. The Winding Ridge entrance was the obvious choice over Broad Run for other reasons, too: Broad Run had no field to use as a parking area for the many cars and trucks that would come for the gathering of the militia, no nearby boardinghouse for the men to stay in while building the cavern.

With a sigh of relief, McCallister turned right onto the old logging road. He hadn't passed anyone else after reaching the road to Winding Ridge. He continued driving up the mountain road past Myrtle Landacre's cabin, which stood a little more than two miles below his own. He rolled through the parking area that had been created by all the trucks, campers, and cars that had come and gone during the militia's assembly a couple of years back. McCallister was not familiar with the new entrance because the assembly had been held during the years he was in jail for child trafficking. He looked for and then spotted the large rock formation that he had been told marked the lane that led to the door.

McCallister left his truck and moved through heavy brush, knowing he would find the smaller monument of stones that he knew both concealed and marked the beginning of the footpath to the large, heavy, steel door hidden deep in the rocky face. Finding the first and smaller mound of stones, he stepped around it, immediately saw the base of the much larger rock formation, and stole through the brush to the concealed door. The lock was broken and lay at the side of the path.

Someone had deliberately broken it . . . *but who? The men working for Al Qaeda wouldn't leave the opening unsecured.*

McCallister opened the door. "Damn!" he swore, as the interior was lit.

Unswervingly and with frightening speed, something soared out of nowhere, passing within inches of his head.

"What the—?"

CHAPTER

AFTER THE LAST BELL, THE HALLWAYS vibrated with the racket of teenagers on the move. Shouts of "What're you doing tonight?" "Meet me after practice." "Call me later." "Can't. Got to do my homework," rang out. In the fray, Patty was inadvertently pushed into another student, dropped her favorite pen, and accidentally stomped on it, rendering it useless.

"Sorry," Patty apologized to the teenage girl she had unintentionally shoved into the wall unable to stop her momentum.

"It's okay," Isabel smiled. "Like I'm so-o-o used to it. I've been pushed around all my life."

Seeing the mischievous smile warm the girl's face Patty laughed, holding her damaged pen up for the girl to see, "This was my favorite pen in the world."

"Oh, do you need help!" Isabel pantomimed a hocus-pocus. "So un-cool, being that attached to a fountain pen," she wisecracked.

"Really. Aren't you the funny one?" Patty playfully pushed Isabel, and both of them grinning, they moved on.

The girls slowed down as they drew nearer to the heavily crowded front entrance where the homebound students propelled them more rapidly toward the three huge , walnut, double doors that looked large enough for a train—clanging, wobbling, and choo chooing—to speed through them.

"I've seen you around lately, but for some reason we've never met." Patty said, taking the five steps that led to the landing ahead of Isabel. She turned, prancing backward and forward, long hair swinging around her shoulders as she bounced on her toes and motioned for Isabel to follow,

"Oh, my gosh! Can't you stand still?" Isabel giggled and joined Patty on the landing at the foot of the steps.

Patty resumed walking forward, anxious to get out of the stuffy school and onto the tree lined school grounds. "I'm glad we did, though," Patty smiled.

Isabel paced her steps to match Patty's. "Me too, but I guess I needed to wreck your pen to get your attention."

Pressed by the jostling mass of students, the two girls were steered through the doorway to the far right, where they were propelled into the sunshine along with the others.

"I'm a loner, I guess," Isabel smiled. "Like, I don't have many friends."

"Really?"

Isabel shrugged. "I guess it's my mother. We're so close; I don't have much time for friends. Like, we spend a lot of time doing stuff together."

"I wish I'd've gotten to know my mother," Patty said. "She died while I was being born."

"Oh, my gosh! I'm so sorry," Isabel said. "That's tough, too. You see, like, actually I'm adopted, and don't know anything at all about my birth parents. My stepmother doesn't even seem like an adoptive mother. I wonder about my real mother, but I never talk to my stepmother about it."

"Really! That's too bad," Patty said, wondering if Isabel's life without her mother was as bad as her own had been without a loving mother all to herself, but from the looks of Isabel, Patty didn't think the girl was raised in poverty as she herself had been.

"In that regard, we're in almost the same situation. My half-sister and half-brother's mother stepped into my mother's place in raising me."

"Sounds as if there's a story there," Isabel raised her eyebrows showing interest.

"How'd you know I'm a closet writer?" Patty grinned.

"Oh, my gosh! Like, you want to be a writer?"

"Really, I do. Anyway, what's wrong with that?" Patty asked, knowing that the lawless and out–of-the-ordinary people who led to her extreme life experiences—from hopelessness to happiness—would help her create many colorful characters for her stories.

"Nothing!" Isabel said. "Like, I just think it's uncanny, I meet my first new friend and we have the same interests. Anyway, it's too cool."

"Really! You want to write too?" Patty asked.

"Yeah, I do."

"I like it," Patty said, "our having the same interests."

"You know what? I've always kept a journal."

"Really, Isabel, so have I!"

"Cool!" Isabel said.

"What are you going to do this summer?" Patty asked as they started down the path leading across the grounds to the street.

"Nothing special," Isabel shrugged. The wind caught her dark, shining hair, blowing it across her cheek when she turned toward Patty. She turned even farther, walking completely backward to face her, disregarding her hair whipping into her face and stinging her eyes. "I'm taking some summer classes. Like I need to be prepared if I'm to get into a good college. I started to school a year late. It had something to do with my adoption, but I never knew exactly what."

The two girls continued to get more acquainted. They giggled and talked the length of the tree-lined walkway and somehow managed to reach the street without Isabel taking a spill as she continued in her backward gait. As they passed in and out of the shaded area into the sunshine, the rays caught the highlights in the girls' hair.

They figured the difference in their ages was eleven months, with Isabel the older. Still they looked the same age.

"I'm going to summer school too," Patty said, "I want to take extra classes. I'm glad we met. It'll be nice to have a friend in a totally new school this summer. You're going to take your summer classes at Whitman, aren't you?"

"Yeah, like it's the closest one."

"For me too," Patty said, "I live on Lee Street."

"Oh, my gosh! I don't believe it," Isabel said, "I live on Berry Street. It runs parallel to Lee."

"Five hundred block!" Patty guessed, and stopped.

Isabel smiled and shrugged. "Seven hundred block."

"I so can't believe we haven't met before now," Patty said.

"You know, along with my being a loner, my family has only lived here for the past six months. My father is a consultant for a big contracting company, and he was transferred here from St Clairsville, Ohio."

"Really? That's just across the river," Patty said, "but as far as getting acquainted, it might as well have been across the country."

"That was where my adoptive parents lived when I was adopted when I was two- and-a-half years old. I so wish I knew where my real parents live."

"You don't know?" Patty touched Isabel's arm and they began walking toward their homes.

"No."

"You were never told?"

"Adoptions are sealed and kept secret as far as I know," Isabel said.

"Really? I didn't know that. I'm sorry, though, because I know how it feels not to know anything about your actual, birth family."

"I intend to find out someday," Isabel declared passionately. "Like, I don't talk to Mother about it. You know, it'd make her feel like I was ungrateful or something," she said, shrugging unhappily.

"I only recently found who my maternal grandmother was and where she lives. Also, I found out who a few others in my family are," Patty confessed. Her deep brown eyes sparkled with the determination to find out more about them. "Keep it under your hat, but that's what I want to write about. I know there's a story there, that's probably why I've always kept a journal. There's even been criminal activity in my family, and a bunch of cool stuff, and I don't know all the details about it, but I'm going to find out, and write my memoir."

Patty was ignorant of how great the curiosity had been about her father during the period following the attack on the World Trade Center. So had no idea that a memoir from the notorious Jacob McCallister's daughter, depicting her point of view, would be of major interest. She was also unaware of many events that had gripped her family and through the years kept it torn apart, and neither did she understand that only Aunt Aggie knew all the assorted parts and was the only one who would be willing to tell her about them one day. Patty had no idea that there was much more lawlessness and impoverishment that she didn't know about than that she did, but she did intend to get details from her Great Aunt Aggie for her memoir. Patty remembered the stories Aunt Aggie had told the children as they grew up on the remote mountain, and she always felt that there was a great deal of truth woven through the tales.

"Not to hurt your feelings, or to burst your bubble, but if you're not famous or something no one would want to buy it," Isabel said.

"That's just it," Patty explained. "What my pa's done is—like they say—in the air. You hear stories every day now about a missing child, and later it's found out that the child was sold or worse. That's just what my pa is known for, and as far as I know now, he sold his own children."

"Oh, my gosh! I can tell there's more."

"Except for the fact that he did time for child trafficking, I don't want to get into it all now, but I will. Really, I need to get to know you better."

"Patty, like that's so scary," Isabel said, her deep brown eyes reflecting the same sparkling intelligence as Patty's. "I don't know what to say."

"Really?" Patty raised eyebrows that suited her face naturally, without waxing or plucking. "We just met, but I just can't imagine you speechless."

Isabel laughed aloud, confident in their developing friendship.

Patty continued, "He'd be stupid to get involved in the same crime. Anyway, my stepfather is a detective, and because my pa would like to get back into Tuesday's and my life, believe me, my stepfather—with the law behind him—keeps an eye on him."

"I understand what you're saying, and I want to help," Isabel offered. "I admit I'm a little scared, especially after what you just told me, but you'll notice I haven't run from you as fast as I can."

"We can talk about all that later. For now, would you like to walk to summer school together this summer? We can do some research on both our families, and we can study together after school," Patty suggested.

"Yes, I would love that! Working together will be fun. Just think, like, we may actually become famous one day!"

"Why not? Famous people have to start from being anonymous at one point in their lives."

Isabel has no idea how far it really is from where and how I was raised to famous, Patty thought, not realizing that families like her own were just the thing that people watching the news channels looked for. *Pa's been on the news at different times for the many crimes that he's committed over the past years. And he's still under suspicion for the murder of Tommy Lee Hillberry.*

The media loved showing her father's darkly handsome face.

"True," Isabel said. "Anyway, I so need a diversion from worrying about my dreams."

"Really! Nightmares?" Patty stopped walking, mouth agape, surprised that Isabel had actually mentioned dreams in the same sentence as worry.

"No, it's not like that," Isabel said. "It's more like reoccurring dreams."

Patty stopped in her tracks and turned to face Isabel. Her hair was blowing across her forehead and she pushed it out of her eyes, which had lit up at the possibility of intrigue. "Really! Like something that happened or will happen?"

"Like dreams about people and places I've never been. Like, somehow they're too real. You know? It's so like memories."

"Isabel, do you ever dream about something and it happens?"

"I don't know why you're making such a big deal about my dreams. I don't want to go into detail about them now. I don't even know why I mentioned them. Like you said about talking about your father, when our friendship gets more comfortable with time we can share our outrageous secrets."

"You may think I'm only making this up because of what you're saying," Patty said, "but I have dreams too. They're about something that has happened in my family's past or is going to happen. Nightmare-like—well, sometimes they are—but only when my father's in them, then they . . ." Patty trailed off.

"They what . . . ?"

"Like we said, let's talk about it some other time," Patty said.

"Okay, but for the record, some would call what we're talking about psychic phenomenon." Isabel leaned into Patty and whispered as if someone were close enough to hear what she was saying. "People make money calling themselves psychics, and it's nothing but wrong!"

"Really, I know all that, and agree," Patty bristled, pushing her hair back from her face again. "I'm not into that garbage of fortune telling—and all the other crap those people do—or am I interested in making money on other people's heartbreak, only warning them if I can. But we are psychic whether you like it or not. It was a good thing when I helped my stepfather find the twins my father sold."

"Oh, my gosh!" Isabel said. "Like I'm not either, but people will call us witches if we talk about this in public."

"I never intended to be public about this, making people believe I can conjure up help for them. I just want to tell the story about my father. Believe it or not, my grandmother and mother have been called witches for years. As for me, my entire life, people thought I was strange. The woman who raised me got nervous every time I mentioned my dreams, and would change the subject by telling me to get my chores done and to stop talking nonsense. I think she knows something more than she has ever admitted to me or anyone else, and I intend to confront her about it and find out the truth for myself."

Isabel could not hold in her laughter, although there was obviously nothing humorous about the conversation they were having.

"What are you laughing about?" Patty could not imagine what was so funny.

"Oh, my gosh! I'm so sorry, but you did 'chores'?"

Patty blushed. After being in the city for the last few years she knew people did not use words that she had grown up using.

"Isabel, you have no idea how I was raised. It's like another world from here, a very harsh world."

CHAPTER 8

McCALLISTER DUCKED OUT OF THE way of the bat. He had been temporarily stunned by the suddenness of its startled flight, at first thinking he was under attack. In reality, he was alone in the cavern— with the exception of the family of bats that had taken up residence there.

Although McCallister knew the cavern had been constructed by the militia, instead of walking into the tunnel as he expected, he had stepped into the cavern. Light filtered into the huge room from the door McCallister had not closed behind him. The sudden, unwelcome light was the cause of the startled bat.

McCallister could see that the area had been taken over, in a big way, by someone other than the militia, who had been forced to disband and had abandoned the hideout long ago.

McCallister was not familiar with the additions that the militia had made to the tunnel. He had discovered the tunnel many years before, but he had never had much use for it. He didn't know what equipment the militia had set up or what Al-Zarquwi's people had installed to adapt the cavern for their use. All he knew was what Abu-Musab had told him: that Al-Zarquwi had had the connection from the cavern into the tunnel sealed off.

During the militia years the militiamen kept the cavern stocked with piles upon piles of crates filled with provisions that would have kept a small army alive for years. Now the crates were stacked twenty feet to the ceiling, covering the sealed opening that had once led into the tunnel that ran north and south from state to state. When the militia was using it, the opening connecting the tunnel and cavern had been expertly camouflaged from both sides.

Arranged across the huge area not taken up by the mountain of crates were four desks. Each desk had a computer, a phone, and a quadruple tray with ledgers and legal-sized binders piled in them. McCallister went to the nearest desk and picked up the phone. To his surprise, there was a dial tone. As far as he knew these were the only phones on the mountain above Winding Ridge—ever. Unnerved, he put the handset back in its cradle. He pulled out one of the ledgers and opened it as he took a seat in the leather chair.

Listed on the ledger, from top to bottom, were names. Each name was followed by a Social Security number, a phone number, a birth date, and an address, filling the width of the page. He used his forefinger to scan the full length of one ledger and then another. After going through several, he still had not found one name he recognized.

McCallister looked around the huge room and realized that there had been a great deal of work done by Al Qaeda's people. They were up to something big.

CHAPTER 9

OUTSIDE THE MORAN HOUSE, USING THE mailbox to support their notebooks, Patty and Isabel exchanged phone numbers, planning to get together soon. Finally, with a goodbye wave, Patty ran up the walk and disappeared into the house. And Isabel, smiling, happy to have met a new friend, continued walking toward her own street.

Patty was awfully curious about Isabel's dreams and wondered if it was fate that the two of them had met. It seemed too much of a coincidence that they were both contending with similar life issues, neither one ever having known her birthmother, her mother's background, or her mother's extended family.

"What are you doing home so late?" Tuesday called to Patty. "Mary Lou has been here for an hour."

"Sorry! I walked home with a new girl from school. We just met this afternoon. She's only lived here for six months. I guess we talked more than we walked."

"Oh, that's nice," Tuesday said. "You need to make more friends. I've worried that, unlike Mary Lou, you keep to yourself too much."

"Mary Lou has a boyfriend, and I don't," Patty reasoned.

"Oh! I've been known to say that the two of you are opposites, except that both of you had a crush on Paul Frank Ruble. But, Patty, she's moved on and you haven't," Tuesday raised her brows, relieved that Patty never asked who Mary Lou's boyfriend was.

Patty smiled. "I like to write, and I'm not ready to get my heart broken again. Anyway, my new friend is going to summer school too. It'll be nice to have a friend from the start. It can be lonely not knowing anyone. Having a friend to hangout with from the first day will be too cool."

"What's her name?"

"Isabel Brown."

"Not to change the subject, but I heard you up several times last night," Tuesday remarked. "Something bothering you?"

Patty shrugged, feeling uncomfortable; she sat at the piano and, running her fingers across the keys, picked out a popular tune.

"Patty! Don't do that when I'm talking to you." Tuesday turned for a better look at the girl. "Don't keep anything from me. You know we need to stick together and be open. After all, that's how we got this far. You've been having dreams again, haven't you?"

At Tuesday's command, Patty removed her hands from the keys and subconsciously reached for her doll. It had been positioned on the polished surface of the piano where she always put her when she intended to play. She placed the doll on her lap and stared defiantly at Tuesday.

"Oh, Patty, don't look at me that way. You know I think you're too old to be playing with dolls. And I can't understand why you won't let Winter Ann play with it."

"Tuesday, you know why. Summer is not just any doll. She and I have a connection with the past. You and Cliff both know there's more to it than simply having a dream that comes true, and you need to look past the fact that Summer is a doll. I know she is, but she's also a medium of some sort. You know, she's a way for me to get information about things that I don't understand."

"Oh, I know all that. I'm sorry." Tuesday put her arms around Patty, encompassing both the girl and the doll. "I just can't wrap my mind around all that's happened. Now that we're so far removed from it, I can hardly believe it happened at all. I simply want you to have a normal life for a change, just like other girls your age. That's all."

"Really, I know how you feel, but all that really happened, Tuesday. It did."

"I know, I know, Patty, it's so unreal."

"But . . ."

Tuesday shushed Patty. "Oh, Patty, I believe about the doll. I just can't help it, but on an everyday level I can't understand it. I know you live with it, and experience it, but you know it's not the same for me."

"I know you want me to try to forget everything. My dreams, my love for Paul Frank, and my old life," Patty said, "and I am. Really."

"Oh, Patty, that's not exactly right. You must never forget about your ability to predict danger through your dreams, and I never want any one of us to forget Paul Frank. Finally, you can and will learn from your old life."

"You don't like me to go there."

'You're talking about the mountain above Winding Ridge, aren't you?"

"Yes, I am."

"No, I don't. I'm afraid something will happen to you."

"I must find out about my family," Patty said simply, and Tuesday knew it was true.

"Tell me. Are you having dreams again? You've been looking worried lately."

"Really, Tuesday, I'm okay. Don't worry so much. It makes me feel bad."

"I don't want to make you uncomfortable, Patty. You know that. I just want what's best for you like any mother does."

"I understand that, but lighten up, okay?"

Patty didn't want to alarm anyone and therefore was not about to say anything just yet. Really, there was nothing to tell, except that she kept having this unsettling dream about Winding Ridge and witchcraft. She was also having vivid dreams about Paul Frank in which she could see him—as big as life—standing on the cobblestone road outside the sheriff's office. She could believe then that he wasn't really dead.

What was in truth calling her to the mountain—her recent dreams, and not her desire to write, or was it both? She could not talk about it to anyone. Paul Frank was gone, and thinking about those earlier days was too painful. Although two years had gone by and the grief had dimmed a great deal over the last year, she still couldn't talk about him without feeling the deep pain of loss. And still, she hated it when her birthplace was in her dreams—as always, it could only mean trouble. Not only that, her dreams eventually happened or turned out to be visions from the distant past that affected her life now. *How could dreaming about Paul Frank Ruble and witchcraft fit into past and present events?* she thought. The events that affected her in a negative way invariably took place on the mountain where she was born. What was with that?

These recent dreams about witchcraft had influenced Patty to dig into her old notes from school where, a few years before, she had done a paper on witchcraft. At that time, she had had a great interest in witchcraft, inspired by her history of prophetic dreams and the fact that she was often shunned by her peers and family because of the bizarre dreams she talked about. Most of all, it was because they were a forecast of future events. Conversations with her newly found grand-mother, about the history of family members being burned at the stake those many years ago, had inspired her even further to learn all she could.

"Patty! Aren't you listening to me?"

Patty was brought back to the present, "Really, you worry too much, Tuesday. Plus, I'm not in the frame of mind to get into all that now. Anyway, the dreams I'm hav-ing these days are not about my father. I know Jacob's ex-actly what comes to your mind whenever the subject of my dreams comes up."

Saving Patty from further questioning, Winter Ann ap-peared at the top of the stairs. Seeing Patty, she hurried down the stairs, wanting to be involved in whatever was going on in the house. The curls that she hated bobbed with each step.

Mary Lou was right behind Winter Ann, and the distrac-tion of the newcomers ended the conversation Tuesday and Patty were having.

"You're home! I knew you were," the eight-year-old said as she flung herself at Patty, "I heard you playing my favor-ite song. Were you playing it for me?" Winter Ann asked hopefully.

"I sure was," Patty said.

"Why did you stop?" Winter Ann asked.

Patty took the girl's shoulders and whispered, "Our mother made me."

Winter Ann gave Tuesday a frowning look.

"How was your day?" Patty asked Winter Ann and hugged her, while smiling at Mary Lou, whom she could see over Winter Ann's curls.

"It was the best. I love school, and my friend Karen and I have the best time. Know what?"

"No. What?" Patty asked, amused at Winter Ann's standard question, wondering when she'd ever grow out of it.

"We're the smartest ones in our class!"

"Oh, Winter Ann!" Tuesday admonished. "It's not polite for you to blow your own horn."

"Mom, that's so uncool."

"Oh! What's uncool?" Tuesday grinned, knowing exactly what Winter Ann was referring to.

"Blow your own horn!" Winter Ann exclaimed. Whoever heard of that?"

The girls got a good laugh at Tuesday's expense, and Mary Lou questioned Patty about Isabel. "I heard you talking about your new friend, and I'm glad to hear that you have someone to pal around with, Patty. You spend too much time alone. Or with that doll." Mary Lou rolled her eyes, grinning.

Patty stood up, clutching the doll. "I wish everyone would let up on me about Summer. You know it just makes me so angry, and I can't understand why you all don't just humor me—since I'm not giving up the doll!"

"I'm sorry, Patty," Mary Lou apologized. "I guess we just can't resist teasing you."

"I am, too," Tuesday said as she reached out and hugged Patty.

"Know what?" Winter asked.

"What?"

"I like Summer, but I have my own dolls, Patty doesn't have to give me hers."

Patty stooped and hugged Winter Ann. "You are a good sister."

Tuesday and Mary Lou looked at each other and shrugged.

CHAPTER 10

"I WAS STUDYIN' 'BOUT JEB ALL TH' DAY yesterday, so I was," Aggie announced.

"So what's new about that?" Annabelle grumbled.

"Don't get pert with me. Ya an' me have some things to sort out, so we do."

"Y'are goin' to tell me whether I'm wantin' to knowed or not," Annabelle said.

"I knowed ya been thinkin' 'bout 'movin', so ya have. But ya ain't thought 'bout some of th' problems I've been studyin' 'bout, so ya ain't. Such as, how it's goin' to be, all of us together in one cabin.

"Y'are just thinkin' 'bout seein' him again, so y'are. That's all ya think about, Jeb, Jeb, Jeb."

"I do think 'bout him all th' time, but that's not unusual," Annabelle said. "He's my man. I'm missin' 'im everyday. What's your excuse?"

"I knowed he's your man, same as for th' other women, so I do." Aggie looked smug. "But right now that's not th' problem, so it's not. With me, ya, Jeb, an' Sara there's goin' to be four adults an' a child in one place. Ya knowed I'm used to livin' by myself. Why before Jeb took ya an' th' other ones, him an' me lived in th' same place, just th' two of us. That was nice, though, so it was."

"Ya knowed, when it comes to Jeb, there's been more than five of us livin' in this four-room cabin at one time. It's been up to eight as I recall. Maybe where he's takin' us is goin' to be big as Frank Dillon's cabin where we stayed when Jeb was in jail."

"Ya callin' a one-room log cabin big? It ain't much bigger'n this cabin with its four rooms. His'n was one big room, an' had a woodburner in a corner, table in th' middle of th' cabin, rockin' chairs 'round th' potbelly stove, an' a bed in 'nother corner. Jus' 'cause it had a loft didn't make it bigger, so it didn't. Just a place for his women to crowd together an' sleep, an' I can tell ya, I didn't much like sleepin' on th' loft where a body could fall off, so I didn't.

"If ya ain't seen such a cabin, I can tell ya haven't traveled much in your lifetime, so ya haven't."

"Traveled more than ya have, ya weren't one of us taken to Wheelin' to testify 'bout Jeb, an' where we stayed wasn't anywheres near th' same as Dillon's cabin."

"Wouldn't testify against my nephew, so I wouldn't. I've got loyalty, so I do."

Hearing her great aunt's voice in the kitchen Kelly Sue appeared at the opening in the tattered curtain that divided the kitchen from the bedroom that she and her mother shared.

"Kelly Sue, don't hang on th' curtain, go see ya aunt," Annabelle said.

"Hi, Aunt Aggie," the young girl mumbled, and crossed the room and stood at the rocking chair where Aggie sat.

"Ya can go on an' play now," Annabelle said. "Ya all ready had your breakfast."

"There's no one to play with," Kelly Sue whined. "When's Ma comin' home?"

"She just left for th' store, ya knowed it as well as I do," Annabelle said. "Now go play for a while 'fore ya have to go an' do your chores."

"Kelly Sue, give ya old aunt another hug a'fore ya go."

Kelly Sue reached out and Aggie leaned forward and gave her a hug. Aggie lifted her up onto her lap. The little girl loved the attention. She missed her cousins whom she used to have around all the time to play with, and any diversion was welcome.

Before long, bored with the older women, Kelly Sue jumped from Aggie's lap. After playing with the cat for a while, she disappeared beyond the tattered curtain to play in her room. She enjoyed playing with the homemade toys, but even more, she liked the ones Daisy had bought for her and the twins at The Company Store in town before she left the mountain for good.

Two years ago, when Daisy had left the cabin in the dark of night with her twins in tow, she had carried her savings in a box, tucked under her arm. The money had been earned by waiting tables in the town bar. That and the clothes on their backs was all she had in the world. She had no thought of the children's toys or any other of their meager possessions. She thought only of finding Detective Cliff Moran, whom she knew to be conducting an investigation from the little town of Winding Ridge that spread out at the foot of the mountain. She was seeking the safety that he and the town represented. For her children's and her own safety, she had been bent on getting to Winding Ridge before Jacob McCallister woke from his drunken sleep.

"It's hard for th' child with no one her age 'round," Annabelle sympathized. "She surely misses Daisy's youngins."

"I know, an' it's th' first time since I can remember that there're no squallin' youngins runnin' round, so it is. Why, Jeb was always havin' his women droppin' a baby as often as possible, so he was."

"Aggie, what kind of talk is that? Why, y'are worse than Jeb talkin' like women're baby machines."

"We got a history ya don't even want to knowed 'bout, so we do. I suppose Jeb an' me mean so much to one another, we think alike. We've gone through so much together just to survive, so we have."

"Forevermore, I've heard all that before, an' ya knowed it's been a hard life for me without Jeb these past two years. I knowed all of us need 'im, but he don't treat any of us with respect. So, like ya say, I don't treat 'im an' Joe with respect, it ain't due 'em, an' that's why. But I just don't knowed what we'd've done without first, Joe, then Daisy, and then Sara, helpin' out after Jeb'd gone off to who'd knowed where. Since Joe's gone sometimes, Sara's talkin' 'bout gettin' away. I don't knowed what we're goin' to do without her if she goes," Annabelle worried. "She's been talkin' 'bout leavin' me just like all th' other'ns done."

"She's not got th' guts that 'em other'ns has, so she don't. I can't see her goin' anywhere on her own, so I can't." Aggie leaned forward till her fingers gripped the tin can she used for a spittoon and spit into it, once again unmindful of the spittle left to drip down her chin, darkening even more the brown stain that was already there.

"Well, I'm glad she's workin' at Th' Company Store, 'stead of th' town bar like Daisy did."

"But she's not makin' th' money like Daisy, so she's not. Ain't no tips workin' in Th' General Store. An' not as likely she'll save any money to amount to anythin' or meet a man, so it ain't."

"She spends her money on food an' such for us," Annabelle said.

"That's just why she ain't goin' anywhere, so it is."

Annabelle sat in the rocking chair across from Aggie, who, heedless of the tomcat's weight in her lap, subconsciously massaged its ears while it purred in appreciation. They were quiet for a time.

Each of the women was mesmerized by the fire in the stove, lost in thoughts of Jeb. The flames leapt through the grate in the potbelly's door, warming their faces and legs, as bright sparks fell into the ashbin and then burnt out, reduced to a fine powder. Soon it would be warm enough that they would no longer need the potbelly to warm the cabin in the early morning and evenings.

"Do ya think Jeb'll really come back and move us to another place?" Annabelle sighed, breaking the silence between them.

"Ya knowed I do, so I do. Said he was, so he'll come walkin' through that door like he always ends up doin', so he will. Only this time it'll be to change our lives forever."

"Well, I guess it wouldn't hurt none to change out lives—can't imagine it bein' worse. I've seen better when I was in th' city."

"Oh y'are a liar. Ya wouldn't leave here for any reason, 'less Jeb's takin' ya away, so ya wouldn't."

"I hope it ain't goin' to be like when he knew he was goin' to jail an' he moved us to Frank Dillon's place." Annabelle ignored Aggie's insult. "I can't abide bein' bossed around again by th' likes of Big Bessie."

"Don't think it's goin' to be like that this time, so I don't. 'Cause he's goin' to be there. Ya knowed he likes worldly comforts, so he does."

"Do ya think he'll go after Tuesday an' Patty again?"

"Nope, so I don't." Aggie made light of the idea that Jeb would be so careless. "It ain't as if they can't find their way back home, an' Tuesday' knows her way around th' mountain since Paul Frank an' Patty helped her an' Mary Lou get away, so she does. It ain't like when he brought Tuesday here drugged an' she had no idea where she was, so it ain't. She'd not seen anything like it. An' Patty was just a little girl at th' time—had never been off th' mountain. He knows th' time's past when he could keep them against their will. He told me so, so he did."

"I hope y'are right 'bout that." Annabelle rose to lay another log on the fire, in the already too-warm room. She got the mitt from the wood box and, gripping the handle, pulled the door open. She chose a log, threw it into the fire, and slammed the door against the immense burst of tiny sparks.

"I usually am, so I am."

"Do ya think Patty or Tuesday'll come back to th' mountain ever again?" Annabelle asked, as she settled her large form into her rocking chair once again.

"Ya ask that all th' time, an' th' answer's th' same. It's yeah. I do think so, so I do. Patty's already come tryin' to find her family once an' she ain't done with that. She'll not be satisfied 'till she learns who her family is."

"Forevermore," Annabelle lectured, "I can't think why you'd think she'd come back here after what happened th' year Paul Frank was murdered. She's already found out who her grandmother is."

"You'll see, so ya will."

"Look where it got her," Annabelle quarreled. "It almost got her killed. And like I said, Paul Frank got himself killed helpin' her."

"I knowed that, but that girl's set on findin' out 'bout her family. Anyway, I'm cravin' to see Winter Ann. She's Jeb's daughter an' th' only one of his children I ever got close to, so she is."

"Hogwash," Annabelle spat. "There never was but three of his children he let us keep 'round long enough to get close to, an' ya never got close to them; even though Joe, Sara, and Patty helped ya with your chores, kept ya company. Not only that, th' youngins' made sure ya had what ya needed when Jeb was gone. How can ya sit there an' expect me to believe ya have a hankerin' to see Winter Ann—a child ya ain't never been 'round. Th' child ain't old enough to go traipsing round th' mountain with a teenager no how."

"Was too 'round Winter Ann, so I was. I helped take care of her th' very first days of her life. Ain't got to do that with any of th' others, so I didn't."

"Ya expect me to buy that?" Annabelle quarreled. "Ya was present at every birth that went on in this cabin. Ya could've taken care of any one of them as much as ya wanted. Why we was even beggin' help, an' I ain't hearin' ya givin' one ounce of breath frettin' over where those youngins're an' worryin' if ya'll ever see one of them ever again!"

"This one is different, so it is." Aggie stubbornly stuck to her declaration of fondness for Winter Ann. "An' I—"

Whatever Aggie was going to say was cut off by the slamming of the screen door. She and Annabelle gave a gasp.

CHAPTER 11

IT WAS THE LAST DAY OF SCHOOL, AND FINALLY the bell rang, signaling the end of classes. Patty and Isabel gathered their books, and along with their classmates, shouldered their way to the door. After reaching the hallway, Patty invited Isabel to dinner that night. She had already cleared it with Tuesday. "After we eat, we can go to the mall. Even though I've lived in Wheeling for the past six years, I can't get enough of the excitement at being in the mall. So many people, and there's stuff from the smallest piece of jewelry to great big boats in the hallways."

Isabel looked at Patty with an expression of skepticism. "I'll call my Mom from your house, but what's the big deal of a mall to you? To anyone else, it's so-o-o not a big deal, like kids hangout there every day."

"I know, but never mind right now," Patty smiled. "That's part of what we'll talk about after dinner."

"Oh my gosh, your enthusiasm about going to the mall is almost more weird than you being so interested in my dreams, like you're starting to creep me out."

"Really! Don't be so melodramatic. You know I have a reason to be interested in your dreams."

"Okay, Isabel said, "I just never met a teenager so excited about simply going to a mall. That's just something we do. Anyway, I don't get it.

"I have to go to my locker before we leave," Isabel remembered. "I need to clean it out. There's a pair of gym shoes and a couple of books that I need to get."

"Me too." Patty agreed.

All around them kids were spilling from their various classrooms, filling the hallways, going to and from their lockers, shouting their plans, anxious to get to their afternoon activities, all the while with the idea looming in their minds of freedom from homework for the next three months. The din of young voices, rising to the high, domed ceiling hallway, drowned out any chance of having a real conversation.

Later, strolling along the sidewalk, in the quiet of the tree-lined streets, Patty and Isabel found themselves talking about their dreams once again. It was a subject they had seemed to skirt around ever since they had met.

Now that their relationship had moved to a new level, Patty had invited Isabel to dinner that night so that she could reveal a special secret to her new friend. This thrilled Isabel because she knew that Patty was going to share something with her that she had never told anyone outside her family.

As they moved beyond the early stages of becoming best friends, they were becoming even closer, as generally only sisters can be. And they walked and talked with arms linked, two extremely pretty, dark-haired teenagers about the same height, each blessed with olive skin, and deep, dark, brown eyes.

As they moved on, Isabel revealed to Patty more of her own unusual and oddly familiar dreams. The dreams brought to her images of a way of life she could not have knowledge of unless it was memories from an extremely young age, she explained. But that could not be. No one remembered from infancy.

Patty was overwhelmed by what they had in common and what it could mean. It was like having someone other than Tuesday understanding her, easing her past experiences of being an outsider and the feeling that everyone saw her as abnormal.

Now with some reservation, each of them sensed that the other felt the same close kinship.

Stopping under a huge silver maple tree, Patty waited until Isabel noticed and stopped too.

Fearing she had told too much, and misinterpreting Patty's expression of relief for revulsion, the new sense of kinship Isabel felt was about to dissolve. She turned away with a hurt look on her face. Except for her parents and Patty, to whom she had dropped only tidbits here and there; Isabel had never told a soul about her dreams.

"Really, Isabel. Don't look so solemn," Patty let herself smile at the worried girl. "I know how you feel. People have made fun of me my entire life for having dreams I could not explain."

"You've been laughed at?" Isabel asked, hardly daring to acknowledge the feeling of empathy from someone who'd had the same experiences. The warm sensation of kinship washed over her once again.

"I have, and believe me a psychiatrist is not the answer."

"I don't think that Mom thinks so anymore, either," Isabel offered.

"And they're not," Patty said decisively. "I want to take you someplace, Isabel. Would your parents let you go visit my childhood home? We'd be gone for the weekend."

"Sure, I'd love to go with you, but why? A minute ago, you were all agog about going to the mall. You're sounding so mysterious about everything." Isabel wore a curious look on her face.

"Going to the mall is tonight, and I'm still wound-up about going. Really, it'll be fun, but when you were telling me about your dreams, I was reminded of a particular place, the place I grew up. I want to see if where I grew up reminds you of the place your dreams are coming from. That's all," Patty answered. "Do you think your parents will allow you to go?"

"Oh, my gosh!" Isabel gave Patty a blank stare. "Why wouldn't they? I'm not a child."

"No reason." Patty continued walking, and Isabel followed.

"I thought you were overly interested in my recent dreams the first time we met and I mentioned them to you, and you are. Why? Are you saying, like, you think we were raised in the same town?"

"No. Families don't leave the mountain. It's like they can't. Anyway, that would be too much of a coincidence. But where I was raised could trigger memories for you, because when you describe your dreams, I'm reminded of my growing up years. Isabel, I've admitted that I have dreams of my past, but I also have some that are even more frightening when they're of the future—and they come to pass. The dreams of the past are of people and events that can be traced back to my ancestors."

"Oh, my gosh! I'm speechless," Isabel said.

"Really?" Patty could not help grinning as Isabel kept chattering.

"Like I've had dreams and they happen, but I've been afraid to tell anyone. Even you." Isabel glanced at Patty. "I know for someone whose speechless, I'm going on and on about it. Most of them, though, I've always sensed were really memories of my very early childhood, but, get this, for some reason I haven't told my mother, or anyone, of the ones that have actually happened. Maybe I believed I would be laughed at, like you were."

"You haven't been speechless since we met!" Patty said after Isabel wound down, unable to stop a fit of laughter.

"Like you've ever been speechless, I sure can't attest to that either," Isabel giggled. "Tell me more about your dreams, Patty. Like why you were not afraid of people thinking you had lost your mind, and told your family your dreams were going to happen."

"Really, I was, but I wasn't smart enough to keep them to myself, like you did. And the fact is, had I not talked about them, some very good things would not have happened."

"Like what?"

"I was waiting until after dinner, and before we went to the mall, for us to talk in my room where we can be relaxed and share our stories. I know we both will have a lot of questions for each other."

"You've gotten me curious. Tell that one while we're walking to your house."

"I told you a little of it, and I don't remember what."

"That's cool, just tell it," Isabel said.

"Okay. The twins." Patty was a little nervous about telling Isabel about the event, but she knew it needed to be told to her new friend. "They were born to Daisy and my father. My father sold them when they were only two years old. A few years after that, he kidnapped Tuesday, keeping her in the cabin against her will. I would sneak into the room where she was and talk to her. I was so intrigued—I had never seen anyone like her except in a Sears catalog, modeling clothes. Really, I thought she was a fairy godmother, like in the stories my Aunt Aggie told.

"Anyway, to make a long story short, I told Tuesday that Pa sold many of his children through the years, and that included the twins, who I was having dreams about. And she understood, and told me there were studies about people who had my gift. I think that's when I fell in love with her. She was the only person that understood—ever.

"Tuesday knew Cliff was working the missing children division, and he was the detective who found Linda, Cora's daughter. Cora is Tuesday's closest friend. After Cliff rescued Tuesday and me from the cellar house, she told him about the twins during the ambulance ride to the hospital. Because Cliff is a detective, she believed he could help.

"One interesting thing is, because the twins were sold by their own father, it explained why they were not reported missing. Well, during the investigation into Tuesday's disappearance, Cliff had found twins he couldn't trace, and because they had not been reported missing, he made the connection.

"Anyway, the twins were found with a family who mistreated them. That's why I told Tuesday about them, I saw that in my dreams too. After all they were my brother and sister, and because of the information I was able to give, they were taken away from the people who had them. Cliff's boss and his wife adopted them, you know, because Daisy could not take proper care of them. Anyway, to return them to her would put them in danger because she lived with the man who sold them in the first place."

"Oh, my gosh, what a story that's going to make. I'm speechless."

"Yeah, right," Patty laughed. "Speechless."

Enjoying a glass of iced tea before the girls got in from school, Tuesday and Cliff were having a rare moment together at the kitchen table, as this was a time in the day that Cliff was not normally home from the office. Accordingly, they were taking advantage of the quiet time, before the girls got home and the house filled with the laughter and chaos as they did their assigned chores and helped with dinner. With the four girls, including Isabel, there was always plenty of happy chatter and rowdiness, but now even more than usual because they were excited, looking forward to the summer break that loomed just ahead of them.

"I want to talk to you about something before the girls get home," Cliff said, breaking the mood. "There's word at the office that McCallister is being investigated by Homeland Security concerning the attack on 9/11 and new threats of terrorism."

"Oh! What could he have to do with terrorism?" Tuesday was put out by the sudden change of atmosphere.

"Apparently Johnny Michael was conducting an unrelated investigation and found something interesting in a transcript detailing an interview with someone named Buddy Dean Howerton about his activities on 9/11, I'm concerned about that."

"Are you saying Jacob is connected with this man?"

"Yes, and a more dangerous one, Al-Zarquwi, who is a known terrorist. More worrisome is that in the transcript there's an interview with Howerton concerning his possible connection with Al-Zarquwi. Howerton denies it, of course, but Howerton has been seen with Al-Zarquwi's right-hand man, Abu-Musab, and on one other occasion Howerton was seen in a bar with McCallister."

"So, if this Howerton knows both Abu-Musab and Jacob, you're thinking it ties into Jacob being at the World Trade Center when it was attacked."

"It fits," Cliff said. "But most important there continues to be some connection."

"It's Jacob McCallister all over again!" Tuesday moaned, frowning. "Will I forever live in his shadow?"

Cliff took Tuesday's hand. It was well known that she felt she was to blame for their family living under the constant threat of Jacob McCallister, not fully recognizing that she was the one victimized, and apparently forgetting she had saved Patty from a life of poverty.

"Should I be frightened?" Tuesday asked.

"I really don't believe he has any way of knowing about the suspicion brought on by the transcript, but if—on the off chance—he did, there might be cause for worry." Cliff ran his fingers through his unruly hair. "You and I know he knows we want him locked up for the rest of his life. He wouldn't want us finding out and getting involved in something that could get him arrested again, knowing we'd be more than happy to get him back behind bars."

"Oh, he'd be right about that," Tuesday said. "That's exactly what I want. He's dangerous. Cliff, he's a constant threat to our family."

"Has Patty been having any dreams lately?"

"If she has, she's not talking," Tuesday frowned again. "She's been acting worried lately, and I came right out and asked if she was having dreams again. She denied it."

The sound of female voices came sing-songing from the front of the house, and Tuesday took Cliff's hand. "We need to talk later." She was unsettled by their conversation and wanted to find out more but knew she would have to wait. The girls demanded their attention as they came into the room.

The girls rushed in, changing the mood back to a happy one, as Cliff and Tuesday knew they would. Patty was pleased that Cliff was there and introduced him to Isabel.

CHAPTER 12

ANNABELLE AND AGGIE EACH WORE LOOKS that changed from bewilderment to glee and back again, having not expected to see Jeb so soon after learning he was coming back to take them away from the only life and shelter they'd ever known. Neither of them was over hashing back and forth about him and what was going to happen. In truth, although they wanted him home, they feared moving to a strange and new place.

"Don't the two of you have anything better to do than rock in those damn chairs of yours all day?"

"Jeb, what on earth're ya doin' here?" Annabelle asked, grabbing her chest, in the excitement of seeing him and the dread of what was coming next in a life filled with bending to his will no matter what. Although for days they had talked of nothing except his return and what it would mean to them, both Aggie and Annabelle were completely taken aback by his abrupt appearance at the kitchen door.

"This cabin happens to belong to me, and when I see fit, I spend time here or not," Jeb said as he strolled in, as though he hadn't been gone for two years, and took his usual place at the table, making himself at home. "What do you think?"

For a long moment, he held Annabelle's gaze with his dark, brown eyes. "You know I always come home in the end. I told Joe to let you all know to expect me, and I know that he did. So what's all the fuss about?"

He fixed the women with a penetrating stare.

Annabelle could see no love in Jeb's piercing eyes. There was only his need shining through. Need for her to do as he wanted, which meant keeping his house and keeping food on his table.

Although all she and Aggie wanted to talk about from the day Jeb went away was his return, she now had the most hopeless, sinking feeling in her gut. She was sure that he was up to something that—in the end—would only bring unhappiness and trouble, ending the tranquility she had enjoyed these past few years with the radio as her companion. She now realized—with clarity—that her longing for Jeb was simply a habit. She'd never learned the hard fact that life was better without him—as she ought to have—all through the days that Daisy took care of their needs, and especially now that Sara was such a trustworthy provider. She provided what they needed with love, not just out of necessity as Jeb had always done, as if he were tending to barnyard animals.

Nevertheless, each of the women—had acts of affection been permitted —would have jumped up and hugged Jacob, but overtly showing affection would likely get Annabelle at least slapped. Jacob seemed not to have the inclination to use force with his aunt. As far as Sara was concerned, as was the case with her siblings long gone, she would never consider, or have any desire whatsoever to hug her distant, unloving father.

"Annabelle, I'm hungry," Jeb said. His aura and magnetism commanded attention. That was the thing Tuesday had noticed when she had agreed to have dinner with him that fateful day years ago—his charisma. Had he been so inclined, and had he not chosen to lead a life of crime, with his looks and allure he could have become an actor and gone on to stardom.

Moving to the woodburner, Annabelle adjusted the flue. She added wood in preparation for cooking Jeb's meal. She had many questions that begged asking, but knew her man would not reveal anything to her unless he wanted to.

"What's goin' on?" Aggie asked in a low voice, believing he would tell her with Annabelle's attention focused on the preparations for the meal.

"Not a thing. Not a thing,"

"Ain't ya wanted by the law?" Aggie was put out by her nephew's refusal to tell her what she wanted to know. "Last I knowed, ya was wanted in connection with Paul Frank an' Tommy Lee's deaths, an' for fakin' your own death, so ya was."

"No proof. And you well know that the Rudd boy was charged and convicted of Paul Frank's murder," Jacob spat this out through clenched teeth. "As far as I know there's nothing known as to who killed Tommy Lee and why."

"Well, they're watchin' ya, so they are."

"Aunt Aggie, there's no reason for the law to be interested in me. The only thing they were bent on finding out was why I was at the World Trade Center when it was attacked. Just because I wasn't seen by anyone for months after 9/11 doesn't mean I was faking my death. No one collected on my life insurance, so there's not any fraudulent intent, and if they couldn't find me after the 9/11 attack, so what? Who did I have to report to? No one!"

Annabelle as usual could not hold her tongue. "Are ya sayin' your family's no one. What 'bout me an' your youngins? What 'bout your aunt?"

"Shut up, Annabelle."

Without another word, Annabelle turned back to the stove. In spite of all his selfishness and cruelty, she wanted to be with her Jeb and was willing to put up with anything to have him. She had been with him since she was a mere child.

"So y'are back here 'cause y'are free from th' law now?" Aggie asked.

"That and I have a new outlook. I'm going to use my education and my new connections to make big bucks."

"How's that?" Aggie prodded.

"Oh, you'll see, so ya will," Jacob said, heartlessly mocking Aggie's tendency to confirm her own statements.

Not knowing he was making fun of her way of speaking, she ignored his unkind tone of voice as she would with no other. "I'm happy to know y'are smart enough to stay away from kidnappin', so I am."

"You've got that right. The main thing I learned behind bars was that what I was doing was penny ante stuff. But I must say it kept me in big money and worked while it lasted.

"Have the two of you ever heard of Al Qaeda?"

Annabelle and Aggie gaped at him. They knew what he was talking about. During 9/11 and the years afterward, they had religiously followed any newscasts detailing the attack on the World Trade Center.

They had heard all the talk about Al Qaeda and the other terrorists creating havoc around the world and, like other American's, feared that another violent attack was sure to come.

Later that evening, Annabelle and Aggie were quarreling as usual. They were free to do as they pleased with Jeb gone again. Aggie was preparing to return to her own cabin when, with a slam of the door, Sara entered the kitchen. She had caught the last of Annabelle and Aggie's disagreement about their respective and rightful places in Jeb's life, as each of them boldly voiced her own idea of what he was up to.

"Ma, ya always see Pa with rose colored glasses. Ya just don't knowed what he's capable of," Sara said.

Hearing her mother's voice, Kelly Sue cantered through the doorway; leaving the bedroom she and Sara shared. Getting tangled for a moment in the ragged curtains that hung in the doorway, easily shaking them off, she ran to her mother. Sara scooped her small daughter up into her arms and gave her a kiss on the cheek.

"Ya getting' uppity, girl, so ya are. Rose-colored glasses? Who'd ever heard of such a thing?" Annabelle asked.

"Aunt Aggie, ya an' Pa're like two peas in a pod," Sara said. "Th' two of ya only think 'bout yourselves."

"That's no way to speak to me or your aunt," Annabelle snapped.

"You're right, Ma. I'm sorry, Aunt Aggie. I've had a bad day, but I get sick an' tired of hearin' th' two of ya, talkin' about Pa all th' time. He's gone, an' I say good riddance."

Aggie stood and, drawing herself up to her full height of five feet, said, "I won't hear of ya talkin' 'bout my nephew, Jeb, thataway, so I won't."

"I'm sorry, Aunt Aggie, but ya an' Ma just refuse to see him as he is," Sara said.

"Ya don't knowed everythin', so ya don't."

"I know enough." Sara hugged her daughter tighter. "An' sometimes I wonder why ya take up for him."

"Sara, your pa's in town, he'd come back home," Annabelle intervened.

Sara's face fell.

CHAPTER 13

IN PATTY'S ROOM AFTER DINNER, ISABEL AND Patty sprawled across the bed talking, with Summer propped between them. "I haven't ever told anyone outside my family about my doll." Patty picked up the doll as she talked.

"This is the secret you planned to tell me?"

"Yes, Isabel, this doll is very important to me."

"Oh, my gosh, you still have a doll?" Isabel was not surprised at Patty having a doll, but was shocked that she handled it and kept it on her bed. Isabel herself had dolls from her childhood that she didn't want to part with, but she kept them in boxes at the top of her closet.

Patty could see in Isabel's face and hear in her tone of voice that she did not understand about the doll. That was no shocker she knew that it was inevitable for people not to understand. How could they?

"I know it is strange to you that someone my age has a doll, Isabel, but Summer has helped me understand my dreams as no one ever has."

"Her name's Summer?" Isabel asked, only to have something to say and try to lighten the mood.

"Yes, didn't you name your dolls?"

"I did, but I put them away a long time ago." Isabel raised her eyebrows.

"This doll is different," Patty explained as if she were talking to a child. "It is some sort of medium."

"Oh, my gosh. That is spooky," Isabel gushed. "Like, who'd ever believe a doll could have the ability to communicate with you, or anyone for that matter."

"Really! She is like a medium, and I know it's spooky. Tuesday won't even talk about the doll, except to ask when I'm going to put it away or give it to Winter Ann, and she knows that I have foresight in my dreams. She has seen first-hand how when I tell her of dreams and . . . they happen just like I tell her, time after time."

"Winter Ann's an inquisitive child," Isabel said, changing the subject, "It's so cute her asking 'Know what?' each time she's going to tell you something."

"Really, and she won't go on until she's asked, 'No, what?'"

"Is there something special about her being named Winter Ann?"

"Yes," Patty held the doll up. "Winter Ann Summer."

"Oh, my gosh. I get it," Isabel smacked her forehead with the palm of her hand.

"Anyway, after everything you've told me, I still don't understand," Isabel said, "and I really don't think my dreams are like yours. Like, I don't know, except for a few strange ones where something—clearly not as notable as in yours—comes to pass, but most are familiar, like memories are."

"Really!" Patty raised her eyebrows. "Like I've said, just maybe you're remembering your life before you were adopted in some. And other dreams are a foretelling."

"I guess so, and I thought of that, but as for the memory-like dreams, people just don't remember back to infancy."

"Really," Patty mused. "Everyone's not the same. All the time, you hear of unexplainable events of the extraordinary involving people."

"I suppose, but it'd be pretty cool happening to me if it wasn't so scary," Isabel worried.

"Remember I told you that I'm writing a memoir? And you said you were too. Maybe we could tie them together some way."

"Yeah, like using the psychic and paranormal connections."

"It's going to be about my family," Patty explained. "The fact that we met I think is part of it."

"Like our divine destiny."

"Something like that," Patty frowned. "You're not making fun of me, are you?"

"Oh, my gosh, no."

"Really, there is so much mystery, past and present. So much we don't know about our real parents. Most importantly for public interest there's my father's life. And, like you, I really don't know much about my mother, except she was sold to my father against her will. There's so much more to learn about her, I'm sure, besides what my grandmother—who I came to know as my grandmother only two years ago—has told me."

"What do you mean 'as your grandmother'?"

"I knew her as the witch who lived at the edge of the forest. She lived two miles below the cabin I was born and raised in."

"I can see where we're going with that," Isabel said, remembering the conversations about Patty's ancestors being accused of being witches.

"Where are we going to start?" Isabel asked, sitting up straight. All this new information whet her natural curiosity and motivated her to get involved, as she had not been before.

"Really. You're going to help?"

"Oh, my gosh! You have me so curious, like how could I not?"

"That's why I've asked you go with me to my hometown for a weekend."

"Yeah. I said I'd go. But I'm still scared."

"I am too, but we must." Patty squared her shoulders.

"You don't seem like you're frightened at all."

"Believe me, I am," Patty admitted, "but before we start summer school, we're going to take our first trip to Winding Ridge."

"Winding Ridge? You mentioned you were raised there, but I never heard of it before you," Isabel said.

"It's where I was born. Well, actually in a small cabin on the mountain about four miles above Winding Ridge, that is."

"Sounds cool. I asked my mother when we talked about it before," Isabel said. "She wants to meet your mother first, but she said if it meant so much to me, I could go. I didn't tell her about your interest in my dreams or in writing. I think my dreams freak my parents out, and I haven't told them the whole of it."

"She'll like Tuesday and Cliff and say yes."

"Like who wouldn't like your adoptive mother and father?" Isabel said.

"They're cool, aren't they?"

"My mother and I are not apart much except for school, but she's always wanted me to have my own friends."

"Are you afraid, since I told you about the crime in my family?" Patty asked, teasing.

"Oh, my gosh no! For all I know my birth parents are in a prison, or worse, themselves. There's got to be a reason they didn't keep their own child."

"Okay. We'll plan on going next weekend. That will give us time to do some more research on my ancestors."

"Yes, and there are three more weeks before summer school," Isabel said. "That will give us time enough."

"We've got a plan," Patty grinned. "And I'll tell you more about my life as we travel to my place of birth. I think it'll be more intriguing that way."

"You really are going to be a writer," Isabel said, rolling her eyes. "Like with that ability to be so melodramatic. . ."

"And you're not?" Patty raised her brows.

"Maybe not as much as you."

"That's your opinion."

"Let's go to the mall," Isabel said, needing to clear her head.

It was the day before Patty and Isabel were to leave for Winding Ridge. It had taken some doing to get their parents to agree to the trip when it had actually come down to it. They had reluctantly agreed, though, especially now that the girls were eighteen, and Isabel would turn nineteen in a month. She had never seen her birth certificate because her adoption was closed, according to the attorney, George Cunningham, and the names of her parents were to be kept undisclosed. And there was no birth certificate for Patty, her date of birth had been chosen by Tuesday using process of elimination, and by calculating Sara's and Joe's ages, which were not known precisely, either.

Since Patty's most recent visit, during which she had found her parental grandmother, and all had gone well, Tuesday and Cliff were a little more confident that there was no reason for Patty to be afraid of her father, who no longer lived on the mountain.

During Patty's trip two years earlier, McCallister was not the one who had kept her hostage—it had been Tommy Lee Hillberry. He had been a schoolmate who was obsessed with Patty. Her brother, Joe, had kept him away from her through intimidation and a reputation for whipping to submission anyone who crossed him.

That was the fateful year Paul Frank was murdered—and Patty refused to let fear of a heartless father control her life. Anyway, he knew there was no way he could get back into Tuesday's, Patty's, and Winter Ann's lives, and surely would realize that he would be the first one blamed if harm came to any one of them.

Regardless, Tuesday and Cliff were married now, and she and Patty had the Moran name, a protection they had not had when Tuesday and Jacob McCallister met. Tuesday's parents and grandparents had died at young ages, leaving Tuesday an orphan, which had made it easy for McCallister to step in and take advantage of her.

The greatest pull to the mountain for Patty was her newly found grandmother. So far Patty had not brought her grandmother to the city to live as she had promised. Patty felt the need to keep her grandmother informed about the details she was working out for them to live near each other. There was no phone service to the cabins on the mountain above Winding Ridge, plus Patty's grandmother had never learned to read—so the only way for them to communicate was for Patty to go there.

Having never held a job, Patty's grandmother was totally dependent on her son for her needs, as she was not collecting Social Security or any governmental help. Knowing all this, Patty fantasized about how great her grandmother's awe was going to be at her first experience with modern conveniences. She conjured up mental pictures of her grandmother learning to use a phone, watching a TV show for the first time, and having indoor plumbing for the first time in her life. Moreover, Patty got joy from how those things would change her grandmother's life, knowing how they had changed her own and how blown away she had been learning something new and up-to-the-minute almost every day.

Patty could not help smiling at the memories of Annabelle, Sara, Daisy, and the others when they had been introduced to the many modern conveniences four years ago when her stepfather, Cliff Moran, had them transported to Wheeling as witnesses to Jacob McCallister's crimes of child trafficking. And that exposure was only a cheap hotel room in a small city.

CHAPTER

14

"WHERE'S SARA?" JEB ASKED. "I'M taking you all to my new place, and we're going now."

"What 'bout me an' my cats?" Aggie asked.

"I don't care about your damn animals one way or the other, but I'll need your help. The house is going to need the two of you to keep it up. Why are the two of you avoiding my question?"

"What question?" Aggie asked, showing off her position as his confidant. As such, she had a firm belief she could test Jeb's temper as no other could. He chose, though, to put his aunt in her place and directed his question toward Annabelle instead. "Where are Sara and the child?"

"Sara ain't goin' to like movin," Annabelle said stubbornly. .

"That's not what I asked you!" Jeb's temper was audible in his voice. "And I don't give a damn what she likes, and you know it."

"She's right, so she is," Aggie said as she puffed out her chest, determined to hold her position.

Jeb gave Aggie and Annabelle looks of warning.

"I have to tell ya th' truth, Jeb. Ya knowed Patty an' Daisy ran away from ya because y'are so cross to us," Annabelle said incredulous. "An' ya thinkin' Sara's just goin' to say, 'Oh, goody,' when ya tell her we're movin'. Why she's got a job at Th' General Store in town. She ain't givin' that up.

"How'd ya thinkin' we got all this good food?" Annabelle continued. "Ya an' Joe sure don't keep us in th' fresh food, an' snacks an' such."

Jeb slapped her. "So that's where she is. That's going to stop."

Annabelle's face stung at the slap, but even worse was the indignity of his behavior as Aggie looked on.

"Where's the child?"

At the mention of her mother's name in connection with the ringing smack of a sharp slap, Kelly Sue had come into the kitchen. She ran quickly for the safety of the hem of Aggie's dress, using it to cover her face.

"Shush, child." Aggie tugged the hem of her dress from the frightened girl's grip and lifted her onto her lap, causing the cat to jump to the floor.

"Well, that answers my question. Aggie, quit fooling with that child and tell me when Sara's going to be home."

"Jeb, Annabelle just told me 'fore ya came in, Sara should be here anytime, so she should."

"Where's th' new place that your takin' us?" Annabelle asked, hiding her anger at being slapped. In light of the fact that the women often quarreled about who was his favored one, it was especially embarrassing that he had slapped her in Aggie's presence.

"You wouldn't know if I told you, Annabelle. All I need is for you get yourself and the child ready. Do it now! Aunt Aggie, you come with me. I'll take you to your cabin to get your things together. After that, we'll come back for

Annabelle, Sara, and the child. If Sara's not here, we'll go without her."

"Ya can't do that!" Annabelle cried. "Sara'll be heartbroken if'n ya take her baby from her."

"She should be where she belongs then."

Without another word, Aggie and Jeb left.

CHAPTER 15

As they drew closer to Winding Ridge, Isabel grew uneasy. "We're like getting real close aren't we?"

"Yes, the turnoff to Winding Ridge is just a mile more." Patty glanced over at Isabel. "Looks familiar, doesn't it?"

"I don't know."

"Really?" Patty asked.

"Yes."

"Really, are you saying that you don't like what you're seeing?"

"No, but it's like really remote, and I'm sure it's not familiar."

"You've got the remote part right," Patty grinned. "And, I guess even if you were remembering this area in your dreams, this wouldn't be familiar to you. You were very young when you were adopted and would have been too young to have explored the area you originally came from. You know Pa never took his women or children anywhere. The children, the ones he did sell, spent their entire lives inside our cabin until they were sold."

"Patty, it's too far-fetched that my adoptive parents got me from the same place you came from so forget it. Anyway, like, I want to hear about you, and you agreed as we were traveling to fill me in on your early life. I want to know more about your life here," Isabel said.

"Then I'll tell you, and I've all ready told you a lot more than I've ever told anyone. And as for the rest of it, now's the time, if there ever is going to be one.

"I was raised on the mountain up ahead in a small four-room cabin with—at the least at any given time—three women who shared my father as a husband. He fathered their respective children. My father sold the women's children for profit, with the exception of Joe, Sara, and me. We were kept around to do the work. I suppose had I not been rescued by Tuesday, I would have been having babies like Sara. I don't really know how old I am, because there are no birth records, and Pa's women had no way of knowing or recording the date. They've never learned to read or write. Tuesday and Cliff guessed my age from what Annabelle and Aggie told them about my birth, and they assigned me an official birthday." Patty grinned at the last thought, and then continued telling Isabel everything she could remember.

Isabel sat beside Patty, listening wide-eyed at Patty's description of life on the mountain, being raised by multiple women, and her father when he was there. Also, she described living with her half-brother and half-sister. Isabel could hardly envision Patty's life as she characterized it.

"So now you know some of it," Patty concluded. "I have countless half-brothers and sisters I'll never see or know about, really, simply because my father sold his children for profit."

"Countless?" Other than this one word, Isabel was speechless and did not ask for more information. The ramifications from the story Patty was spinning were numerous, and she needed time to digest what she had just learned.

"You look like you were struck dumb," Patty said, startling Isabel from her pensive state.

"Oh, my gosh!"

"Is that all you've got to say?"

"Are you kidding me? Like, I don't know what to say."

"Really? Come on," Patty probed.

"Patty, are you thinking what I think you are? Like, if you are, it's too much of a coincidence."

"Really!" Patty tilted her head toward Isabel.

"Watch the road," Isabel shouted.

"You know it could be true. Even Cliff thought we looked alike. I've always been told that I favor my father, who has dark hair, the same olive skin coloring, and deep brown eyes. Just like us!"

"Let's reserve judgment," Isabel said. "We have a long way to go before I buy into your idea."

Patty glanced at Isabel, grinning. "From the look on your face, I think you already have the same thoughts that I have. Tonight before we go to bed, we can compare notes in our journals."

"Like what specifically do you think we'll find by comparing our notes?"

"That's what we're here to find out."

"I'm getting nervous," Isabel confessed.

"Me too, I guess," Patty admitted.

"I'm anxious to meet your family."

"And I'm anxious to see them again. I know my life was appalling by most standards, but I miss some of it," Patty confided. "You know, my sister and brother, and the women who raised me."

"Nostalgia." Isabel recognized the sentiment.

They were four hours into the drive, and Isabel had fallen asleep, the cascade of her dark hair hiding her face as her head rested against the window. When they came nearer to the road leading up to the town of Winding Ridge, Patty nudged Isabel awake. She wanted her to get the first impression of Winding Ridge, beginning at the foot of the road that had given the town its name. It wound steeply toward the town that was nestled at the foothills of the mountain range where the little cabin had been Patty's home.

Isabel sleepily pushed her hair back from her face and became attentive as they reached the side road. She looked at a sign unlike she had ever seen, with an arrow pointing to the left. Above the arrow, large block letters proclaimed "Winding Ridge, Population 932." Someone had marked through the "932" and written "991" above it in red paint. It, in turn, had been marked out and replaced with a different number, as was a succession of other numbers. "Apparently when the population changes here there's no time to have a new sign painted," Isabel giggled. "I guess the mayor has his own system. You can plainly see the population changes over time."

"Not the mayor," Patty grinned. "I think that's Jess Willis' doing. It's just the kind of thing he'd do. Anyway, whoever it is tracks deaths and births as they happen."

"Who's Jess Willis?"

"The sheriff. When I lived here he was a deputy. Cliff told us that Sheriff Ozzie Moats—he was the sheriff when I lived on the mountain—got himself in trouble with the law and is doing time."

"That's interesting. Maybe there's a story there."

"Yeah, there is. I found out just recently that Ozzie Moats is my uncle, and you can bet when he finds out, he'll have no intention of acknowledging it."

"Why not?"

"He's embarrassed about my grandmother, because people say she's a witch. As a matter of fact, the mountain children used to taunt her about it. Remember, I told you about the woman that the people refer to as the 'witch who lives at the edge of the forest.'"

"Oh, my gosh. Does he know about your dreams?"

"I don't think he knows specifically, but I'm sure he's heard the buzz. Of course, although he never would acknowledge or admit to it, he has always known we're related through my mother, Betty, and my grandmother, Myrtle Landacre."

"Myrtle's your grandmother, and Ozzie Moats is your uncle, right?"

"Right, and I think that he wants to distance himself from anyone associated with my grandmother, or anyone living on the mountain. He always called them mountain trash. Anyway, the funny thing about it is my other uncle, Ozzie's brother Aubrey Moats, was sent to prison for kidnapping children. Some time after that, my uncle, the sheriff—a man whose job it is to uphold the law—was involved in cockfighting, which is illegal. Also, he was convicted of allowing the unlawful assembling of the militia, which involved stockpiling weapons and obstructing justice. The obstruction charges involved the cases that spanned the years when my father was being investigated."

"Oh, my gosh, it sounds like he was trying to protect his brother and in the process was actually protecting your father," Isabel correctly guessed.

"Really, but the sheriff was also as ashamed that his brother was in jail as he is of his sister being thought to be a witch. He also despised my father, as he did anyone who lived on the mountain. It seemed to me that the sheriff's real intention regarding my father was to ignore him like he did everyone else who lived on the mountain.

"Here we are," Patty said as she turned to the left. The road wound steadily higher with every curve, climbing the foothills that led to the base of the mountain.

Isabel's eyes grew large as she looked from side to side as they continued up the steep incline.

"You are about to see a town lost in time," Patty said, smiling at Isabel in an attempt to lighten the mood in the car.

Annabelle was at a loss as to why Jeb wanted to move his Aunt Aggie out of the cabin she had spent her adult life in and crowd them in together, particularly after the cabin had been modernized by Booker. Booker, who had been the head of the militia, was doing time and would likely never return. Annabelle knew there was no reckoning with Jeb; he would not tell her his reasons for moving Aggie anyway.

The back door slammed, startling Annabelle from her dark thoughts. She looked up from her sorting and sighed with relief that it was Sara rather than Jeb returning.

"What're ya doin', Ma?" Sara asked, looking wide-eyed at Annabelle's possessions heaped alongside her rolled-up quilt, which was stretched out across the table. At the same time, Sara swooped her daughter, whose outstretched arms begged for attention, up into her arms.

"Your pa's back, an' he wants to move us."

"Where to?" Sara's disbelief and fear showed in her face.

"Ya knowed he don't tell me nothin'," Annabelle said.

"Ma, why do ya put up with it? Ya can live with me. I want you to."

"He won't let us stay here an' ya knowed it. How would we live anyway?"

"I have a job. We can move to town."

"Now y'are soundin' like Daisy," Annabelle said.

"I knowed ya wouldn't want to live without Pa, but I'm not goin'."

"Sara, don't be silly, of course y'are goin' with us, your pa won't stand for it, ya not comin' along. Ya have to, 'cause he's goin' to take Kelly Sue even if ya don't go."

"I bet I knowed where he's takin' ya, to th' big house we heard he was fixin' up for Tuesday back when we thought he'd been killed in th' attack in New York City. Jess told me all 'bout it."

"I didn't think of that," Annabelle said. "I guess I had in mind he was takin' us to a place like he took us before, ya knowed, like when he took us to Frank Dillon's cabin. I couldn't abide somethin' like that again."

"Maybe its worse," Sara said. "Ya have no idea who's livin' there already."

"Ya don't know anymore 'bout it than I do!" Annabelle insisted. "Ya just get ready afore he comes back. Jeb ain't goin' to like it if he has to wait for us to get ready."

"I'm not goin' nowhere with Pa," Sara shrilled. "What about my job?"

"Ya don't have to yell. I ain't hard of hearin'. Anyway, ya knowed your pa don't want ya a-workin', an' I knowed ya don't want to leave Kelly Sue."

"I don't care what my pa wants. I have a few friends now," she cried. "Ya knowed I never got to have friends. I ain't goin, an' neither is my daughter."

Not willing to take a chance on being there when her father returned, Sara quickly disappeared behind the curtain that led to the room she and her daughter shared. In mere minutes, she was dealing with her own quilt, rolling it as tightly as she could to hold her and her daughter's meager possessions. Leaving much more behind in fear that her father would come back and force her to go with him, Sara scooped her daughter up in her free arm and was out the backdoor, beside herself with fear, struggling with her load, in a frenzy to get safely away. She was terrified that her father would keep her from her job and destroy her first chance at happiness in her newly begun life in town.

"Sara, who's goin' to watch Kelly Sue when y'are at work?" Annabelle shouted out the backdoor.

"Jus' so ya won't worry, I'm goin' to Jess Willis, but don't ya dare tell Pa," Sara called back over her shoulder. "He's my new boyfriend. I was scared to tell ya, 'cause ya'd tell Pa, now I've no choice. Now mind ya, don't tell Pa. Ya knowed he'd kill Jess in a minute, not thinkin' twice, if'n he knew 'bout Jess an' me."

"Well, he's goin' to be mad 'cause I didn't keep ya here."

"Won't be th' first time he's been mad at ya." Sara and Kelly Sue's hair whipped in the wind as she continued away from the cabin. "He'll get over it, but don't tell him about Jess. If Pa kills Jess 'cause ya told, I promise ya'd never see me again. Ya hear me?"

Regardless of her load, Sara appeared to be growing smaller and smaller quickly as she began to descend down the mountain, using the footpath where she and Kelly Sue would not be spotted if Jeb drove by.

Annabelle let the screen door slam and walked down the two steps from the stoop at the back door and yelled, "I don't have to tell him. Ya knowed he's goin to find out. An' if ya go, y'are goin' to pay th' price. Ya knowed Jeb'll not settle for ya havin' a man any more than he'd settle for ya livin' an' workin' in town. He's goin' to say y'are too young for such things." Annabelle abruptly gave up, knowing that by now she was shouting to the wind.

In fact, they both knew that Sara's father could not afford to stir up trouble over getting Sara and Kelly Sue back, and they knew that he knew it.

Sara was out of sight and out of Annabelle's life.

A tear ran unbidden down Annabelle's cheek.

When Ozzie Moats was arrested for obstructing justice, failure to uphold the law, cockfighting, and numerous other infractions, Jess Willis went from deputy to acting sheriff until he was voted in unopposed. Being sheriff was his lifelong dream. From his first day as Ozzie's deputy, witnessing that the sheriff spent his time looking at *Playboy Magazine* while expecting Jess to empty the trash, sweep and mop the cells and the front office, and dust the furniture, Jess had not approved of Ozzie Moats. He was opposed to the way Moats had allowed the militia to take hold on the mountain and especially to how he had turned a blind eye to Jacob McCallister and his child trafficking. Moats had cared only about the town and its people, forgetting that he was elected to enforce the law throughout the county. It did not take Jess long to figure that Ozzie Moats' reasoning was that the mountain folks could not read and therefore did not vote.

Jess Willis' finest day as sheriff was the day Cliff Moran and Randy McCoy came to Winding Ridge for the sole purpose of congratulating him on the fine job he was doing. They even took him to dinner. Then there was the day Jess and Sara realized they were hugely attracted to one another and wanted to marry. They had known each other for years. She knew him as the deputy who kept disrupting their lives, chasing after her father; he knew her as one of Jacob McCallister's ragamuffins. Until she began working at The Company Store and they became attracted to each other, he hadn't for one minute allowed himself to dream of finding a wife in this sparsely populated town.

Not until Sara.

Although Willis looked a lot like Don Knotts, who portrayed Deputy Fife on "The Andy Griffith Show," he was not a timid or inept man. When it came down to it, he was an intelligent and dedicated law enforcer,

Jess loved his job of keeping the peace. Without the former sheriff getting in the way of law enforcement, sweeping what he did not feel was worthy of his attention under the rug, Jess was intent on creating a new atmosphere in the town between the townies and the mountain folk.

When Moats had been in charge, there had been those who knew they could live under the radar of the law, knew he had no interest in what happened on the mountain above the small town of Winding Ridge. It was a perfect climate for the mountain men who wanted to join the militia, rule their too-large families, and sell their children off to one another. That was, until Cliff Moran, through the search for Tuesday Summers, had learned of the lawlessness. Then, working with Moran, Willis had learned something about himself—he discovered that he actually had a backbone, and at long last he defied Sheriff Moats. It was a great improvement that the former deputy was the sheriff now that Moats was doing time. For one thing, unlike Moats, Jess cooperated with outside law enforcement when necessary to keep the law.

Now, in Jess Willis' charge, the entire county was free of child trafficking and the influence of the militia. Under his authority, the entire area was monitored day and night. He and his deputies, Orval Frank Henderson and Mark Allen Michel, cruised the county, as one or the other was on call or manning the office. Jess cringed whenever he thought of all the time, he had spent sweeping and mopping the office and jail cells, under Moats' reign, while crime prevailed across the county.

Jess Willis was aware that Jacob McCallister once again had become a threat to the county Willis was elected to protect, as well as to the neighboring county. He and his deputies were working with other law enforcement agencies, monitoring McCallister's movements. The investigation was being kept very quiet. Few knew of McCallister's involvement in the undertaking to bring the very heart of terrorism into the two counties. As always, he was looking for yet another way to feed his greed, using any means at hand to garner a fast, unearned, and huge windfall of cash.

The girls topped the hill, looking open-mouthed, right and left, through the windshield. The girls stared, Patty because it had not changed one iota, Isabel, because she had never seen anything like the small, quaint town, except in a few of the old movies she had seen during her lifetime. As Isabel was getting her first glimpse of the little town, unfortunately, she also spotted the notorious town drunk, Andy Hillberry. He was staggering from the town bar as the two girls slowly drove over the cobblestone street.

"Watch out!" she shouted. "There's a man in the road, and he's not about to get out of the way."

"I see him! Oh, no! That's Tommy Lee Hillberry's father."

Patty braked, skidding a bit on loose cobblestones.

Andy Hillberry stood his wobbly ground, weaving back and forth, trying unsuccessfully to keep his hands on hips that seemingly would not support them, and looking anything but friendly.

Having been forced to stop, Patty and Isabel both got out of the car.

"Are you crazy?" Patty cried aggressively. "I could have killed you."

Andy Hillberry lurched toward Patty as she stood with one hand on the open car door for support.

"Answer me!" she shouted, as if it were not the first time she had witnessed the man drunk and reeling his way home in the center of Main Street. "What are you doing walking in the middle of the road?"

Stuck in time, specifically the day of his son's murder, Andy Hillberry was quick to recognize Patty.

"Ya killed my son," Hillberry accused.

Isabel looked at Patty, clearly startled.

"Now there're two of ya," Hillberry said as he leaned in toward the girls, moving forward with uncontrolled, staggering mini-steps, and squinted at them. *Was he having hallucinations?*

Isabel remained wide-eyed at the confrontation.

"Stop!" Patty extended her arms, palms out. "Are you crazy, as well as drunk? Tommy Lee was arrested for taking me against my will and locking me in an old shed. As you well know he was murdered as he sat in his jail cell."

"Ya led 'im on, an' ya knowed it."

"Seriously! Don't kid yourself. I wouldn't have been able to get to and from school safely if it weren't for my brother, Joe. Tommy Lee stalked me day and night, and you know it." Patty shook her finger in Andy's face. "Your son was the one who kept me hostage for days and days. Now! Get out of my way!"

Andy Hillberry swayed back and forth until one foot lost its purchase and, making involuntarily, toddling steps, he staggered toward the car. He locked his arms at the elbows to try to stop his fall. When both hands found the hood of the car, the solid hit brought his forward momentum to a sudden end. But the heat coming from the hood of the car caused him to rear back suddenly. Without fanfare, he landed on his rear end. Too drunk to feel much pain, he sat staring, legs outstretched on the cobblestone road.

"Patty, so far I don't find anything familiar about this town," Isabel declared. She stood with her arms folded at her breasts, attempting to look unafraid, trying to ignore the drunken bum. In truth, she was frightened by the pitiful old man—and the things he had said, but she was determined not to back away from him. He looked like an overgrown child, refusing to go any further.

"You okay?" Patty asked.

"Oh, my gosh, Patty," Isabel hissed in a low voice, not wanting Hillberry to detect fright in her voice. "I'm scared, but as you can see, I'm not turning tail and running away, even though that man accused you of murder. You don't seem to find that out of the ordinary."

"Not here, it's not."

"I think it's a downright dangerous situation you've gotten us into."

"'Downright dangerous'?" Patty mimicked inquiringly. "Come on, Isabel. He's just a scared, drunken, old man who lost his son at an early age."

"He thought he was seeing double!" Isabel said.

"Really! It's about time you noticed we look alike."

"Oh, my gosh, I don't know what to do."

"So we look alike, I don't mind looking like you. Really, I could find worse- looking teenage girls for me to look like."

"Okay—okay—but, Patty, like he threatened us!"

"Really, Isabel, he's harmless. He's just a wretched drunk."

Isabel swung her arm in an arc encompassing the town, including Andy, who was still sitting in the middle of the road.

"Oh, my gosh. What are we getting into? I don't think being here is a good idea."

"Really! How about the fact that, number one, we do look alike and two, I think this place is the place of your dreams, and you don't want to admit it. You've got to quit seesawing back and forth, Isabel. First you want to be here and then you don't.

"Let's help him up," Patty groaned.

"Oh, great. Let's do." Isabel rolled her eyes, ignoring Patty's comments about her lapses in and out of fear and about their similarity.

Although Andy was still angry with Patty for her words about rejecting his son, he had been stunned by his fall, so he allowed himself to be supported between the two girls. Still, he resented them for having pulled him from his happy, booze-induced haze, which was the state he much preferred to be in. They got him on his feet and, as they released their hold on his arms, he began to lurch down the street—mumbling that there were two of them and Tommy Lee would like that. He stumbled toward the lane that led to his cabin partway down the mountain.

Watching the man go, Patty and Isabel could not keep from breaking into fits of laughter. As the harmless old man grew into a small speck, tottering his way toward home, Isabel finally noticed the majestic mountain range. Now that the excitement was over, she had a great appreciation of its beauty.

"Here we are," Patty said, taking notice of Isabel's look of wonder at the imposing mountains she herself had always taken for granted. She spread her arms in a wide arc, twirling around in the road. "I would ask what you think, but it's written all over your face."

They had a laughing fit again.

"Oh, my gosh," Isabel gasped. "Like, I don't even believe what just happened. But this town is unique."

"Oh, really. Believe it!" Patty laughed. "And yes, the town is unique, isn't it? Let's check into the boardinghouse first thing."

"All right, lead me to the boardinghouse, but it seems odd to me that you don't stay with your grandmother."

"When you see the mountain cabins my family lives in, you'll understand."

They climbed back into the car and Patty drove the half-block to the boardinghouse.

"Is this the only street in this town?" Isabel asked.

"It's the main street with all the business establishments." Patty nodded left and right. "You are now in downtown Winding Ridge, consisting of one boardinghouse, one bar, a movie theater, post office, and The Company Store where you can buy anything from food to a bag of nails. The school is up that side street about a quarter mile," Patty said, pointing to the street off to the right next to The Company Store.

"That's interesting," Isabel shrugged. "Who're the men on the boardinghouse porch?"

"The locals, they sun themselves and gossip, I suppose. The proprietor, Melba, barely tolerates them, as I noticed the time I stayed here when I found my grandmother and when Paul Frank . . ." she choked.

"It's okay," Isabel said, "I understand, you don't have to talk about him."

"Anyway, the boardinghouse porch is where they entertain themselves by watching the activities along Main

Street," Patty regained her voice. "They stuff wads of tobacco in their jaws. It's disgusting, seeing them chew and spit."

Isabel was taken with the quaint way the rocking chairs spanned the length of the front porch. "I think it's charming, the men gathered there in the chairs."

"The men aren't interested in the porch in the winter, though," Patty continued. "That's when they gather at The Company Store, loafing around the potbelly stove inside, warming themselves where they can be at the center of the community activity. The thing is, in both places it's the same scene. Rocking chairs, community gossip, and spittoons."

"What a picture," Isabel said. "I'm sure that's a page out of your book. Anyway, like, what's a spittoon?"

"I can't believe you don't know what a spittoon is," Patty feigned surprise. "It's something one can spit in. Really, you don't know anyone who rubs snuff or chews tobacco?"

"No, I don't."

"Well, you're in for a treat," Patty chuckled.

"I'm sure." Isabel looked right and left, and grinned, letting her gaze move upward toward the skyline. "We're surrounded by towering mountains," she commented.

"Really," Patty chuckled at the obvious statement. "You know, I never really appreciated that before. Its fun seeing the town through someone else's eyes, you know, someone who didn't grow up here."

They stopped in front of the boardinghouse and opened their doors at the same time, stepping onto the cobblestone street.

"Seems like everyone we see stares at us," Isabel complained.

"There're hardly any strangers coming to this town. I guess we're a treat."

The lobby was as Patty remembered it. The memory of Paul Frank was overwhelming, and tears filled her eyes.

"What's wrong, Patty?" Isabel asked, alarmed.

"You know, reminds me of Paul Frank Ruble?"

"Yeah," Isabel answered. "And we would have to be welcomed by Tommy Lee Hillberry's drunken father."

"Yeah."

"He blamed you, and that's scary. I guess I don't understand why he holds you responsible."

Patty shrugged. "There's no real reason, except he needs someone to blame, other than himself for not being there for Tommy Lee. You know, being drunk every day all day, and all, Andy Hillberry sure wouldn't have won any father of the year award."

"I can see that," Isabel said.

"The sad thing was the old man allowed Tommy Lee, since he was old enough to walk from their cabin to the bar, to tag along with him and—the way I heard it—he'd put a shot in Tommy Lee's cola."

At the reception desk, Melba pushed the register toward them, letting the girls know that they were lucky to get a room, what with the uncommon activity in town. Patty was surprised; strangers in Winding Ridge were a rarity. She scrutinized the names listed, not recognizing any of them, and both girls signed. Melba handed them a key to a room with double beds.

"Ya've been here before," she said, nodding toward Patty. "An' ya got ya self in all kinds of trouble. I trust ya've learned to mind ya own business by now."

Melba was as fat and nosy as ever. Of course, she said or asked whatever was on her mind, but would not tolerate questions directed at her. She was known to say straight out when questioned about anything at all, "That ain't none of your business an' it ain't none of mine." She was one who operated by a double standard if there ever was.

"Excuse me," Patty said. "I'm sure you know very well that I was a victim, so I don't understand how you could accuse me of making trouble."

"Wouldn't've been trouble if'n ya'd stayed where ya belonged.

"Now there's no one here to show ya your room right now, an' my arthritis won't let me," Melba complained, effectively dismissing the two of them.

"That's okay, we can handle it," Patty said, realizing by Melba's tone it was useless to continue the discussion about how she was victimized.

Although Melba never employed a bellboy, not wanting to pay the wages, she told every new guest that there was no one to carry bags at the moment. She believed the guests would be happy thinking that she had hired help and that her boardinghouse was a high-class establishment. It really didn't matter, as she had no competition in the town. And anyway, to her way of thinking, if people wanted rooms, they could carry their own bags.

And so Patty and Isabel carried their bags up in two trips, and when they were finished they surveyed their new temporary home.

"This room is so quaint," Isabel gushed.

Patty propped her doll on her bed, "It is, isn't it," she said. "My stepfather, Cliff, told me that during the years of the building up to the notorious assembly of the militia, the men paid in advance and they paid a high price for the rooms, to be sure to get a place to stay. Up until then, though, the only business she got was when there was trouble at the mine, and men were brought in to take care of it. Otherwise, she was lucky to have any guests at all.

"Anyway, with all that money coming in from the militia, Melba remodeled. What had been a dreary boardinghouse, with fifteen rooms and two outhouses, became ten rooms, each equipped with a bath and sitting area. I'm glad that she kept the look of the past. This place makes you feel like a favored family member in your great-grandmother's guest room."

"Aren't you the up-and-coming author?" Isabel said. "Like, if you can do prose like that; you're going to be a hit."

"Really!" Patty laughed. "I wish. You know I have a long way to go. But one thing I do have is a story to tell."

"You can call it '*Patty's Story*.'"

"Do you really think people will buy that?" Patty tilted her head in a questioning look.

"Why not?" Isabel asked.

"Really, Isabel, nobody knows me. I think I'll have to use my father's name in the title."

"I suppose so," Isabel yielded.

"There's enough time for that. I haven't got all the information I need yet. All I have to do is get Aunt Aggie to talk. My guess is she knows . . ."

"That makes shivers run down my spine," Isabel said.

"You know, it just dawned on me, what Melba said."

"What's that?" Isabel asked.

"Remember, she said we were lucky to get a room—that she was almost booked up. Booked up never happens. The only time I know of is when the militia gathered here about two years ago.

"Something's going on."

CHAPTER 16

S SARA HERE NOW?”

“I told ya she’s gone, an’ she ain’t comin’ back.”

“Get the girl then. We’ll take her, and Sara will come around soon enough.”

“Said she ain’t goin’ to move, an’ grabbed up Kelly Sue an’ run off.”

“How could you allow her to take the child?” McCallister was furious.

“Can’t stop a mother from takin’ her child, Jeb. Sara’s a woman now an’ she’s too fast for me to run down.”

“That doesn’t answer where she is.”

“I don’t know where she is.”

“You’re trying my patience, Annabelle.

“Your rocking chairs are loaded in the truck, so are you finished packing yet?” Jeb growled, knowing he was getting nowhere fast with Annabelle. “I’ll deal with Sara later. I know where to find her when I’m ready to deal with her.”

“Ya leave her alone or y’are goin’ to see th’ last of me too.”

He laughed. “You? You wouldn’t dare.”

"I'm ready as I'll ever be," Annabelle answered. "I don't knowed 'bout Aggie, but I'm sure she's still at her cabin workin' on it."

"I didn't ask you about Aggie, I asked you about Sara."

"Jus' tryin' to make conversation," Annabelle said with hurt feelings. "I already told ya all I knowed 'bout Sara's whereabouts."

"Did you now?"

"Yeah, I did. I don't knowed where Sara is. Just knowed where she's workin', an' I tol' ya that. Ya'd best remember ya don't want th' law on to ya. If'n ya go after her that's just what's goin' to happen."

"I could kill Cliff Moran just for taking you women to the city. Since you've been there, you think you know everything, using big words you don't understand, and getting ideas in your heads about working and making money. You'd not know what to do with it even if you had it."

"I ain't th' one ran away to town or th' one moved to th' city with money earned at th' town bar. An' ya knowed I've been listenin' to th' radio, an' I've learned from listenin'. Ain't nothin' to do with th' detective." Annabelle wanted to say much more, really give him a piece of her mind, and tell him she knew more than he thought, but she knew she would be asking for his wrath. She settled with giving him a view of her back.

"You are determined to try my patience aren't you?"

"Jeb, I'm th' only one here. Sara run off at th' mention of ya takin' us somewhere else to live. An' I knowed all th' time ya was stayin' away these past years, ya was hopin' Daisy an' her twins had come back, wasn't ya?"

"I was, so what? I can't believe that you women can't appreciate being taken care of and stay where you belong. Daisy will never make it in the city on her own. I still believe she'd come back if she realized that I'm not going to punish her for outright disobeying me and working at the town bar. You know, I've even thought of looking her up and telling her she can come back without any fear that my intention's one of settling scores.

"You know she always prided herself on the fact that she thought she was my favorite."

"What ya tellin' me ya wantin' her to come back for? When ya find her, tell her your own self. I guess ya haven't noticed that I'm th' only one still here. I ain't gone an' run off somewheres. I'm th' one always does your cookin' an' cleanin', an' puttin' up with your temper an' womanizin'."

Jacob couldn't help laughing. She was right—it must be the radio. He didn't know she knew so many words. "All right, all right," he said, laughing.

He smiled as joy lit her eyes on hearing his laughter.

"Let's get going. We need to get Aunt Aggie. She shouldn't need much time to gather the little she's got to take with her."

"Wish she could take th' nice furniture an' stuff she has now. I'd like to have such as she got."

What he saw as her ungrateful attitude brought on his disfavor again, changing the light mood of a minute before.

"I guess you don't know as much as you think you do. You think because you've seen that seedy hotel room in Wheeling that the city provides to house its witnesses, you've seen the best. It not only doesn't compare to Aggie's cabin, it doesn't begin to compare to my place. Not only that, the place I'm taking you to will make Aggie's place look like the small, primitive cabin that it is."

Not really believing she would prefer another place of Jeb's choosing to Aggie's modernized cabin, Annabelle took one last look around. She was saddened by the empty space left where her rocking chairs had stood during the years the babies had come and gone. This cabin had been her home from the day, when she was very young, that her father had sold her to Jeb for two hundred dollars. The cabin was her only connection to the many children born there. Some were her own; others were born to Jeb's other women. Now that she was leaving for a new home, they felt even more forever lost to her. She wiped her eyes as the tears ran uncontrolled down her cheeks, and she tucked her most valued possession—her radio—more securely under her arm.

The drive to fetch Aunt Aggie was a short one. Aggie standing on her back porch, waiting impatiently. "There y'are, thought ya'd never get here, so I did."

It was well known that Aggie would do anything for her nephew, and Aggie and Jeb's tight bond had always been a mystery to Annabelle. *Why would he bond so closely to his aunt—even given the fact that she raised him—and yet he had no ties with his children whatsoever?* She had no idea they were bound by their evil deeds.

Jeb jumped from the truck and, telling Annabelle to stay put, began carrying Aggie's things across the hard-packed dirt that served as a parking area and tossing them in the bed of the truck.

"Don't forget my rockin' chairs," Aggie reminded her nephew, noting Annabelle's tied near the rear window, "I left th' two I'm wantin' by th' door."

They were not taking any of the furniture from either cabin, except for two rocking chairs each. Although Aggie's cabin had inherited the rich furnishings that Benjamin Booker had furnished it with, she had chosen her two, aged, scarred, washed-out wooden rocking chairs to take with her to her new home.

Annabelle's cabin never changed from year to year, containing the barest minimum of furnishings which—except for the four-poster bed, potbelly stove, and woodburner stove—could hardly be called furniture. In the kitchen was a wood plank table, the living room housed an old, wine-colored, horsehair couch, the children's room held the full-size bed Sara had purchased, and the room the women slept in had the four-poster bed.

Unknown to the women, the huge mansion had been richly appointed little by little over the past three years. Jeb was sure that after the women finished with the cleaning, dusting, and polishing, the huge house would be a showplace straight out of a Sears Catalog, like they never could have imagined.

At Jeb's instructions, days before the scheduled move for Aggie and Annabelle, Joe had cleaned the windows until they sparkled. He'd also hired a gardener to take care of the grounds. The man had worked wonders on the overgrown jumble of weeds.

With the cab loaded with women and cats, Jeb headed the truck down the winding mountain trail, came out on Main Street, and continued down Winding Ridge Road to Route Seven.

On the way down Annabelle, riding shotgun, sat bolt upright as the sheriff's Jeep moved up the hill. "Who in tarnation's that?" she asked. "It looks for all th' world like Paul Frank a'sittin' in th' passenger seat."

"The one that looks like Paul Frank is Orval Frank Ruble, so he is. The one drivin' is Mark Allen Michael. His brother is Johnny Michael, an' those two're Paul Frank's cousins. Orval Frank is th' uncle of th' three of them, an' Orval Frank was th' second youngest of six children, an' Orval Frank's brothers an' sisters were pretty well grown when Orval Frank an' their sister Karen were born. When Johnny Michael an' Orval Frank were babies they was treated like brothers, so they were."

"How come I didn't knowed that? Annabelle asked.

"'Cause ya don't knowed everythin' so ya don't."

"Ya old woman, ya just forgot 'bout 'im bein' deputy an' don't want to admit it," Annabelle accused.

"Will the two of you shut up," Jeb warned. "You sound like an audio of a family tree."

"Don't ya talk to me like ya do to your women, I won't stand for it, so I won't. Just 'cause ya don't like comin' so close to th' law, ya take it out on whoever's close enough for ya to vent your anger. I suppose ya didn't knowed there was more lawmen than ya can shake a stick at now that Ozzie Moats's doin' time in prison. I for one think ya' need to knowed what y'are up again', so I do."

A complete and ominous silence hung in the cab of the truck. Jacob broke it.

"You'd better curb your mouth, Aunt Aggie. You're asking for trouble, I know about those boys. I'm smart enough to keep in tune with my surroundings. I know much more than you think I know! A couple of years back in a conversation with Paul Frank, when I moved Tuesday and the others to Broad Run to keep her from Moran. He told me that due to a stroke of luck, Herman Ruble's brother-in-law, Orval Wayne Henderson, got a job in Wheeling years back. Orval and his wife, Mabel, were among the few that managed to move off the mountain and away from their life of poverty. I'm familiar with more about them and their children than you'll ever know."

"I don't knowed about that, so I don't. Joe told me that Orval Frank, Johnny Michael, and Mark Allen, hearing of Paul Frank's murder, went through th' police academy to become lawmen. Mark Allen an' Orval Frank got hired by Jess Willis, an' they're Winding Ridge's prize deputies now, so they are. Johnny Michael's livin' in Wheelin' now."

"Yeah, Aggie," Jeb sneered, "I know all about it, especially that Johnny Michael got a job with Homeland Security."

"Ya sound like ya got it in for Johnny Michael, so ya do."

"Maybe I do." Jeb was not a bit happy that the two deputies may have recognized him. He did not want anyone to know of his whereabouts. *Just maybe they hadn't paid attention. They didn't acknowledge that they recognized the passengers in the truck. Too damn bad—I have family here and own property here. It's not as if I'm a stranger sniffling around.*

"Ya need to stay on th' good side of th' law, so ya do. Not going around sayin' ya have it in for them."

"Just shut up, both of you!" Jacob snapped.

After an extended silence provoked by the women's hurt feelings, and a few miles before reaching the mansion, Jeb began telling the women a little about the history of the place. He said he had found very old newspapers and, always interested in history, he had spent a lot of time reading everything in them about the immediate area. Years ago there had been stories about the people who had originally built the mansion being accused of witchcraft. He told them about stories of a few women who were kidnapped and taken to town where they were burned at the stake.

The nearest town to the west was Weston, and the nearest town to the east was Salem. The latter was named for Salem, Massachusetts—and called little Salem—where many of the inhabitants' forefathers had originated.

Annabelle, who had been quiet as she listened to Jacob's stories, now had to add her own spin. "Th' nearest one is Salem, ain't it?"

"They're 'bout th' same," Aggie answered, "but Weston might be a little closer. I knowed that, so I do."

"Can't the two of you agree on anything?" Jeb growled.

"Who was they? Annabelle asked.

"Who?" Jeb asked, having lost the train of the conversation.

"Ya don't want to knowed, so ya don't."

"Forevermore," Annabelle said, "If I didn't want to knowed, I wouldn't've asked."

"Who're you talking about, Annabelle?" Jeb asked.

"I want to know the name of th' people what used to live in th' house y'are takin us to."

"Their name was Hathorne," Jacob answered.

Aggie and Annabelle were both struck speechless for once.

"What's going on with you women? I've never heard so many questions from the two of you. It's no wonder I never take you on outings."

Annabelle found her voice. "Had no idea ya knowed anythin' about th' witch stories, let alone their history or their name."

The two women fell silent again, watching the unfamiliar landscape speed by—a blur of trees, streams, and a few houses scattered in the valleys.

CHAPTER 17

"YOUR NEW HOME IS COMING UP AROUND the next bend. There'll be a straight stretch, and then you'll see the house on the right."

Seconds later, Aggie and Annabelle gasped as the mansion came into view.

"Oh, my word, it's not that one is it? If it is, we'd get lost in it for sure, so we would."

"Ya can say that again!" Annabelle said. "It's so big, it's like th' hotel that city detective set us up in when he took us to Wheelin' for questionin' for your trial, Jeb.

Annabelle saw his face change and quickly added. "It's much grander though."

"It's not quite as large," he said angrily. "And I don't want to hear about Cliff Moran. How many times do I have to tell you women to forget you've ever met the man? He's nothing to you, not anything but trouble."

"If'n you'd stay outta trouble, it wouldn't matter 'cause he'd not have any interest in ya, so he wouldn't."

At the end of the driveway, paying no heed to his contrary aunt, Jeb stopped at the edge of the road, leaving the truck to open the gate.

"Here we are," he said gleefully. He climbed back inside, kicking aside the cats, who went right back to crawling over Annabelle and Aggie. He put the truck in gear and, with a lurch, moved forward onto the circular drive, bringing them directly to the huge double doors.

With a hand down from Jeb, the women, each carrying a cat under her arm, climbed from the truck onto the grounds that were now spectacular. He led the women to the door, enjoying their bug-eyed faces as they struggled to take everything in.

The first thing that Aggie noticed, shining in the sunlight, was the newly polished pentagram hanging at eye level in the center of the great door.

"What's the matter with you, Aunt Aggie? You look as if you've seen a ghost." Jeb demanded.

"Th' door's mighty big, so it is."

"Don't give me that crap. You don't turn white at the sight of a door. I don't care a damn how big it is."

"All right, if ya' wantin' to knowed . . . that thing on th' door is witchcraft, so it is. It's th' mark of th' witch family, Hathorne."

"How'd ya knowed that?" Annabelle asked.

"Jeb told us who used to live here just a minute ago, so he did."

"I knowed that," Annabelle said. "I'm wantin' to knowed how ya knowed the Hathorne family was involved in witchcraft."

"If ya'd paid attention to anyone but ya self, ya'd knowed that Betty's grandfather's name was Hathorne, so ya would. Many years ago her ancestors settled here from Salem, Massachusetts.

"Stop that bickering," Jeb snapped. "I'm tired of your bad tempers. Neither of you know what you're talking about."

He unlocked the door with a flourish and waited for a reaction from the women, who looked as tattered and frightened as the lion, tin man, and scarecrow did in "The Wizard of Oz" when they stood at the entrance of the palace.

For the time being, Aggie forgot the pentagram as she got her first view of the inside of her new home. The foyer alone was as large as Aggie's cabin, and the ceiling was higher than she ever could have imagined one to be—and would not have thought it necessary, anyway. The floor was a black ceramic tile with a hint of white and gold swirls. The walls were the purest white marble. Also, there were marble tables with various statues and candelabra. Arranged above the tables were various works of art, which meant nothing to the women. They saw simply pictures of people and scenery. The art was displayed at tasteful intervals, creating a very formal atmosphere.

The women released the cats, allowing them to run free, and then stepped inside themselves. The animals scattered, spooked by the sound of their claws clicking on the hard, polished surface. They skidded on the marble floors and slid aimlessly with their hackles up.

Purchasing the artwork was McCallister's master plan to conceal his ill-gotten gain, a result of the accounting education he'd gotten in prison. Jeb knew to invest part of his leftover stash from the bungled sale of Winter Ann.

He was happy with his earlier investments in collections of art, diamonds, and gold, thus never having capital and accumulated cash to report to the IRS. Now he was working on investing the first installment, collected from the self-important Abu Musab. There was nothing like learning from past success.

To help with the laundering of his stash, Jeb had hired Buddy Dean Howerton to do the footwork and visit various art galleries and jewelers, spreading his tax-free wealth as thin as he could so as not to call attention to any large expenditure.

"Oh, my!" Aggie turned about, trying to see everything at once. "I never seen such a place, so I ain't. An' I thought my place was as good as it got, so I did."

"It's too big," Annabelle whined, peering down a hallway that looked to her to be large enough to drive a herd of two-hundred cattle the length of it.

Annoyed with her whining, Jeb, who had started on his way down the corridor to show them around the first floor of the mansion, stopped. "I never saw such ungrateful women. You've been complaining about the hardship of living in a cabin that's too small, and I bring you to a home fit for a king, and you say it's too big!"

"Ah, Jeb, she didn't mean it thataway, so she didn't," Aggie elbowed Annabelle, irritated with her constant crabbiness. "She's just surprised, that's all. Ya knowed she ain't never dreamed of a place such as this, so she ain't."

Jeb relented and continued his commentary. Walking along the hall toward the back of the house, he pointed out that the ballroom was to the right, and on the left was the formal living room. Continuing farther, he pointed out the dining room on the right, and across from that the library, which doubled as his office. Not only could the kitchen, dining room, and ballroom be accessed from the grand hallway, French doors—an interior access—connected the dining room and ballroom, as they ran side by side along the right of the grand hall. This setup allowed easy passage for guests to mingle freely in the dining room and ballroom. There was also a connecting doorway from the servant's pantry through the dining room and the kitchen, giving servants easy access to each room.

Jacob stopped them where French doors led onto patio gardens at the back, and the kitchen opened to the right. From there the corridor ran left, creating an L shape. That corridor extended past two bedroom suites to the right and left, continuing on a good twenty feet to where it ended at a wide double door, which led into the largest suite at the far end of the hallway.

"My bedroom is on this floor at the end. It's behind those double doors," he said as he motioned toward the impressive doors "We can use the smaller two," he continued, gesturing to the doorways halfway down the length of the hall, "for guestrooms. The two of you can choose from one of the many rooms on the second floor."

My word! Who in th' world's goin' to visit us? Why, we ain't had no visitors except for th' law in my lifetime, Annabelle thought but didn't say aloud. She knew she had said enough that day.

"Wouldn't it be better to have th' guests outta th' way on th' upper floors? The guests wouldn't want to be 'round th' kitchen an' such, so they wouldn't."

"What on earth do ya knowed 'bout guests, Aggie?" Annabelle huffed.

"I said to stop the bickering!" Jeb had lost his temper again but refrained from acting on it.

"All right, the two of you can pick the one you want, but if you don't stay out of my way, I'm moving you both to the upper floors. And, beyond that, I'll let you know when I want my rooms cleaned. Otherwise, stay out!

Jeb pushed each woman on the small of her back in the direction of the kitchen. "Now, let me show you how to turn the stove on. I don't want the two of you trying to build a fire in here."

"My word," Annabelle exclaimed as the top of the range turned bright orange. "Is it hot?"

She held her hand a few inches above the unit and quickly jerked it away. "My word that's hot. How'd that happen?"

"It's electric," Jeb answered, "but you don't need to know how everything works—only that it does. Besides, between the two of you, you'd never figure it out. All you need to know is to clean and cook. When you need heat, low or high, you just turn the knob that corresponds with the unit you want to use."

CHAPTER 18

IN THE BOARDINGHOUSE ROOM, PATTY AND Isabel put their belongings in the drawers provided, getting ready to explore the town before visiting Patty's grandmother, Aunt Aggie, and Annabelle.

They crossed the lobby and noticed a few strangers who were dark skinned, and Isabel recognized them as being of Middle Eastern descent. "Who are they, Patty?"

"I don't know. I've never seen them before. They're not the usual sort you see on the mountain. It's too strange if you ask me."

"You think they're something to do with Melba saying the rooms were being taken fast?

"Yeah, I do."

The two girls stepped into the sunshine. Strolling along the sidewalk, they were an enigma. The teens and adults alike in the little mountain town and those living far above were not nearly as up to date in the styles of dress in the more populated areas, neither did they have the funds to buy such items, particularly the mountain folks. Therefore, the two girls invited stares as they went from place to place, chatting and laughing. They were having great fun, Isabel exploring a new and unknown way of life and Patty in a time of remembering.

Isabel loved the old sign that hung on chains, proclaiming The Company Store. "I guess they couldn't think of a hip name," she laughed, "but it's quaint, and it looks as if people have no choice but to shop here. I haven't seen any other store of any kind. It's a monopoly."

"Really, that's just what is. The men work in the coal mines, and the company owns the store. Families can buy what they need and it's taken straight from their paychecks."

"Like that song, '*I owe my soul to the company store.*'" Isabel wrinkled her brow in concentration. "The song's an old one and I can't remember who recorded it."

"I don't think I've heard it at all. Anyway, since I've lived away from here for the past six years, I've come to see the town in a new light. It's actually adrift in time, and like that song, I've missed so much," Patty mused.

"That's just the thing, although at our age it's not so unusual not to have heard that old song, you have missed what other teens take for granted."

"We each have had experiences that will indirectly or directly influence our lives," Patty said.

"How true," Isabel agreed, smiling, as they strolled between the narrow overstocked isles, sidestepping the items that blocked passage in some areas.

"Look at this!" Isabel tried to pick up a feedsack bag filled with cornmeal, but found it too heavy and climbed over it. "Do people really buy in bulk like this?"

"Sure. It's a hard trip to town for them, especially in the winter months, so they have to. There's no electricity on the mountain, except for Aunt Aggie's cabin. As I understand it, when the militiamen took over her cabin they installed a generator so they'd have electricity for their appliances. Otherwise, the families grow, kill, and preserve their food themselves. That's all we ever knew."

"Like, how do the people preserve the food? All I've ever known is mass produced food that you pick off the shelves or out of the cooler in the grocery store, and it's brought in by eighteen-wheeler delivery trucks."

"Yeah, those trucks bring loads of stuff to The Company store, too, because the townspeople buy it, but for the mountain people cold packing and sugar curing, for the most part, is the way they keep food preserved," Patty explained. "Each spring and summer, the woman and children preserve their kills and garden produce and store it in the cellar house."

"Like, that sounds like work to me," Isabel said.

"Really, you haven't heard anything yet. The women make dresses from the feedsacks after they're emptied." Patty smiled at Isabel's openmouthed reaction.

"Oh, my gosh," Isabel said, "I don't know if I'd want to live your experience. But, you know what? I'd like to read about it."

"That's why I'm counting on people wanting to hear about the infamous Jacob McCallister's life and times."

"That's too corny," Isabel said as she wrinkled her nose.

"Let's go back outside. It's stuffy in here," Isabel suggested and walked past the empty rocking chairs gathered around the potbelly stove. The girls stepped out front and surveyed the town.

"Is that a movie theater?"

"Yes, can't you tell by the marquee?" Patty loved watching Isabel's reaction to the antiquated, stuck-in-time town.

"Oh, my gosh!" Isabel cried.

"What!"

"Look who's watching us. How good looking are they!"

Patty looked in the direction Isabel was pointing. Then she fainted.

CHAPTER 19

SOON AFTER JEB BROUGHT AGGIE AND Annabelle's chairs, crates, and quilts to the kitchen, having no further interest in their reaction to their new surroundings, he left without a word.

Annabelle and Aggie found themselves alone in the huge mansion. They moved around the huge hallways and rooms, feeling small in comparison to their surroundings.

"I feel lost, so I do."

"Y'are more used to these new-fangled gadgets than I am," Annabelle huffed.

"Y'are th' one always braggin' 'bout your trip to th' city, so y'are."

"Ya, but y'are th' one with th' cabin with all th' new-fangled stuff."

"Compared to this, that's an over-declaration if I ever heard one, so it is."

"I knowed. Ya've been listenin' to th' radio," Annabelle said her eyebrows raised. "All of a sudden y'are usin' those big words an' all. Ya can't tell me ya ain't been listenin' to it more than y'are admittin' to."

"Ya don't knowed so much, so ya don't. Anyway, we got work to do. We don't have time to quarrel an' such, so we don't."

In short order, the women had chosen their respective rooms and carried their belongings to the room of choice. The task of choosing rooms had been no trouble as both were more than acceptable. Each of the rooms off the grand hallway beyond the kitchen area had a master bath, dressing room, walk-in closet, and lovely oak furniture.

They ran back and forth from one room to the other, sharing newly discovered closets, drawers, and cabinets behind mirrors. There was more storage space than the women could ever imagine having personal items to fill.

Their explorations took them to the end hallway where the double doors to Jeb's bedchamber stood. The women—having no regard for Jeb's demand that they stay away from his room unless he wanted it to be cleaned—made an effort to open the huge doors and found that they were locked. From the hallway side of the doors, they could not see the ceiling-to-floor windows that gave the occupant a panoramic view of the grounds, including the narrow road leading to and from the property.

With no means to explore Jeb's room, they went back to their own. To the right, Annabelle's room overlooked the gardens and expanse of lawn at the back of the house. Aggie's room was straight across from Annabelle's and faced the front of the mansion, with a full view of anyone coming to or going from the mansion. The women were happy with her respective rooms as they were an equal distance from the coveted kitchen.

Aggie and Annabelle, although yearning for home, were content with the huge house they would be living in now, as it brought out the adventure in them. They had never seen such creature comforts. Neither of them could comprehend the numerous comforts that her new room afforded her, and both were secretly overwhelmed.

Aggie loved the fact that her room overlooked the front gardens and the gracefully curved driveway. With one of her beloved rocking chairs placed in front of the window, she would be able to see anyone coming or going in keeping with her habit of staying in the loop of everyone's business.

"Annabelle, come in here," Aggie demanded, sticking her head in Annabelle's open doorway. "I can't figure what to do with my housedresses, so I can't. There ain't no spike nails for hangin', so there ain't."

"I knowed where ya can hang your things," Annabelle bragged as she crossed the hallway. Seeing that Aggie had placed her rocking chair in front of the huge window, she said, "That's the very place to have one of your chairs. I'm goin' to put mine by my window too." Annabelle beamed.

"What about my housedresses? I already figured where to put my chair, so I did. I'm asking what to do with my housedresses."

"When I was in Wheelin' we had a closet in our hotel room. Let me show ya." Annabelle plucked one of Aggie's dresses from across her arm and opened the closet. She removed a clothes hanger, slipped the dress on it just so, and returned the hanger to the rod, grinning smugly at Aggie.

"Well, ain't ya th' one," Aggie declared.

"That's a far cry handier than th' spike nails we're used to havin'," Annabelle boasted. "Keeps th' room from lookin' messy."

"Ya suppose folks really have dresses enough to fill closets such as these?"

"I can't imagine, Aggie, but when ya look at th' Sears catalog there's so many pages showing all kinds of clothes, folks with big money must be buyin' 'em. That's just th' thing that got Daisy and Patty wantin' to go off to th' city. Sittin' in th' outhouse daydreamin' over th' catalogs. No never mind to them that th' catalogs was for wipin' yourself clean.

"Speakin' of that, Aggie, let me show ya' th' outhouse what's in th' house. That's one thin' that militiaman, Booker, didn't fix up in your fancy cabin." She led Aggie to her own private bathroom.

Aggie and Annabelle stood over the toilet, watching as the water swirled around and disappeared down the narrow opening and just as mysteriously filled back to the exact same level.

"My word, I knowed what this is all 'bout. When ya' do your business, ya pull that handle an' th' water takes it away, so it does. I'm not goin' to ask 'cause I knowed ya don't knowed anymore than me how that can be, so ya don't."

"I do too," Annabelle bragged and reached for the end of the toilet paper and pulled, tearing off a piece. "This is what ya use to wipe yourself. Ya don't need to keep a Sears catalog handy no more, unless ya can read it," Annabelle laughed. "I'll show ya," she said as she tossed the tissue into the toilet bowel and flushed.

Aggie watched in fascination.

"I've always told ya that Jeb never had a thought for our welfare. After being in th' city those few days, I knowed in my soul that Jeb was takin' pleasure, in all these niceties what we didn't have, in his place in Wheelin'. That's why he always liked spendin' his time there an' not with us."

Ignoring Annabelle's unkind commentary on her nephew, Aggie interrupted, "I'm ready for th' kitchen, so I am."

They left the bathroom, and Aggie took another quick, appreciative look around her bedroom. The room was larger than her entire cabin back above Winding Ridge. Even with the conveniences that could only give her comfort, she was going to have a difficult time getting used to living in the gigantic space. It was not only the huge rooms and hallways but also the eighteen-foot ceilings that especially made her feel small.

In the kitchen, Annabelle immediately found a place to set her radio and turned it on, not realizing there was a built-in TV enclosed in the cabinetry beside the refrigerator. She had no experience with a television and did not realize that there were channels that carried the news, in full color, twenty-four hours a day. Annabelle valued her radio for entertainment. It was all she knew.

"Are ya goin' to play that noise all th' time? How're we goin' to talk? I have somethin' to tell ya, so I do."

Annabelle reached over and turned the radio off. She was too excited about the prospect of having Jeb living in the same house to pay proper attention anyway. She thought that she was going to miss her familiar life style in the cabin, and her greatest sorrow was in the hard fact of not having her daughter Sara with her, but wasn't it the way? Jeb had sold many of her children over the years, only allowing three to live at the cabin with them, her daughter, Sara, and her son, Joe, and Patty, who was actually Betty's daughter. Betty had died giving birth, leaving Annabelle to raise the little girl with a birthmark marring her face.

Although she would sorely miss Sara, Annabelle liked the idea of her daughter being with Sheriff Jess Willis. With the women living in the mansion, though, it would be impossible for Sara to come for a visit. Annabelle realized too that, unlike Patty who had Tuesday and Cliff in her life to teach her so much, Sara had never had the opportunity to learn essential new skills like driving a car.

It had not occurred to Annabelle that, because Sara was now with Jess Wills rather than under the influence of her father, she had a better chance of learning to drive by simply having access to a car, as well as a partner to teach her.

Not that Annabelle was used to it yet or even wanted it; still, she was pleased that Sara was with a good man, especially one that she knew. Coming from the mountain, it was an unheard-of accomplishment for a woman to be with a man of her choice rather than being sold to one for his and her father's convenience. As far as Annabelle knew, there had never been a mountain girl who had made her life with a townie.

Annabelle could continue having the pleasure of one of her many children living close by, rather than in some unknown place—with unknown people. It was a dream come true to Annabelle just knowing that she and Sara would be living a few short miles apart. She imagined that Sara would bring Jess around for a visit. Everyone knew he was a kind man; he'd fetch her straight to her mother. Annabelle comforted herself with the daydreaming.

"What're ya staring off in space for, Annabelle? I'm wantin' to talk, so I am."

"I was just thinking of Sara. I reckon I'm going to miss her more than anyone I've ever had to give up."

"Get over it. Youngin's get married an' leave home all th' time. I'm wantin' to talk an' look around some more an' tell ya what I'm thinkin, so I do."

"Keep goin'. Talkin's exactly what y'are doin' right now."

"Okay, ya remember, Jeb an' me told ya that this is th' home place of th' Hathorne family, so it is."

"How'd ya knowed that without Jeb tellin' ya, Aggie? Th' Hathorne family was called witches by folks. My ma and grandma told me about it when I was just a youngin'. Why, I reckon they all was burned at th' stake."

"Oh, not all of them, so they wasn't. Don't ya knowed, Myrtle Landacre was a Hathorne?

"No, I didn't knowed that," Annabelle said.

"I just want ya to keep a watch out for anythin' that might've belonged to them, so I do."

"Y'are thinkin' there may be somethin' of theirs left behind?"

"I wouldn't be surprised, so I wouldn't."

They explored the main floor once again, looking in many of the nooks and crannies they had overlooked on the first pass with Jeb. They began in the dining room, which was so large it was intimidating to them. They wandered about the room, avoiding the few boxes Jeb had allowed them to bring along because Annabelle had declared that she could not cook without her kitchen supplies. They had not even thought of unpacking in the commotion of the move. In one box was the tin ware. Annabelle wanted to put it in the china cupboard, but the shelves were already filled with lovely dinnerware, cups and saucers, crystal glasses, and flatware.

"I think th' tin plates're goin' to look outta place in that fancy cupboard, so I do."

"Let's put them in th' lower doors without th' glass windows." Annabelle opened a door and found an empty space, so they unpacked their tin plates, stacking them neatly across the shelf. They took the remaining utensils and wooden crate to the kitchen. There were wooden spoons, two potato mashers, and large pots and pans with dents and discolorations.

"Here,' Aggie said. "There's room here under th' sink for the pots an' pans, so we can put th' utensils in one of th' drawers. Let's leave th' crates for Jeb to tend to. He's not goin' to want them here. He can take them out an' burn them for all I care, so he can."

"That's well an' good for ya to say, Aggie. I've used them crates for shelvin' for years. I should've left them in th' cabin if he's goin' to be burnin' them."

"Ya' ain't goin' back to th' cabin, so ya ain't, so ya may as well get over it an' load up them shelves with our stuff."

"My word," Annabelle said. "Are ya kiddin'? We'd never in a million years fill up all these drawers, an' all the cabinets an' closets in this house."

After they got bored with the downstairs they continued their rummaging upstairs, taking great care not to miss a thing. With huge curiosity, they explored each of the bedrooms, baths, walk-in closets, and dressers, increasingly overwhelmed by the enormity of the house.

Later, alone in her bathroom Aggie lifted her dress and she sat on the toilet seat. Quickly she finished and used the soft paper to clean herself. She stood and let her dress down as she pushed the handle.

"My word," she said out loud, stepping back as the water and toilet paper swirled down with a strong gurgle and disappeared. "I'd heard of this but never thought I'd live to see it, so I didn't."

She watched as the water magically rose to its original level, just as it had done when Annabelle had showed her how to work it.

CHAPTER 20

ISABEL BENT OVER PATTY, CRYING, "PATTY, wake up. What's wrong?"

"I'm okay." Patty turned her head, looked into the familiar dark eyes of Paul Frank Ruble, and felt panic, knowing it could not be her first love before her in the flesh. He was dead. The two young men were no longer across the street watching the two girls. One of them was down on one knee, holding Patty's hand. The other one was introducing himself and his companion to Isabel.

"Can I be of any assistance?" The one holding her hand asked.

Patty blushed. "I'm okay."

"Are you sure? Why did you faint? I mean, it looked like you took one look at me and fainted. I didn't know I was that ugly."

"See what I told you, Orval Frank?" Mark Allen, who had been standing behind him, joked, "You ought to stay away from women."

"You know, he even sounds like Paul Frank," Patty said, just noticing that the other one had crossed the street, too.

"I'm Mark Allen. So you know our cousin, Paul Frank?"

"Yes, we were very close." Patty answered, not too out of it to notice that Isabel had not taken her eyes off Mark Allen.

"I'm Orval Frank," said the one who was the image of Paul Frank, realizing that Patty was still confused. "I mean, I'm Paul Frank's cousin, and this is not the first time someone's mistaken me for him."

"Oh, my gosh!" Isabel said, looking away from Mark Allen for a moment to see Patty's reaction.

"Paul Frank never mentioned you," Patty said, "or if he did, I don't remember."

He extended his free hand and helped Patty up. "I guess I'm not that memorable." He grinned as he held Patty's hands in his until he was confident she was once again steady on her feet.

"Thanks," she murmured. "Seeing you threw me. You look so much like him."

"I left the mountain a long time ago with my nephews, Johnny Michael and Mark Allen here. The two of them used to live in McCurdysville, and I lived near Paul Frank on Broad Run."

"The two of you look the same age as Paul Frank," Patty said as she looked from one to the other.

"We are pretty much," Orval Frank said. "I mean, my mother was older when I was born. So was Paul Frank's.

"My brother, Johnny Michael, Orval Frank here, and I decided to go into law enforcement," Mark Allen said. "Paul Frank felt he needed to stay home and take care of his sisters, so he stayed on at his parent's house on Broad Run, even after they died."

"That's right, I mean, neither of us ever planned to return to the mountain. But as you know, the day Paul Frank was killed; no one was giving Cliff Moran, who had no authority to run an investigation in this county, the back-up to solve the crime.

"I mean to discover what was behind the whole sordid story. It never made sense that Robby Rudd would deliberately kill Paul Frank. There is just no justification for him to out–and-out murder my cousin," Orval Frank said. "Johnny Michael, Mark Allen, and I vowed that we would not stop until we did find out what was behind it all. First, we had to get the sheriff arrested for his crimes, but that's a long story. Johnny Michael joined Homeland Security after 9/11, which ultimately put him in the right place after all this went down."

"All that stuff took place months before the murders of Tommy Lee Hillberry and Paul Frank," Mark Allen said. "After the murders happened, Jess Willis, Orval Frank here, and I got together and found plenty of evidence to prove Sheriff Moats' numerous crimes."

"I mean, after Ozzie was locked up, Jess was voted sheriff. He knew that he, Mark Allen, and I now had a free hand to look into the case and find out what really led to Paul Frank's killing. The town has never been as safe as it is now under Jess Willis. I mean, he has always been underestimated, but not any more."

"Ozzie always had only one deputy," Patty said.

"Yeah," Mark Allen said. "That was then, and this is now. With Ozzie Moats not taking care of business as far as up keeping the law on the mountain, there was no need for more than one deputy. One was enough to sweep the floors and keep the jail clean."

"I'm Jacob McCallister's daughter," Patty said, watching the young men's faces for their reaction.

"Well, I'll be damned . . . excuse me!" Mark Allen said, apologizing for swearing. "But I hope we didn't hurt your feelings saying those things about your father."

"I already knew you were his daughter when you said you were Paul Frank's girl," said Orval Frank. He had noticed that Patty was still a little pale. "Let's go and sit down."

He and Mark Allen led the two girls to the boarding house and had them sit in rocking chairs on the expansive wraparound porch.

"By the way, I'm Isabel Brown," Isabel said, comfortably easing back and forth in the rocking chair. "I'm Patty's friend."

"Nice to meet you," Mark Allen grinned, as she had directed the introduction toward him.

"Do all of the people on this mountain have two first names?" Isabel asked mischievously.

"Sure, why not?" Mark Allen teased back.

Having recovered from the initial shock, Patty could not keep her eyes off Paul Frank's cousin. "Paul Frank and I may have gotten married if he had lived," Patty said without preamble.

"I can see why he'd be interested in you." Orval Frank actually blushed after being so bold.

Orval Frank's interest in Patty did not go unnoticed by either Mark Allen or Isabel.

"From what I know about your father, I mean, what reason could you have for returning to this place?" Orval Frank changed the subject, seeing that talking about Paul Frank was too hard for Patty. "I'd think it could be dangerous for you."

"Really? Now that I'm not a child, my father has no interest in me."

"From what I gather, you never thought that Tommy Lee Hillberry would be a threat to you either," Mark Allen cut in.

"You got me there," Patty admitted, "but my father was behind it all. He was the one who hired Tommy Lee to work at the mansion."

"See what I'm getting at. I mean, why are you putting yourself in harm's way then?" Orval Frank asked. "At the time you couldn't have known your father was behind the whole thing. That could happen again."

"I have family here," Patty said. Tears brimmed, threatening to spill from her huge blue eyes. "That's what got Paul Frank killed. You see, it was my fault. He was helping me find my relatives."

"Don't be silly, I mean, it's only normal for your boyfriend to help you with something like that."

"I still feel like it's my fault."

"Oh, my gosh, Patty," Isabel blurted. "How can you say that? People help others all the time. Like crap happens, that's all."

"She's right," Orval Frank said, "Patty, you've got to know that Paul Frank wouldn't want you to feel that way."

"I know that," Patty smiled. "You sound so much like him, it's uncanny."

Orval Frank grinned. He heard that all the time. "Maybe I can help you find your family. I mean, I'm a pretty good investigator."

"I'm sure you are, and thanks for the offer, but I found my grandmother and she's filled me in on everyone else. I came to the mountain to visit her and I also want to visit the family I grew up with. You know Sara don't you?"

"Don't I though," Orval Frank said. "I mean, just yesterday she went and married Jess Willis. They're as happy as any young couple I've ever seen."

"Really?" Patty returned the grin. "Good for her! I never thought she'd leave the mountain and her mother. I'm glad to hear she isn't going to die an old maid. And I hope he's good to Kelly Sue."

"Jess?" Mark Allen said, "That man is love-struck. How could he not care for her daughter? He's a good man, Patty, don't worry."

"We'd better be about our rounds," Orval Frank said, smiling. "Hope I see you girls again. I mean, there're not many pretty faces in this town."

"First though, can we help you girls out, when you go on the mountain?" Mark Allen asked.

"Maybe we'll take you up on that later." Isabel smiled at him.

"Hope to see you soon then."

"I mean, maybe we could go for dinner soon?" Orval Frank asked.

"We'll see. I need to get past you not being Paul Frank. Really, it just creeps me out," she shrugged.

Sheepishly, Orval Frank tipped his official deputy's hat and followed Mark Allen across the street to the sheriff's office.

"Oh, my gosh! Those guys are so too good looking," Isabel said when the deputies were out of sight.

"You kinda took a liking to Mark Allen, did you?"

"Oh, my gosh, you noticed it," Isabel said. "And I saw how you and Orval Frank looked at each other."

"Really! That's so not true," Patty snapped, loyal to Paul Frank's memory even after two years. But then she relented, suspecting that she was not going to be able to resist Orval Frank. "Mark Allen is just as handsome."

"Like, don't I know it," Isabel said.

"Really! You're interested?"

"I am."

"That's cool," Patty said.

"What about you?" Isabel asked. "Can you let go of Paul Frank and have a relationship with someone who could be his twin?"

Patty looked at Isabel and smiled. "What could be better?"

"Just so you keep them separate in your mind. I know you don't want to forget Paul Frank, and what you had with him. I don't think it would be good for you if you tried to replace Paul Frank with Orval Frank. Like, there's bound to be a difference."

"Really, I won't. Don't worry."

"Patty, the guys seemed truly concerned about us venturing on the mountain by ourselves. What if they are right? Think about it. Murder, kidnapping, and from what you've told me, those mountain men have no regard for women. Oh my gosh, I have this feeling we won't come back."

"Really, Isabel, you're being melodramatic. This is not the first time I've been back since I ran away from here, and I'm still going wherever I want, and no one's stopping me."

"Oh, my gosh, Patty! You're forgetting what happened the last time you were here."

Patty and Isabel had arrived at the primitive, mountain cabin and were sitting quietly in the car as Isabel took in her surroundings. During the ride up the mountain from Winding Ridge, Patty had pointed out her grandmother, Myrtle Landacre's cabin, "We'll stop there on our way back down the mountain," Patty had said.

"Isabel, this is strange," Patty had remarked when they pulled in at the rear of the cabin. "I can't imagine that there's no one coming to the door to see who is out here."

To Patty's amusement, Isabel had been taking everything in with wide-eyed wonderment. On the way up the mountain,

Patty had kept her focus on the narrow, rutted-out dirt road, but she'd still been constantly aware of Isabel's rapt attention to her new environment.

"Oh, my gosh. This is way out." Isabel breathed, stepping from the car and looking overwhelmed at what she saw. "And this is where you were raised? I have to say it's pretty far removed from where you are now."

"Really, you have a good eye for the obvious." Patty laughed, momentarily forgetting the hard fact that there was no welcome greeting. "Do you feel you've ever been to a place like this?"

"No."

"What do you think?"

"It looks so deserted," Isabel whispered.

"Really!" Patty said. "You don't have to whisper, we're not trespassing or anything. Let's go in."

It was too quiet.

"This is strange, Isabel. I can't think of a time when someone wasn't checking to see who had come calling the minute the hum of an engine was heard and the vehicle came into view. Even if someone came walking, like when we kids came home from school, there'd be someone standing on the porch just dying to know who it was. It's not like anyone ever came just to visit us."

"Except, from what you told me, the law, and from the looks of it, visitors would be a rare occasion," Isabel noted.

"What do you mean?" Patty asked sharply.

"Can't you see? Who'd want to come here! Like, you have to know that."

"Really? Well, you're right, especially about no one much ever coming to call unless Pa was in trouble for one thing or another. Then it'd usually be Deputy Jess Willis."

The girls stepped onto the back stoop and tentatively approached the back door. Patty pulled the screen door open and turned the doorknob, pushing the door inward a crack. She jumped back with a squeal.

"Oh, my gosh! What is it, Patty?" Isabel was pushed backward by Patty's abrupt movement.

CHAPTER 21

"WILL YA LOOK AT THIS?" ANNABELLE asked. "We missed this when we was doin' our goin's over th' place yesterday."

Aggie looked over Annabelle's shoulder and for once had nothing to offer. "What is that? I ain't never seen anythin' like it, so I ain't."

"I don't knowed," Annabelle answered. "I ain't ever seen such as that neither."

Huddled together, they were looking at the built-in wall oven. Jeb had shown them how to use the stove but had forgotten to show them how to use the oven. In fact, he had not given a thought to the oven or the built-in TV, and the women had not discovered either of the televisions in their explorations.

Aggie shouldered Annabelle out of her way, opened the door, and turned the knob above the opening. Quickly the heating elements—top and bottom—began to turn red. "Oh, that's gettin' hot, so it is, just like the top of th' stove does where ya set the pots an' pans to cook, but ya can't set nothin' on them. What would ya hang on th' top one anyway?"

"Forevermore, it's th' oven. I can tell 'cause it has a pull-down door. It's not much different than th' one on th' wood-burner, except ya have to build a fire in that one. It's been right under our noses, an' I'd thought we couldn't bake th' bread."

"What do ya mean 'not much different'? It's in th' wall, an' t'ain't safe, so t'ain't. Anyway, I like th' bread Jeb's buyin', so I do."

"I miss th' oven-baked bread. I've always baked."

"Hogwash! Ya stuff enough of th' store-bought kind down your gullet, so ya do. Seems y'are likin' it a little too much."

"Well, there's th' meat," Annabelle said, wanting the last word. "Chicken, roast, an' such is better done in th' oven. It's not just for bread."

The women continued to quarrel as Aunt Aggie moved away to settle into her favorite rocking chair, leaving the work to Annabelle. The chairs looked out of place, but they gave the kitchen a quaint kind of charm. She quickly stood again when the cat she sat on hissed and squirmed free, leaping to the floor, waiting. As soon as Aggie sat, the cat was on her lap, settling to a comfortable sleeping position.

Annabelle commenced to prepare a meal in the unfamiliar kitchen. She found it both handy and inconvenient at the same time. Inconvenient because she was not familiar with such gadgets and appliances, but on the other hand, as she figured out—or was helped by Jeb to figure out—how to operate them, it was fun seeing that everything she needed was near at hand. And as there was no need for kindling wood, there was no messy sawdust or wood scraps to bite into her feet through her ragged, thin slippers.

Annabelle and Aggie jumped as Jeb's voice startled them. *That man just comes and goes without nary a word. He's goin' to be th' death of me, givin' me a heart attack.*

"Do ya have to sneak up on a body? Ya liked to've scared me to death." Annabelle quarreled as she moved in a small circle from oven to cook top to the side counter, setting the food out.

"Don't be so dramatic, Annabelle. Get used to it."

"Used to be able to hear your truck comin' up th' road an' knowed ya was comin' home."

"Like I said, get used to it. Not knowing when I'm going to show up will keep the two of you on your toes.

"I'm hungry. What's to eat?"

"Can'tcha see? Th' most of it's here on th' counter. I'm gatherin' it to put on your plate. I'd've baked bread, but we just now found th' oven."

"I didn't ask you what you don't have, did I? I just want something to eat."

"Ya don't have to be so contrary. Just sit down an' I'll fix ya a plate." Annabelle said, reaching in the cupboard for a plate.

"After you finish serving up my food, I want the two of you to get lost. You can go to your rooms."

"Why on earth ya wantin' us to go to our rooms? Ain't nothin' to do there, so there ain't."

"I have company coming, and I don't want the two of you sticking your noses in my business. I know what happened the time I got put in prison, the two of you knew too much for your own good. Neither of you could wait to spill your guts about what you knew."

"That ain't true," Aggie said, hurt that he would say such a thing. He knew very well she was not involved in the investigation. It was Annabelle and the others that Cliff Moran took to the city to question. "I never told no one a thing, an' ya knowed it, an' that big-feelin' detective knowed it, too, so he did. Ya'd best not forget our pact, so ya shouldn't. Ya'd be under th' jail instead of in it if'n I was a blabbermouth like th' otherons, so ya would."

"Don't you threaten me, Aggie," Jeb said through clenched teeth. His fear of her threat was the only thing that kept him from losing his temper entirely. "You should know that that's one thing I won't stand for. And I know that you weren't involved with the law, like the other women, giving them information to convict me. And I appreciate it, but I'm not getting into that position again."

"I don't like bein' sent to my room, so I don't."

"I don't either, and we have work to do out here," Annabelle joined in. She set the plate, which she had prepared while he and his aunt quarreled about the two of them being sent to their respective rooms, on the table in front of him.

"Don't bother me with your quarreling! Just do what I say."

"Just how long do ya want us to stay in our rooms?" Annabelle demanded to know.

"I'll let you know. Now do as I've said."

"Now, don't ya forget 'bout us. 'Cause I'm not stayin' in my room an' twiddlin' my thumbs all evenin', so I'm not."

"You can watch TV like everyone else does. You each have one in your room," Jeb sighed. When he saw the blank looks on their faces, he said, "Come with me, I'll show you."

He led them to Aggie's room, opened the cabinet that housed the TV, and showed the women how to work it.

"I pondered about what that was," Annabelle said. "It looks like a window ya can't see out of. Why, there's one in th' kitchen behind a cupboard door."

Jeb turned on the TV, and a full-color picture filled the screen. He changed the channels until he came to a news station.

"'Pon my soul," Aggie said. "I've heard of it, but never thought I'd see it, so I didn't."

"It's not so much different from the radio," Jeb explained, "except you can see who's talking, and what they're doing."

He showed them how to use the remote to turn the TV off and on, and how to change channels, and which were the news stations, knowing Annabelle was addicted to the news.

"The remote for the TV in the kitchen is in the drawer beneath it. It works just like this one," he said, indicating the remote in Aggie's hand.

The women recalled seeing the remote in the drawer, as well as the ones in their bedrooms, but had no idea what they were for. There was so much to take in, they had not bothered themselves with such a small thing, knowing they could delve into the matter later.

Annabelle was mesmerized by the moving picture bringing alive the news she loved. The stories were filled with action and bright colors, and she could actually see the person who was talking. It was all so spectacular; she hurriedly crossed to her own room and turned on her TV. Then she moved the chair from the window and placed it in front of her new passion.

Jeb, pretty much forgotten, went back to his food, leaving the women in their respective rooms.

Aggie, unlike Annabelle, didn't let her curiosity of the TV overcome her fascination for who was coming to visit her nephew. She watched, concealed behind the drapes at her patio door, as a car stopped at the gate. She observed as the man reached out and pushed the intercom button to announce his arrival. She could not hear her nephew's answer or the man's voice on the other side of the gate. The gate slowly opened, and the car moved toward the front of the mansion.

Aggie could not keep herself from watching as the man opened the driver's side door and climbed from the car. Noting that he was every bit as good-looking as Jeb, and leaving the TV playing, she hurried to her door and slowly—so as not to make a sound—opened it on the hallway. Creeping along the wall toward the kitchen, Aggie, not one to miss anything, especially if it concerned her nephew, moved to the entryway to the kitchen. She held her breath, listening.

CHAPTER 22

PATTY HAD SLAMMED THE SCREEN DOOR. "There's a wild animal in the kitchen. Annabelle must be gone. She would never allow wild animals into the cabin. They could be rabid."

Patty struggled to keep her composure.

"You okay?" Isabel asked. "You've turned pale as a ghost.

"Yes, no, I mean seeing that wild animal reminded me of what happened to Paul Frank. He got bitten when he was searching for me. He broke into the shed, and the panicked animal jumped out and bit Paul Frank before he could react. I think that animal was probably rabid. Anyway, Paul Frank was killed shortly after that."

"Oh, my gosh! Call out, just in case." Isabel fell back a few more steps until she was at the very edge of the back stoop.

"Anyone home?" Patty called, fearfully opening the screen door and sticking her head in the kitchen just far enough to see the interior. "Anyone?"

When there was no answer, and keeping an eye out for the animal, she pulled the door open, quickly stepping behind it—and just in time. She pulled Isabel with her because, like a flash, a large ball of fur darted from the cabin. They squealed as the weight of the animal hit the screen door, pinning them to the weather-beaten log exterior, as it scrambled for freedom.

Isabel sobbed, watching the animal scamper quickly away.

"It's okay. The animal's gone." Patty put her arm around Isabel's trembling body and steadied her. "It's gone!"

"Oh, my gosh! I can feel my heart beating like a drum in my chest."

"This is creepy," Patty whispered. "Honestly, I've never walked inside this cabin without either a greeting or a reprimand for something or another. Come to think about it, it was more often a scolding that I got."

"Sounds like a glowing welcome," Isabel said sarcastically.

The first thing Patty noticed was that the rocking chairs that always stood on either side of the potbelly stove were gone. *This is beyond strange,* she thought.

"It's so quiet, it's spooky." Patty noticed then that the crates—the ones that Annabelle had nailed to the wall years ago to hold the tinplates and other kitchen utensils–were gone, and so were their contents.

Isabel was barely listening to Patty as she gazed around the primitive room she had found herself in. Realizing that Isabel was lost in thought, Patty watched her closely to gauge her reaction. She realized that Isabel wasn't touching anything or moving about. Apparently attracted to something Patty could not see, Isabel stared wide-eyed into space, as if she were seeing something in her mind's eye.

"What is it, Isabel?"

"Nothing," Isabel denied too quickly, jumping at the sound of Patty's voice. "You shouldn't scare me like that. I'm still spooked by the animal that frantically scurried out when you opened the door."

She leaned into Patty and whispered, "What other wild animal is in here?" "Forget it, there are no more animals. There are only the two of us in here, but you're staring off into space for some reason. Tell me."

"You are so determined to link me to this place, Patty," Isabel shouted angrily, "but I can't make any sense of my dreams, and I don't think I ever will."

"You don't want to, you protest too much, and yes you can. Just relax. Come on, let's see if there's anyone here." Patty looked at Isabel pointedly, "Don't be so scared—I'm talking about my family. There's no more wild vermin going to jump out and scare you.

"Annabelle, anyone, it's Patty. Where are you?' Patty called out. She gripped Isabel's arm and pulled her behind her as they walked directly through the doorway to the living room. Finding no one there, they continued through the doorway to the right that led to Annabelle's bedroom. Empty. Patty led Isabel to the right once again, through a third doorway to the children's bedroom. Replacing the quilts and mats that she and the other children had slept on was a full-size mattress lying in the center of the floor. Except for the tattered curtains hanging at the doorways, there was not one thing left there from when it had been her bedroom. She led Isabel to the right, parting the curtains, and going through the fourth doorway. The circle was complete; they were back in the kitchen.

"Patty," Isabel said. "I hate to encourage you, but the curtains hanging at the doorways, the musty odor . . ."

Patty tugged on the arm she had been gripping, "Go on, Isabel. What?"

"Oh, my gosh. In my dreams, I must've been around twelve months old or so. I'm running in a circle through those doorways. I'm in the kitchen, then the living room, one bedroom then the second back into the kitchen. I'm making a small circle, like we just did."

"Really! It's like my memories. I remember me, Joe, and Sara running and playing—of course it was when Pa was not here—and getting in trouble with Annabelle about being under foot, and pulling the curtains from the spike nails that held them up. But how in heaven's name would you know that when you did that you must have been only a year old?"

"I don't really know, but oh, my gosh, I just do. There were a few other little ones, but there were babies crawling after me. I guess it was a game we played.

"I remember the curtains getting in my way. I'd just push them aside. Aren't they the most smelly, ugly things? You know, I paid no attention to that. We were just doing what toddlers do, running and playing."

Patty watched the expressions on Isabel's face change by the second.

Patty had never seen the place through another's eyes as she was now: The tattered, faded curtains and the poorly fitted wood planks—in numerous places—letting in the outside air and exposing the damp earth below.

"You know what this means, Isabel?"

"Let's talk about it later. The flood of memories somehow makes me nauseous."

"Really? Isabel, my dreams make me nauseous, too, especially when they're of the past. I also break out in a cold sweat. The ones that seem to predict the future are more like nightmares."

"Oh, my gosh," Isabel said. "This is too much."

"It will be dark soon. We'd better go now," Patty said, taking Isabel's hand. "I can't figure why Annabelle, at least, isn't here. She never goes anywhere except church. And I mean never. I'm really worried."

"This isn't Sunday morning so it's not church. So where could she be?" Isabel asked, reeling from the experience of finding the place of her nightly dreams. "You said your Aunt Aggie lived further up the mountain. Maybe she's visiting her."

"Maybe, but I doubt it. It's more likely Aunt Aggie would come here to visit Annabelle."

"I wish I could meet them. I wonder if . . ? "

"If what?"

"Oh, Patty, I have to be honest with you. This place doesn't just remind me of the place of my dreams, like, it *is* the place!"

"Will you tell me about them now?"

"Let's go to the front porch," Isabel said.

"Okay, but it's getting late, and we need to get back to town."

"Like, since when are you afraid of being out in the dark?"

"Isabel, there's no electricity here. That means no street lights, and it gets very dark early on the mountain. The higher mountain range blocks the sun as it goes down. We don't have a lot of time to get to Aunt Aggie's, Grandmother's, and back to our room."

"Okay, let's see the porch, and then we'll go.

Patty opened the front door, and they stepped out.

"Oh, my gosh! Oh, my gosh!" Isabel cried.

CHAPTER 23

Unconsciously, Aggie held her breath. She waited patiently and heard the muted conversation coming from the grand entrance hall. Soon her patience was rewarded when she heard her nephew say, "Come in, come in." Defiantly, she peered around the corner as Jacob stepped back from the open door.

"Am I late?"

"At least this time you've been invited."

"Don't sweat it," Howerton grinned. "I got the message. You want me to call before I show up at your door."

"Buddy Dean, you're never late."

Where Jacob had dark hair, deep brown eyes, Buddy Dean Howerton was blond and blue-eyed. Jacob's skin was dark mahogany while Buddy Dean had a golden tan that he vainly kept up, as he did his muscles. In addition to their disregard for the law, another thing Jacob and Dean had in common was their commitment to body building.

"Yeah, I landed in a Kentucky jail for a while after that."

"Don't tell me you have a trunk load of money." Jacob laughed, closing the door behind Buddy Dean. "That's what got you in trouble the first time."

"The second time, and I do, and as you know, I'm the best there is." Dean grinned.

"Yeah, until you get caught." They both laughed.

"But I don't plan on getting caught." Dean raised his eyebrows as his way of showing that, although he could take the heat and the ribbing, he did not like the way the conversation was going.

"Come in. It's good to see you. I'm sure you want me to tell you yet again that the art you chose for me turned out to be great. The paintings fit in like they belong here."

"Sure, why not? I like hearing how good I am," Buddy Dean pointed out.

"They're just right for the grand hallway, and the paintings are my preferences as a means for investing my money. Better than money in the bank." Jacob slapped Howerton on the back.

"Not better than making your own," Buddy Dean said, leering.

"Too risky!" McCallister shook his head. He believed counterfeiting was unwise. Motioning for Howerton to follow, he led the way the length of the entry hall to the kitchen. "You look like you might be hungry, Dean. I was just having a bite. There's enough for you."

"Thanks. It's been a while since I've had a decent meal."

Buddy Dean tried not to look impressed as he was led down the great hall, getting a view of the posh rooms off from it, and now the extravagant kitchen. He had never been inside farther than the front entrance and had had no idea that McCallister lived like this.

After they'd eaten one of the best meals Buddy Dean had ever had, they talked about the time they had first met and the counterfeiting that had gotten Buddy Dean arrested and imprisoned.

"You know I'm so good at counterfeiting that I can't get it out of my mind. I just know I can make the perfect twenty dollar bill."

"Absolutely not!" McCallister slammed his fist against the table, rattling the dinnerware. "That's not my bag. Howerton. I can't take the chance on getting on the wrong side of the law. That big-feeling Cliff Moran won't give me a break. He keeps tabs on everything I do. I just can't understand why you want to team up with me in your counterfeiting when you know full well that I'm being scrutinized by the law in everything I do."

"Who isn't?" Dean asked, priding himself that he did not as much as flinch at McCallister's outburst.

"Anyway, look around you, Howerton."

"I have! Today. You know this is the first I've been past the front entrance. I had no idea of the furnishings, the ceramic floors, and the rich wood trim that are here."

"Yeah," Jacob said, "but I didn't get this from counterfeiting."

"Oh, you think selling children is noble?"

"Don't be an ass," McCallister hissed.

"Don't be so unbending." Dean leaned his chair back, balancing on two legs as he picked his teeth with the toothpick he always carried in his breast pocket. "You've done time too. With me you could have more money than you ever dreamed, and there's no work involved."

"You've got to be kidding! Howerton, it's not for me."

"I like living dangerously as I know you do," Dean insisted.

Jacob laughed. "What do you really want?"

"I know you're connected with a terrorist plot that's going to make you millions, and I want in on it. I can partner with you, and I have a plan where my knowledge in counterfeiting will benefit you."

"Hell," McCallister said. "They're the ones with the capital. I don't think they need funny money."

"Let me tell you something," Buddy Dean said, grinning.

"Wait a minute!" McCallister clenched his teeth. "The last time you were here, you arrived shortly after I had a visitor. Don't tell me you are involved with him and he's carrying your funny money."

"You didn't mention you had a visitor, McCallister. Who might that have been?"

Jacob McCallister stood his full height, towering over Howerton, who remained seated.

"Just what do you want to tell me, Howerton?"

CHAPTER

24

"ISABEL!" PATTY GRABBED THE GIRL'S shoulders. "What's the matter?"

"I have one dream where I'm outside on a porch—just like this one—with a large man, and he's sitting in a rocking chair with a funny, faraway look in his eyes. He's my father, and I have a sense that I'm more than a little afraid of him. I know I was only a toddler at the time, but it's like he sees me as a thing—not a person, like, you know what I mean."

"Yes, I felt like that too, but I had reasons . . ." Overcome by the hurtful memories, Patty wrenched the door open and motioned for Isabel to follow her back into the cabin.

Isabel ignored the gesture. "It's this porch! I have been here, Patty. Oh, my gosh, oh, my gosh . . . There were rocking chairs and an old swing facing the center of the porch. I remember hearing a car on the road as it drew closer. It stopped near the front steps. Right there," Isabel said, pointing at the steps. "A man and a woman got out of the car, came and put me in it with them, and took me away."

"Do you remember anyone else?"

"No. Like just the man, and me—my father—that's all," Isabel murmured. "Up until the people came, I remember sitting near the steps, at my father's feet, playing with something. I don't remember what."

"I can remember that when Pa sold one of the children, he always did it on Sunday. He'd send the rest of us to church. I guess he didn't want us to see the people or them us."

"I'm only ten months older than you, Patty. If my dreams are true you were a baby at the time I was sold."

"Assuming Tuesday guessed my age correctly. I remember through the years, most of the time Pa sold the children soon after birth. The twins were one exception. They were toddlers, like you must have been."

"Patty, I don't understand, you've just told me that he sold all his children, and you told me why you think he kept the three of you, but I still can't understand why he didn't sell you, Joe, and Sara."

"Like I said before, I don't really know why he kept Joe and Sara, except to appease Annabelle, and probably to help with the constant work that needed done. She was his first wife. As for me, I had that horrible birthmark on my face that I all ready told you about, and I guess he knew no one would want me."

"Well, then what happened to it? Except for a few faint scar lines, your face is as smooth as silk.

"Tuesday and Cliff saw to it that I had plastic surgery."

"What did it look like?"

"It was purple, and it covered the right side of my face from here,"—Patty touched her eyebrow—"to the corner of my mouth."

"Oh, my gosh. How old were you when you had plastic surgery?"

"It took a few years, and a few surgeries. It was healed before my sixteenth birthday."

"Like, aren't you lucky!"

"Really, I am. I was teased for so long I thought that I was ugly and stupid. I tell you, if not for Tuesday and Cliff, I would have stayed on this time-forsaken mountain and hid from the world. I was teased and tormented by the mountain kids and the townies, but it was nothing compared to the teasing I endured when I first started school in Wheeling."

"You do okay now," Isabel said. "Like, I've noticed, though, that some of the girls are jealous of you."

"Really, like they're not jealous of you?"

"Oh, my gosh, Patty. I don't have anything to be jealous of," Isabel said, frowning, "but, on the other hand, you do have."

"Really? People stop and stare all the time. They think we look alike, so if I'm so hot, how can you not be?"

Isabel didn't answer. Once again lost in her surroundings, she felt a stirring of vague memories—and unforgotten dreams.

"Isabel! Isabel!" Patty broke into the girl's thoughts.

"What? You don't have to shout.

"I was thinking, I can understand why your birthmark kept your father from selling you, but what about Joe and Sara and how the three of you grew up together? Do you know the real reason Joe and Sara were allowed to be raised by their own mother? I can't imagine that a man who was cruel enough to sell his own flesh and blood would care about what a mere woman wanted."

"I suppose Pa wanted Joe to do the work, and I believe he wanted Sara to bear children for him to sell. He encouraged me, Joe, and Sara to get close like no sister and brother should. Not one of us knew better, but I always wanted something better for my life. We had catalogs Pa brought us from The Company Store or from the city, and we used them for toilet tissue in the outhouse. I didn't realize how pathetic that was until I moved to Wheeling with Tuesday and Cliff. Anyway, I spent hours leafing through them, and that's how I learned that there was a better way of life."

"Like, you got all that from a catalog?"

"The models, clothing, furniture making up a room like I could've never imagined, and the happy faces the models wore. After all that, I just added a few dreams," Patty smiled.

"That's so cool."

"Well, back to the issue. Where is everyone?" Patty wondered out loud. "Look, Isabel, I can't stop thinking about it. There's always been a rocking chair on each side of the potbelly stove and now they're gone."

"Maybe your aunt knows where Annabelle is."

"That's our next stop, but tomorrow. It's getting dark, and we shouldn't be out so late. Let's go back to our room and head for Aunt Aggie's early in the morning."

"That suits me fine," Isabel said, obviously relieved.

"What're'ya doin'?" Annabelle whispered.

Aggie nearly jumped out of her skin. "Shush, Annabelle! Ya tryin' to get us in trouble? Jeb told us to stay in our rooms an' watch TV, so he did."

"Then why ar'ya standin', here with ya ear bendin' 'round th' corner nibbin' in Jeb's business?"

"Same reason y'are here tryin' to peep 'round th' corner like ya got nose trouble, so I am. I'm worried, Annabelle. Lets go to my room an' talk. Jeb's goin' to hear us an' get in an uproar."

"Who's that man?" Annabelle said, closing the door as quietly as she could.

"I heard Jeb sayin' his name. It's Buddy Dean Howerton, so it is."

"What's he wantin'?"

"I'm scared, Annabelle," Aggie cried. "They're talkin' 'bout workin' with the terrorist, so they are."

"What?" Annabelle felt the hair stand up at the back of her neck.

"Ya heard what I was sayin', so ya did. We've got to stop Jeb, so we do."

"How?"

"I don't knowed, so I don't. Only thing I knowed is we have to watch 'im as close as we can."

"We have to do somethin' or he's goin' to be in big time trouble this time. Why, I listened to every word when th' news was all about th' attack on th' World Trade Towers. I can tell ya th' law will never rest until the terrorists are found, an' as for me, I don't want Jeb mixed up with th' likes of 'em."

"That's what I just said, so it was."

"All we can do is keep our eye on 'im," Annabelle warned. "He's got this big house to take care of, an' that ought to keep him busy. We'll see to it."

"I'll not take fault with that, so I won't."

"I don't want to tell you a thing," Buddy Dean said."You know it all."

"Then, let me tell you something," McCallister said, gritting his teeth as he pushed back his empty plate. "I don't know how you got the idea that I was mixed up in terrorism, but I'm not. I decline your offer to team up in the funny money business. I'm not interested in counterfeiting. I don't know how many times you want me to tell you that."

"What about the jobs I've done for you already? You said yourself I did a great job choosing the paintings."

"You did. You did, but that's done for now. I've never said anything to you about getting involved in counterfeiting or terrorism. Everyone knows I'm against the militia that was gathering here, so why would you think I'd want to get involved with terrorism? It's all the same to me. Dean, did you by any chance use counterfeit money to purchase the paintings and keep the money I gave you?"

"Would I do that?" Buddy Dean grinned showing white, even teeth, and pushed his plate toward the center of the table.

"Actually, I think you would," McCallister said. "I won't be connected with your schemes. Do you understand?"

Buddy Dean shrugged, "I'm fine with that."

"Give me a number to contact you, and if I need you I'll call. Now get out of here. You know it's not safe for me to be associated with you, nor you with me."

Buddy Dean handed McCallister his card and said, "We'll keep in touch."

"Damn right we will. I'll see you out, and I am considering another job for you. How would you like to be my bodyguard? When I'm in the city, you can watch my back. If things work out, I have other jobs you can do. But remember, I don't want to hear the word terrorist come out of your mouth again."

Buddy Dean reached out and shook McCallister's hand, wearing a self-satisfied smile. "I know we can work together, and you couldn't find a better person for a bodyguard."

"Okay then, come back Thursday evening at the same time and we can talk again. I'll have your instructions. I have a great deal to put together for now," Jacob said.

"And Dean, you'd better not be up to something that I'm not aware of. I won't be blindsided. I have ways to keep my people honest."

"What're you talking about? I haven't given you one reason to be suspect when it comes to my work."

"Timing, Howerton, and bad vibes. I don't have time for penny ante schemes."

"Timing? What's that supposed to mean?"

"I think you know."

"Just so you know, I only do big time, McCallister. Don't mess with me."

"Look, you came to me. I can do without the sarcasm," Jacob snarled. "You're lucky that I believe I'm going to need you. If I didn't, I'd kick your ass out the door so fast you wouldn't remember if you were inside or not."

Buddy Dean Howerton left.

Jacob headed for his room, unaware that the women had seen his guest and were worried that he was headed for trouble.

I don't need that asshole, but I've always heard that you should keep your friends close and your enemies closer.

CHAPTER 25

IT WAS FULL DARK WHEN PATTY AND ISABEL reached the boardinghouse. Patty found a parking place along the street with a little more difficulty than when they first arrived. "It seems to be getting busy around here," Patty noted. She did not notice that across the street a man watched the two girls intently as they locked the car and headed for the front door of the boardinghouse.

What do you know? If it isn't my long-lost daughter. He watched until they were out of sight.

What's with the girl? Always forcing me to hurt her.

He moved from the shadows.

CHAPTER 26

As CLIFF MORAN UNLOCKED THE DOOR to his office, his cell phone rang. The caller ID said it was Johnny Michael on the other end.

"What's up?" Cliff answered.

"You aren't going to believe this. The bones that Randy McCoy found in Aggie's cellar house two years ago are the bones of McCallister's dead parents."

"Are you kidding? Don't you need McCallister's parents' DNA to connect them with the bones?"

"Of course we do," Johnny Michael said. "Don't you get it? The bones are McCallister's parents' DNA."

Cliff could hear the grin in Johnny Michael's voice. Johnny usually had that special grin that made everyone like him immediately.

"The way it happened, Randy McCoy had found the bones during the search for Patty two years ago, and kept them in an evidence bag. He sent them off to have a DNA test. I just got the report that someone in the lab caught the match. The bones matched the DNA we have on McCallister. They are his parents, I'm sure."

"I remember from Aggie that his parents," Cliff added, "left McCallister, and Aggie took him in and raised him. According to Aggie, no one knew what became of them."

"I hate to speak badly of dear old Aunt Aggie," Johnny Michael said, "but it looks like murder, and I'm betting on Aggie and McCallister himself."

"Johnny, Aggie wouldn't murder her own sister," Cliff said.

"No, but she would cover up for her nephew, and we both know McCallister wouldn't think twice about getting rid of someone who stood in his way. That someone was his parents that time."

"If that is true, we finally have something to hang on McCallister that will put him away for good."

Up early in the morning, Patty sat staring at her doll while she waited for Isabel to finish her morning shower. Patty held the doll close to her face. *You think my Pa's watching me, don't you, Winter. He wouldn't dare. All he has to do is come near me and he will be arrested. You know that.*

"Are you talking to yourself, Patty?" Isabel came from the bathroom with a bath towel wrapped around her.

"No, Isabel, I'm talking to Summer." Patty looked Isabel in the eye, daring her to make a comment.

Isabel threw up her hands, "I'm not saying a word. Let's get ready to go. I'm hungry."

The girls left the car and Patty led the way to Aggie's back door. Once again it was too quiet.

"Anyone here?" Patty called as she opened the door and walked into the kitchen, with Isabel close behind her.

"Isabel, Aunt Aggie's rocking chairs are gone too. This is too weird!" She turned and faced Isabel.

Isabel let out a sigh of relief.

"What was that for?"

Isabel quipped. "I was never here."

"Isabel, the babies were never taken from the cabin where we were born until they were sold. When that couple picked you up, it was your first time you ever left the place of your birth. Pa never wanted anyone to know about the children he was going to sell, so he kept them in the cabin. There was never a birth certificate recorded either. "

"You're giving me the creeps!" Isabel shuddered.

"That's the way it was."

Isabel waved her hand to encompass the room.

"Why isn't this cabin as crappy as the other one?" She twirled around, taking in everything. Looking up, she noticed the ladder leading to the loft. "What's up there?"

"That's where the children of the family sleep. It saves having to build an extra room on. I've heard gossip that Aunt Aggie and Pa sold Aunt Aggie's stepchildren some years ago, after her husband died. That was when Pa was a teen himself."

Patty started up the ladder. "Let's take a look up there."

"I'm right behind you."

Reaching the top, the girls left the ladder and leaned over the rail that went around the loft, staring down at the living and kitchen areas. Both were impressed by Aggie's cabin, especially Isabel, after the unpleasant experience of visiting Annabelle's disorderly one.

"You didn't answer me," Isabel said, as she leaned on the rough wood that made up the rail. "Why is this place so nice?"

"It's a long story, and I've mentioned it to you a few times." Patty straightened up the covers and got comfortable on the bed, which sat on a pricey oriental rug. "Anyway, when the militia was having its assembly here on the mountain, the man who was in charge of the militia got Joe to rent this place to him. That man fixed it to suit himself."

"What'd he do with Aggie?"

"She stayed with Ma and the others. Aggie wanted to be where she'd hear the first news if there was anything happening with Pa. Otherwise, Joe would never've gotten her out of here. And all that militia stuff happened during the time Pa was in prison, or Pa wouldn't've let Joe get away with it. But you should've seen this place before the militiaman got it. Pa had dismantled this very loft to use for firewood."

"What?" Isabel looked back along the nifty loft.

"Yes, it was a raw wood floor with mats scattered over it," Patty remembered. "The time Tuesday and I were held here by my pa, he partially dismantled the place for firewood. At that time it was pretty much like the cabin we were looking for Annabelle in, except there was never a loft there.

"Anyway, that was when he decided to take Tuesday, Winter Ann, Aunt Aggie, and me to Broad Run to keep Cliff from finding us." Patty frowned. "He took us across the mountain in a sled he had gotten from Paul Frank Ruble. Paul Frank used his team of workhorses to pull the sled."

"I thought Paul Frank was your boyfriend!"

"Not at that time. We had just met. I don't think he knew yet what my Pa was up to or how cruel he really was."

"This is getting scary, Patty."

"I'll tell you more about it in the car. Let's go to see my grandmother before we go back to the boardinghouse," Patty said.

"Okay," Isabel said, knowing she needed to hear it all.

They made their way down the ladder by turning their backs away from the loft, stepping on each rung a foot at a time and holding on to the upper rungs as they went.

"What's that?" Isabel whispered, holding the rungs so tight her knuckles were white.

"Quiet," Patty whispered back, and her feet hit the floor as she let go of the rungs. She moved toward the door and saw that a stray cat had come into the cabin through the door they had left open. *Was it for a quick getaway if someone was hiding, waiting to grab them?* "It's only a cat."

CHAPTER 27

"OH, MY GOSH!" ISABEL SQUEALED upon seeing Myrtle Landacre's cabin up close.

Patty pulled off the rutted out dirt road into the weeds because there was no proper place to park. Myrtle, Patty's grandmother, had virtually no one who was interested in visiting her. Even her son Burl stayed away, almost never taking the time to visit with her. He did visit briefly a couple times a year, merely out of a sense of obligation. Otherwise, he sent a young boy from town, who made the trip on foot to get to her cabin. Once a month, Burl gave the boy a few dollars as his pay, as well as what he allotted for his mother's food for the month. Using a list Burl gave him, the boy made the purchases at The Company Store and delivered them to Myrtle.

The only other visitor she got was Mark Allen, who had a good heart and, as a deputy, went out of his way when he knew someone needed his help. He always brought her a few special groceries that he knew she would enjoy as an addition to necessities her son provided.

"Watch the briers, Isabel. You don't want to ruin your clothes and have your mother down on us about just what we were up to on our trip."

"Like that's possible," Isabel said. "There are briers everywhere, and they're so thick I can't even see the ground."

"Just step carefully." Patty laughed at the look on her friend's face. "I don't think there are any gigantic holes in the ground."

"Oh, my gosh. You think it's funny!" Isabel flipped her hair from her flushed face and stomped off toward the front door.

"Wait up, you're going to—"

Before Patty could get the warning out, Isabel got caught in a tangle of weeds and trash. She fell forward on her knees and mercifully caught herself with her hands.

"Seriously! I tried to warn you."

While Patty was trying to untangle Isabel, Myrtle stuck her head out the door to see what the commotion was. At the same time, the sheriff's Jeep was slowly moving down the mountain. It pulled to the edge of the overgrowth at the side of the road behind Patty's car and stopped. Inside the Jeep were Orval Frank and Mark Allen.

Surprise showed on their faces as they saw the girls struggling in the weeds. "What's going on?" Orval Frank asked as he and Mark Allen jumped from the Jeep, leaving their respective doors wide open.

At Mark Allen's command Buddy, his Jack Russell, stayed in the Jeep at first, wagging his tail furiously, wanting to get to the girls for attention. But Buddy was a young dog and he felt a need to go to the rescue, so he left caution to the wind and dashed to where the girls were. He excitedly licked Isabel's face, wagging his tail for all he was worth.

"Get off her!" Mark Allen got the dog away from Isabel and backed off toward the Jeep, unable to hide the grin on his face.

Buddy squirmed from Mark Allen's arms and ran directly to Isabel for the second time.

Recognizing the two men, Isabel's face flushed a deeper red at being caught in such a ridiculous posture with a dog all over her face.

"What're you grinning about?" She picked up the dog, to keep him from licking all the makeup from her face, and stood up straight. Gaining her balance, she set the dog back on his feet and brushed at her clothing, glaring angrily at the two men. They were both leaning at the hip against the side of the Jeep, grinning.

"What do you think, Mark Allen? I mean, don't you think these young women are as pretty as any you've ever seen?"

"I guess I do," Mark Allen happily replied. "Nice seeing you. Come here, Buddy." The dog jumped from Isabel's arms, ran back, and leapt into the Jeep.

"What's going on out there?" Myrtle shouted. "I don't see so well, an' I don't like it when ya youngins fuss outdoors of my place."

"It's me, Grandmother," Patty answered. "I've brought my friend to meet you, and these two gentlemen just stopped to say hello."

"Oh, my word. Come in here where I can see ya. I've been wonderin' when ya was goin' to get back here!"

Myrtle opened the door wide and, remembering that there were others outside her doorstep, called. "Is that ya, Mark Allen?"

"It's me, Myrtle. Orval Frank's with me. We just stopped to see that the girls were okay," Mark Allen said. He had closed the doors so Buddy could not get out and jump on

Isabel again, and now he was settled back against the Jeep, his legs crossed at the ankles, arms across his broad chest. "The one girl here seems to have trouble running through the brush."

Isabel glared at him.

Mark Allen grinned with a twinkle in his eyes that melted Isabel's anger at his teasing.

"How ya doin', Mark Allen?" Myrtle asked, grinning and showing her snuff-stained snaggleteeth. She nodded to Patty. "They're good young men—ain't many of them anymore, seems like."

"Good to see you, Myrtle," Mark Allen said.

"It's good to see ya too, Mark Allen, an' thanks for th' supplies ya brought for me. It's mighty kind of ya. My own son neglects me, but he's not a good man, no he's not. He's taken after his pa, I'm afraid."

"It's no big deal, Myrtle, I like to make sure you're not doing without what you need and are having a few special treats."

Patty and Isabel each were privately comparing the two deputies to the young men they attended school with in the city. There was no contest. The two deputies won hands down.

It was obvious the two were related to Paul Frank. In fact, Orval Frank looked so much like him that he could have been a twin, and the sight of him tugged at Patty's heart. Mark Allen was as tall and broad shouldered, too, but he had sandy hair and blue eyes, where Orval Frank had dark hair and brown eyes like Paul Frank's.

Isabel was enchanted with Mark Allen's mischievous smile, which showed off his perfect white teeth. And she thought his dimpled chin gave him a potent, masculine appeal.

"Come on, Isabel!" Patty tugged on her arm, bringing her out of her thoughts. Patty had been a little put out at the merriment on the men's faces when Isabel had been tangled in the wild vines, until her grandmother's declaration that Mark Allen looked after her needs. Besides, the truth was that Isabel had looked comical, struggling with the briers. Patty was sure that she herself had looked just as funny in her attempts to free Isabel. "Grandmother is waiting for us."

"Hope to see you girls soon," Orval Frank called, as he pushed himself away from the Jeep.

"We'd better head back to town," Mark Allen said. "Sheriff Jess'll be wondering what we'd gotten into."

With a nod and wave toward the two girls, who were heading clumsily toward the cabin, the guys headed down the mountain toward town. The last the deputies heard from them was Isabel mumbling, "Is this what you call an adventure? If it is, you're nuttier than any writer I've ever heard of."

"Really, so you've read the biographies of a few authors, have you?"

"Don't be funny."

When they reached the door, Myrtle opened it wide, her eyes gleaming at the sight of her granddaughter returning once again.

"Come in! Come in! Who ya got with ya?"

Patty hugged her grandmother before answering. "This is my new and best friend, Isabel. Isabel, this is my grandmother."

"Hi, I'm so glad to meet you,"

Isabel impulsively hugged the old woman.

Over Isabel's head, Patty saw the startled look on her grandmother's face.

"What is it, Grandmother?" Patty put her hand on Myrtle's arm.

"Does she knowed 'bout th' dreams?" Myrtle asked.

"Yes, she does. I told her as much as I understood."

"She's part of us in some way, Patty." Myrtle stared into Patty's eyes.

"How?" Patty knew that it was true, but she wanted to hear what Myrtle had to say about it.

"Ya an' her have ties, an' that's why ya was drawn together." Myrtle hesitated. "It was bound to happen . . . Even with me she has, I knowed it. There's a connection . . ."

"Really? Go on, Grandmother. What are you talking about?"

"You guys are losing me." Isabel rolled her eyes. "Patty, why don't you tell your grandmother what happened at the cabin when we were looking for Annabelle?"

"I will, Isabel, but first I want to hear what Grandmother has to say about us," she said, noticing that Isabel's eyes widened at Myrtle's outlandish use of vocabulary.

"Well th' two of ya believe y'are half sisters, don't ya?"

"We believe that we share the same father, yes," Patty answered, looking pointedly at Isabel.

"I believe it's true that ya share th' same father 'cause ya both look like 'im.

"But 'cause ya both have foretelling powers—an' I can tell—that's what some in th' old days called witchcraft, ya have th' same mother."

The girls gasped—Myrtle knew. Patty had been right about Myrtle having a gift to see much that others could not. Patty gasped. They had been thinking only that they shared the same father, never imagining that they had the same mother as well.

Isabel asked hurriedly, "How could that be possible?"

"I didn't say I knowed how it was possible, I just said it was. Ya each have a gift of dreamin'—that's what Betty always called it—so y'are goin' to have to learn what to do with it."

"Who's Betty?" Isabel asked, her eyes huge eyes. "Like, I don't understand any of this."

"My mother," Patty answered. "Our mother. It makes sense. I'd forgotten it, but now that we're talking about it, I'm pretty sure that I've been told Betty had a child before me. They were surprised that she had so much trouble with me, enough to have caused her death. That's something we can find out from Aunt Aggie and Annabelle. They'd know for sure. It's just a matter of getting them to tell us."

Patty knew enough from her own experiences to realize that what her grandmother said was true. Her own experience of foretelling dreams had led her stepfather, Cliff Moran, to other lost siblings.

"Our mother," Patty said, "is grandmother's daughter. She had the dreams too."

"Oh, my gosh! It runs in the family. Are you two kidding me?"

"No, Isabel, we're not. I don't know if it runs in the family or not, but the four of us have had the same experiences. I don't know what to call it, and I'm sure Grandmother doesn't either. That doesn't matter. It's what we do with our gift that matters."

"Yeah, me an' my Betty've had 'em too. I always called them warnings. More often that not, I don't knowed what to make of th' dreams I'm havin' now."

"Like, is this the twilight zone?" Isabel asked.

Patty laughed.

"That's done with," Myrtle said with conviction, taking the time to grab her spittoon and spit a brown wad into it.

"What're you talking about, Grandmother? What's done with?"

"Not th' witchcraft, but th' baby sellin'. It's done with. Don't see th' baby tradin' in my dreams no more." Myrtle's eyes clouded over with something like fear.

"I don't either," Patty murmured.

"Sorry," Isabel sighed. "I'm lost again."

"I don't knowed it all, but if ya two don't get outta here, you're goin' to get mixed up in th' work better left to th' law."

"You said yourself that you couldn't see anything when it came to your family, Grandmother, so how would you know that?"

"Y'are here an' there's trouble comin'. That's how."

"Oh, my gosh!" Isabel squealed. "What trouble?"

"I reckon I don't really knowed, but I've been havin' troublin' dreams lately an' I'll tell ya when I can. They just ain't makin' sense to me right now."

"Grandmother, I'm not going anywhere. I have questions and I'm going to ask them."

"Y'are a stubborn one."

"That's not it, Grandmother. I'm writing a memoir about my life on the mountain above Winding Ridge. I need to know the history of what happened around me that affected my life so profoundly."

"Patty," Isabel suggested, "maybe you should call it *The Mountain above Winding Ridge.*"

"Or maybe *Aunt Aggie's Story,*" Myrtle said. "There's much ya don't knowed 'bout her an' her nephew—your father, Jeb McCallister. Y'are goin' to learn some things y'are better off not knowin'."

"There's so much to take in," Isabel moaned. "I don't recognize my life anymore. Starting from our room at the boardinghouse to where Patty was born to Aggie's cabin to here."

For emphasis, Isabel stretched her fists out and jabbed her forefingers toward the floor. She looked at Myrtle sheepishly. "I don't mean any disrespect, but it's like I've crossed an invisible time line. You know, like in an Alfred Hitchcock movie."

"I don't knowed nothin' 'bout no movies, child." Myrtle showed her few snuff-darkened teeth in a rare smile. "I do know that y'are a kind soul. I can feel it. I'm glad that y'are, 'cause y'are my granddaughter, too."

Isabel smiled a broad smile showing her quick fondness for Myrtle. *My grandmother?*

"Grandmother," Patty asked, "there's nothing going on here on this never-changing mountain. How would we get mixed up in matters of the law?"

"Oh, child, do ya forget when th' law was chasin' all over th' mountain lookin' for Tuesday, when ya father brought her to his cabin against her will. Did ya forget th' militia? There's more than ya knowed goin' on here. Ya thinkin' th' militia was a bad thing—wait till th' terrorists show their handiwork."

"Terrorists?" Isabel shrieked.

"I know, Grandmother," Patty said, ignoring Isabel's question. "But that was a small period of time in my life. Now, you sound like Annabelle and Aunt Aggie. They've spent so much time listening to the talk shows on the radio they think there's a terrorist behind every door."

"I have my dreams. They don't," Myrtle said.

"Anyway that has nothing to do with what I'm talking about."

"Your gift of dreamin' won't let ya get ya'self in a jam ifn' ya don't let it. But I'm thinkin' y'are not heedin' 'em."

"You know my dreams—as do yours—give me no direction or forewarnings."

"I knowed, but remember your dreams saved your twin siblings when ya used them th' right way, by tellin' Tuesday, an' she got th' law involved. On th' other side of th' coin, they could lead ya to trouble if ya take them on with th' two of ya alone."

"Are you saying that you want me to leave the mountain and abandon my writing plans?"

"Patty, there're other subjects to write 'bout."

"It's going to be a memoir. It's my story, Grandmother. I need to write *my* story."

CHAPTER 28

"I CAN SEE WHY PAUL FRANK WAS SO TAKEN with Patty and was so intent on rescuing her," Mark Allen said.

"Yeah, she's something else," Orval Frank said. "I really want to get to know her, and I can tell you feel the same about Isabel."

Mark Allen grinned." Well, when Buddy likes a girl, she can't be so bad. I think they took to each other."

"I saw that," Orval Frank said as he clipped Mark Allen on the shoulder.

"It was just plain weird when Patty fainted, thinking you were Paul Frank."

"I haven't had a chance to tell Jess Willis that she thought I was Paul Frank, somehow returned, and she fainted when she saw me. He'd get a kick out of it."

"You don't say," Mark Allen said, visualizing Willis' eyes get owl-size the way they did when he was spooked.

"Has anyone ever told you that you were a man of few words?" Orval Frank said.

Mark Allen laughed.

"I mean, I really like Patty," Orval Frank admitted.

"It's as obvious to me as the silly grin on your face."

Mark Allen stopped the Jeep in front of the sheriff's office, and Jess Willis stepped out the door and waved to his deputies.

"Jess is a nerd, but he's a good man," Orval Frank said.

Mark Allen rolled his window down and nodded to Willis. "Evening, Sheriff."

Orval Frank leaned away from his window as Jess placed his elbow on the roof of the Jeep and bent to peer inside.

"Evenin'," Jess nodded. "Heard we have one of our own come back to our humble town." He reached behind Orval Frank to pet the overzealous dog. Buddy jumped on the back of Mark Allen's seat and took a few tongue swipes at the sheriff's face, leaving a wet trail.

"Stop that, Buddy!" Mark Allen pushed Buddy away and the dog fell back onto the back seat, yapping.

"We've met her," Mark Allen said, grinning and pointing a thumb toward Orval Frank. "She fainted at the sight of this one," Mark said gleefully.

"You kiddin' or somethin'?" Jess Willis asked, screwing up his brows in a frown. Surprise showed in his eyes.

"She saw Paul Frank—or thought she was seeing him come back to the living," Orval Frank explained.

"Never thought much about it, but you could be his twin for sure," Jess remarked, his eyes and brows relaxing back to normal.

"So I've been told. I do like her, but I could tell the fact that I remind her of Paul Frank is not a good thing. I mean, it only puts the memory of him out there."

"It doesn't help that you sound like him, either," Mark Allen ribbed his cousin. "What happens, happens."

"There's a girl with her too," Orval Frank reported, nodding toward the sheriff. "I don't know where she came from, but she and Patty look a lot alike. They have long, dark hair, dark brown eyes, same height, and great bods."

"That's an understatement," Mark Allen said with a smile.

"Not to change the subject of beautiful young women, but I've been hearing rumors that McCallister has been seen on the mountain," the sheriff said, sounding worried.

"Going up, we saw McCallister and two of his women on their way down," Mark Allen offered. "For one, I've never seen McCallister bring his women off the mountain."

"Neither have I," Orval Frank said. "I've seen them walk to church, but that's it."

"Maybe you finally got him scared and he's moving away," Mark Allen said.

Jess saw the laughter in Mark Allen's eyes and gave him the look that he had developed since being elected as sheriff. Even when he was deputy to Sheriff Ozzie Moats, Jess Willis had liked to project a look of importance. Knowing that Jess believed he could stare with a harsh look on his face, head tilted, as a reminder to the offender that he was boss, encouraged Mark Allen to provoke him just to see "the look."

"I'm sorry, Sheriff," Mark Allen apologized, trying unsuccessfully to hide his desire to rib Willis. "No offense intended."

"One day I'm goin' to get you for insubordination, Mark Allen," Willis said.

All three of them laughed, as each one of them knew that in reality they had great respect for one another.

"Seriously, though, I've always heard that where there's smoke there's fire," Mark Allen said. "I wouldn't take the rumors lightly. There's got to be something to the saying: 'The guilty always returns to the scene of the crime.'"

"Can't argue with that," Orval Frank said. "Now we know he's back on the mountain, we'll keep an eye out, Sheriff."

"You should've followed him," Jess said.

"He would have noticed," Mark Allen said. "And if he was up to something, he would've led us on a wild goose chase."

"You're right, but we need to keep tabs on him starting now."

"Look, Orval Frank," Mark Allen said as he pointed to the boardinghouse. "The girls are back."

"What do you say we go over and ask them out to dinner?" Orval Frank proposed.

"I'm with you," Mark Allen answered.

They left the sheriff standing on the street with his thumbs in his belt and his jaw dropped open.

"Are you girl's hungry?" Mark Allen asked.

"We are," they answered at the same time.

"We know where the best food in town is," Orval Frank said, holding his arm out to Patty. Mark fell in behind, and Isabel took his arm.

"Lead the way, Orval Frank," Mark said.

CHAPTER 29

THE BEST (ONLY) RESTAURANT IN WINDING Ridge was ran by Fran Rudd. It was located in the back of the town bar, which was owned by her husband, Humphrey Rudd—best known as Hump. The only entrance to the restaurant was from the side street. Fran would never submit her customers to the atmosphere of the bar and had sealed off the entrance connecting it to the restaurant, separating the habitual drunks from her clientele. The bar's regulars included Andy Hillberry, who to this day turned himself in at the sheriff's office for public intoxication when he got too drunk to make it home on his own. The practice had started when Hillberry, envious of McCallister's lifestyle, would stop at the sheriff's office after a few too many at the bar and lay blame on Ozzie Moats, the former sheriff. He would accuse Moats of failing in his job, saying that McCallister was selling his own children to the city folk and it was the sheriff's job to put a stop to it. In order to discourage Andy, Ozzie would simply lock Hillberry in a cell to sleep it off.

The group found a booth in the rear of the restaurant and pored over the menu.

"Everything here is good, girls, so pick your favorite food," Orval Frank said.

"I like the Texas steak burger and the French onion soup," Mark Allen suggested.

"Sounds good to me!" Isabel smiled at Mark Allen, who sat next to her.

"Not me," Orval Frank said. "I'm having the roast beef and mashed potatoes smothered with gravy." He tossed his menu aside.

"I think I'll go with Isabel and Mark Allen on this," Patty said. "Mashed potatoes and gravy have too much fat for me."

Mark Allen laughed.

"What's the matter? Did I say something wrong?" Patty asked.

"Wait till you see the size of the steak and the cheese, peppers, and onions it's smothered with," Orval Frank said.

They talked about the usual stuff that young people talk about when they're getting to know one another. The conversation finally came back to what was on all their minds: the reason for Patty and Isabel's being on the mountain at all.

"I mean, I don't understand after all that's happened, why—although it thrills me that you are here—you girls even want to be here," Orval Frank said.

"I agree," Mark Allen said. "It makes no sense."

Patty and Isabel looked at each other, and Isabel nodded.

Looking across the table at Mark Allen and then at Orval Frank, who sat beside her in the booth, Patty began to talk about her dream of writing about her life on the mountain. "I have a lot to learn about my father's effect on my life and my siblings' lives. I want to know where they are and why my father chose to sell his own children for profit."

"He did his time for that," Orval Frank noted.

"Yes, he did, but that's not what I'm about. I know he's been punished for most of his crimes–and I'm using 'most' lightly. You don't know the half of it. The children who were sold suffered, and so did Joe, Sara, and I. What happened there will affect me all my life, and I've already paid the price more than once because of my pa and his disregard for others, including his own children. I don't even know who my family really is. Isabel doesn't want to believe it, but I think she's my half-sister." She glanced at Isabel and continued, "Maybe more than that."

"Yes, I know, but we really don't know for sure! At least, you should know that I don't. I keep telling you . . ."

"Where's your head been, Isabel? From our conversation with our grandmother, I believe that you are Betty's child too—and so does she. The time frame is right, you're eleven months older than I am, and Betty was given to my father two or three years before I was born. I'm going to find out if my mother gave birth to a child before she died while giving birth to me. Aggie knows, and I know how to get her to tell."

"Patty, you're making my head spin. This is just too much of a coincidence."

"Is it, Isabel? We look like our father, and—more important—we have the same gift as our mother and grandmother."

"What gifts?" Mark Allen asked, totally unaware of what the girls were talking about. "Well, other than your good looks."

"Yeah," Orval Frank said. "I mean, I'm more than lost."

"You would've thought we as detectives could follow a simple conversation," Mark Allen said as he crossed his arms and raised his eyebrows at Orval Frank.

"You're not talking about that doll!" Orval Frank asked. "I've heard about the doll people say you communicate with."

Mark Allen sat with his chin propped on his open palm, looking from one to another of his dinner companions. "I hate to say this, but the conversation is getting too weird for me."

"That's what I've been trying to tell you all along," Isabel said.

"Don't give me that crap, Mark Allen," Orval Frank said. "My sister—your mother—was the same way. You just don't want to talk about it."

Mark Allen grinned. "There was no doll."

"That's not the point," Orval Frank said.

"What about my doll?" Patty asked.

"Word is that you keep a doll with you that you talk to, or something."

"Kinda," Patty admitted.

"What's that supposed to mean?" Orval Frank asked.

"It's part of how I know that Isabel and I are related. First of all we look like sisters, even more that most sisters do. We have dreams that are about the past or about something about to happen. As for the doll, she agrees that I'm right."

"The doll agrees!" Mark Allen raised his eyebrows, not bothering to stifle his grin.

"Yes, Mark Allen," Patty said defensively. "The doll agrees."

"I've heard of weirder things," Mark Allen said.

"You've got to admit, Mark Allen, your mother was respected for the times she had dreams that predicted something was going to happen, and sure enough it did."

"I do, but that was a little different. She couldn't decipher them until afterward. "

"I have the same problem," Patty added to the conversation.

"Right, it's the same thing," Orval Frank said. "I mean, Carol's experiences were similar to what these girls are talking about. The only difference is your mother did not come from a clairvoyant family such as what Patty and Isabel did."

"I don't know about that," Mark Allen said, smiling. "Not that we knew of. Anyway, Orval Frank, some call it witchcraft."

"Oh, my gosh, you guys." Isabel was not ready to accept that she came from this isolated mountain. "Like, I haven't accepted that I am Patty's half-sister, sister, or whatever."

"Really, Isabel, what more do you need to convince you?

"And it's not witchcraft, people just think it is. It's a kind of sixth sense."

"I don't know." Isabel looked defeated.

The waitress brought the food, and the four immediately began to eat. Having not had a meal all day, they were hungry.

"Patty, you mentioned that you were going to ask your Aunt Aggie about your mother giving birth to another child, I thought you said you didn't find her at her cabin. Where are you going to look?" Mark Allen asked. "We saw Aggie and Annabelle with McCallister, and he was driving off the mountain."

"Like, I have an idea," Isabel said.

CHAPTER 30

ANNABELLE AND AGGIE WERE TAKING A break, relaxing in their rocking chairs. The women had arranged them near the wall oven and range in a carbon copy of the way they had been around the potbelly stove and the woodburner inside their cabins.

"Ya been talkin' like y'are homesick, Aggie," Annabelle noted.

"I am, a little, so I am. Livin' here's not th' same as havin' my own place. When Jeb was a youngin', I was in charge. Now he don't want anythin' to do with what I'm thinkin', so he don't."

"Now, Aggie, that's not unusual. A man doesn't cling to his parents when he's of a man's age an' particularly one as stubborn as Jeb."

"I suppose y'are right. I just don't like it, so I don't."

"That's just because you're just as stubborn as he is. I never saw such as th' two of ya."

"'Cause we have a history, so we do. We're like two peas in a pod."

"Hogwash," Annabelle said and changed the subject. "What ya thinkin' he's goin' to think 'bout th' tunnel we found?"

"I don't knowed what he's goin' to think, so I don't."

"I reckon ya do, Aggie, I guessed ya already knowed somethin' 'bout it from th first time we'd gone in th day we was unpackin'."

Aggie and her nephew did know about the tunnel, and Aggie was pretty sure from stories she had heard that there was access into it from the mansion. The Hathorne families, who had been known as witches for centuries, had built and lived in the mansion. Over the generations, there were records of women in the family being burned at the stake. The tunnel was where they hid the women when the men knew that they were being charged with witchcraft. They could not live in the tunnel indefinitely, though, and some were eventually arrested and put to death.

"I want to explore it," Annabelle said, "but I want ya to go with me."

"I told ya when we found it that it creeps me out, so it did. I ain't goin' to explore that dark, evil, witch's place, so I ain't. An' ya knowed Jeb won't like it a'tall, so he won't."

"He ain't goin' to knowed 'bout it. Anyway, we have to, Aggie. We can't sit up here not knowin' what's lurkin' under foot."

"I can, so I can." Aggie stubbornly crossed her arms. "Ya knowed no one's been in th' tunnel near th' entrance to this place. Why th' dust was two inches thick on th' steps, an' it was undisturbed till we went nosin' down there, so it was."

"There might be evidence of th' witches livin' here, Aggie. Don't'cha want to knowed?"

"Nope!"

"I'm goin' by m'self then," Annabelle announced.

"That's okay with me, so it is. If ya don't come back in a couple of hours I'll call th' sheriff's office, so I will."

"Ya don't even know how to use th' phone, Aggie, so how ya goin' to do that?"

Annabelle plucked her shawl from the back of her chair and wrapped it around her shoulders.

"Jacob showed me how to get th' operator, an' she can look up th' number an' ring it for me, so she can. When ya goin?"

"Right now," Annabelle said and turned toward the kitchen at the back of the mansion. At the corner of the kitchen, she entered the pantry and opened the door leading into the dark and damp basement. A wine cellar was off to one side, an old coal bin on the adjoining wall, and near at hand an updated laundry room looked out of place in the gloomy recesses.

Using a flashlight she'd found on a shelf outside the laundry room, Annabelle crossed to the area where she and Aggie had found the opening leading down and into the tunnel. Annabelle pulled the shelves away from the wall and opened the trapdoor.

CHAPTER 31

"WHAT'S YOUR IDEA, ISABEL?" MARK Allen asked.

"The house Patty told me her father was restoring right before nine eleven. I think that's where they've gone. It makes sense unless you guys have any better ideas."

"Patty, what about you? What do you think?" Mark Allen asked.

The two couples were walking off their large meal and showing Isabel the town at the same time. There was more to the town than Isabel had first realized. Walking the side streets and alleys gave the young woman a better perspective of the place. As for Patty, the tour brought back unwanted memories of the days before and after her abduction by Tommy Lee Hillberry and of Paul Frank Ruble's death at the hands of Robbie, the town bar owner's son. No one, including the bar owner, Hump Rudd, had any idea that his son was a leader of one of the towns few gangs.

"I don't have any idea," Patty said. "But what Isabel says is possible, I guess."

"Patty," Isabel asked, "isn't that the house you told me you dreamed about before the incident with Tommy Lee?"

"The one my father bought to take me, Tuesday, and Winter Ann to live with him in?"

"Yes."

"That's it. I was actually there once and recognized it from my dreams."

"Maybe he took your aunt and Annabelle there since he couldn't carry on with his plans to live there with Tuesday."

"Why would he do that?" Patty questioned. "It always was to impress Tuesday, not Annabelle and Aunt Aggie."

"Like, he can't take Tuesday there, so maybe he has other schemes going. Maybe it beats living in the cabin."

"You could be right. The mansion has all the modern conveniences, it's huge, and I know he absolutely hated to spend any time in the cabin."

"And if not for the two of you," Mark Allen said, "maybe no one would have thought of him being there."

"Sure, that's it. I mean, he's not wanted for anything that I know of," Orval Frank said. "And he probably hasn't a clue we're watching him. His MO has always been to stay out of sight. Living in the mansion, he can come and go as he pleases, and not likely to cross our paths like he did earlier."

"Yeah, I'm sure he wants to stay out of our radar," Mark Allen said.

"Oh, my gosh, why's that?" Isabel asked.

"I think he killed Tommy Lee." Mark Allen answered, "And McCallister apparently lives by 'out of sight, out of mind,' as the saying goes."

"Do you girls want us to help you check it out?" Orval Frank offered. "I mean, we'd be more than happy to give you a hand."

"It's going to get dark soon," Patty said. "Can we go tomorrow?"

"How about it, Mark Allen, can you go? I mean, I'm okay with tomorrow."

"Count me in," Mark Allen said, grinning broadly.

They walked to the boardinghouse and the girls went inside, after having agreed to meet in the lobby the next morning at seven and to have breakfast at Fran's.

The door creaked as it had the first time she and Aggie had opened it, but having heard it before didn't stop Aggie from feeling a chill down her spine. Annabelle propped the door against the wall where it leaned on its own weight. She made sure there was no danger of its banging shut while she was inspecting the depths of the tunnel.

As she carefully descended, each step creaked as her weight settled on it, and the unaccustomed noise disturbed the perpetual silence that had inhabited the underground for many years. *Ya old fool,* Annabelle told herself, *this ain't like ya goin' into th' bowels of th' earth. Ya just can't be satisfied with mindin' your own business. Y'are gettin' too much like Aggie, an' th' other 'uns!*

Reaching the bottom of the stairs, Annabelle stepped on solid ground. With the brightness her flashlight showing the way, she could see hard-packed dirt at her feet, spreading out to the walls left and right. The beams overhead were six feet high in most places. She could see that, as the tunnel went on north and south, the ceiling lowered to about four or five feet in height.

She spotted a trunk to the right of the foot of the steps. Shining her light on it, she saw it was covered with dust and dirt, and it looked a bit rotten. Annabelle turned back and set her flashlight on the third step with the light pointing toward the trunk. She lifted the rusted latches. The lid came open with a loud squeak that caused Annabelle to jump.

"My word, it's filled with black dresses!" She lifted the top one so she could see it in the light, and tucking a few of the dresses under her arm, she rustled around and found, stacked on one side of the trunk, leather pouches tied with leather strips. She picked up a half dozen of them.

Annabelle couldn't wait to show her find to Aunt Aggie, and picking up her flashlight, she hurried to the steps. It was difficult climbing with her arms full, but when she topped the stairs, there was Aunt Aggie, peering down into the depths of the basement.

"Oh, I reckon you couldn't wait to find out what I discovered," Annabelle bragged. "Ya just didn't want to make th' effort to deal with th' stairs. Y'are wantin' me to bring what I find to th' comfort of ya rocking chair."

"Y'are right on that, so y'are, but as ya can see, I'm not relaxin' in my rockin' chair, so I'm not. I've been waitin' right here for what seems like hours to see what ya been down there for so long doin', so I was."

Annabelle plucked a dress from the crook of her arm and held it up so Aggie could get a good look at it.

"Oh, my word! Oh, my word!"

"It's not just th' dresses. Look at this." Annabelle held out one of the leather pouches for Aggie's inspection.

"I got word that McCallister is heading home following a meeting with Abu-Musab," Randy McCoy said, rushing into Johnny Michael's office. His red hair had been tousled by the wind, and a few curly strands sprinkled, untended, on his forehead,

"Howerton hasn't said a word about it."

"No, and I'm told that it's scheduled for today. The girls are on the mountain as we speak, and knowing where McCallister is is imperative to their safety.

"I'm getting bad vibes about Howerton."

"I don't like getting that information pretty much after the fact," Johnny Michael said.

"Exactly," Randy agreed.

"There's something going on," Johnny Michael said. "The chatter is all over the wires. I think Al-Zarquwi is stepping up his plans to attack."

Assigned to work with Johnny Michael at Homeland Security, McCoy had been concerned about the chatter as well.

"I think we need to find someone other than Howerton to keep an eye on McCallister. That man's just got to be working both sides. Otherwise, we would've heard it from him and not have learned about the step-up in the threats for the first time on our own."

"I agree. Howerton is smarter than we've given him credit for," Johnny Michael said. "He's not keeping us up to date on McCallister's Al Qaeda activities. Randy, you're going to have to get involved and begin keeping a twenty-four hour tail on Howerton. We have to assume he can't be trusted. Since you're so familiar with the mountain and McCallister's dealings, you're the obvious one to take over the tail on him. And I mean stick to him like glue."

"I agree that, according to the chatter, Al-Zarquwi is planning an attack, but where?" Randy asked. "That's the question. Howerton's been able to get pretty involved with Abu-Musab and must know some of what's going on with Al Qaeda."

"I think that's the case, and I don't like it." Johnny Michael frowned, looking at the reports on his desk."

"That's true. If he was being straight with us, he would be pounding on our door with this information," Randy said, gesturing toward the paper trail on Johnny Michael's desk. "That's the only reason for Howerton not to be reporting to us—double cross!"

"You'd better get packed."

"I'm out of here." Randy saluted, making Johnny Michael grin. They were not military, but before his assignment to Homeland Security, Johnny Michael had been an officer in the National Guard for years.

"Are you okay with the possibility of running into Patty?" Johnny Michael asked, switching to a lighter topic. "She's on the mountain now, I'm told, and doesn't know you and Mary Lou are seeing each other."

"I don't think she cares. She was always too busy, and Mary Lou and I just happened," Randy said. "I'd go to the house to see Patty, or call for her on the phone, and I'd end up talking to Mary Lou. Over time she and I realized we had developed a huge attraction."

"One of you should tell Patty," Johnny Michael said in an offhanded manner.

"You're right. It feels like we're being dishonest."

"That's what I mean," Johnny Michael said. "She probably doesn't care or she'd be spending time with you, but everything needs to be out in the open. I wouldn't normally say anything–I don't like to get involved in other people's business–but I know Tuesday is worried about it. And since you work for me, I'd like you to clear the air."

"Yeah, yeah. I hear you."

"Then get going, Randy. Time's a-wasting. I'll be working to crack the code to get me into some of this chatter. That seems to be the fastest way to find out just what's going on."

"Thanks for the advice, and keep me posted if you learn anything at all," Randy said as he left Johnny Michael's office.

CHAPTER 32

AFTER LUNCH ON SUNDAY, JUST HOURS before the girls were to return home, along with the deputies they finally made their trip to the mansion to find out if Aggie and Annabelle were there.

"There!" Patty pointed. "That's it."

Shaded by the mountain, the huge house looked every bit as impressive as a castle.

"Where should I park?" Mark Allen asked.

"Let's go on past and walk back," Orval Frank said. "I mean, we're not even sure whether McCallister's here or not."

"I don't see his truck," Mark Allen said.

"You know what he drives?" Isabel asked.

"Yes, I do. Orval Frank and I saw him going off the mountain. He was driving a Ford extended cab pickup."

"What about the garage?" Isabel asked."

"I don't think he parks in the garage," Patty said. "Look at it. It's not large enough for a big truck. You couldn't park anything in that one, except for the smallest vehicle."

"Yes, it looks as if it was built in the days of the Model T Ford," Orval Frank said. "You'd never fit his truck inside it."

Mark Allen found an abandoned lane a half mile away from the mansion, and he pulled the sheriff's Jeep far enough into the brush not to be seen.

Getting out of the Jeep, Patty had a flashback to one of her recent dreams. In it, she was standing in the very lane Mark Allen had just parked in. She was wearing a black dress with a hood. As Patty recalled the dream, a chill ran down her spine. She broke out in a cold sweat, became nauseated, and felt faint. As the four walked back to the house, the overwhelming clairvoyant feeling faded as quickly as it had come.

"What is it?" Orval Frank asked. Walking close to her, he had noticed she had turned white as snow for a few seconds.

"I'm okay, just a flashback to a dream." Patty continued walking toward the house and the enormous front door. "It always makes me so sick I think I'm going to pass out."

"I remember my sister describing her experience the same way," Orval Frank said.

"Really!" Patty said.

"Patty, just tell us!" Isabel had noticed how nonchalant the guys were about Patty's dreams. She didn't feel so weird after all about having her own mysterious dreams, which seemed to worry her adoptive parents so.

"Okay, okay. I don't remember exactly when I had the dream, but that lane we parked on was the setting for one dream I've had. In it, I dreamed I was standing along the lane. I was wearing a black dress with a hood. Really! It's creepy."

Mark Allen and Orval Frank, who were walking alongside the girls, looked at each other and shrugged.

Mark Allen opened the gate, leading to the walkway that ended at the front door, and the foursome cautiously moved through the opening.

"What is that?" Patty asked, pointing to the brass, five-pointed star on the door, just as they were midway to the house and she could see the door clearly

"It's a pentagram. I mean, I think that's what it is," Orval Frank said.

"That's a symbol for witchcraft!" Patty exclaimed as she hurried to the door—with the others close behind—to get a better look.

"Wonder why it's on your father's door?" Isabel asked, fearful of touching it.

Wanting to lighten the mood, Mark Allen grinned and said, "I'm sure it won't bite you."

Patty rolled her eyes in Mark Allen's direction.

"I have no idea why my father left the pentagram on the door—and more importantly—why someone cleaned and shined it as they have obviously done. I'm going to find out, though. I remember that it was so tarnished I couldn't tell what it was."

She looked steadily at the group.

"I've had many dreams about women being burned at the stake. In school I wrote reports on witchcraft so I could study it. You know, Grandmother says we come from a family that's been accused of witchcraft over the years."

"Are you sure it's the same doorknocker that was there before?" Mark Allen asked. "Maybe it's not the one you saw."

"I didn't pay much attention to it," Patty answered. "I'm pretty sure it's the same one, but it was so tarnished then it blended in, like a plain old, useless doorknocker. I'd have to have inspected it more closely to be sure, though."

The shrubbery to their right moved, and the group turned in the direction of the disturbance. each of them was startled by the unexpected movement.

"What's that?" Isabel grabbed Mark Allen's shoulders and hid behind him. He and Orval Frank quickly rounded on the intruder. Patty grabbed Isabel's hand and stepped behind the guys, her eyes darkened with fear.

Early on Sunday afternoon, Tuesday and Cliff were relaxing on the front porch, looking forward to Patty and Isabel's return that evening.

"Oh, I can't wait to hear how Patty and Isabel's trip went."

"Me either," Cliff said, putting his arm around Tuesday. It rested on the back of the porch swing, and the swing moved back and forth, aided by his leg movement.

"Has there been any more on Jacob and the investigation into his possible connection with the men who were responsible for the terrorism on 9/11?"

"A little," Cliff said, "although it's not enough to bring him in for questioning. We don't want him to know there's a probe into his activities."

"Oh?"

"You know he must believe he's in the clear. It's been years since the attack."

"At least it won't involve me and my family." Tuesday sighed.

"I hope not," Cliff said. "One thing I didn't tell you is in the past year he has completely restored the mansion he had planned for you, Patty, and Winter Ann to live in with him. Since his name has surfaced in the investigation into the terrorist act, Johnny Michael at Homeland Security has his men watching the place."

"Oh, and the other thing you haven't told me?"

"All right." Cliff ran his fingers through his dark hair and stopped the swing as he turned to face Tuesday. "It's about Buddy Dean Howerton. Remember, I once told you about the man connecting McCallister to the plot to blow up the White House and the World Trade Center Towers. Well, he has been seen around Salem and McCallister's mansion.

"I heard from Johnny Michael this morning. He's assigned Randy McCoy the job of tailing McCallister. Randy's a good choice since he knows the mountain and McCallister's history. Randy and Johnny Michael are pretty sure Howerton has double-crossed them and is acting for both sides."

"Oh, no!" Tuesday squealed.

"Tuesday, there's no reason for you to worry."

"Then why are they stepping up their investigation on Sunday? Furthermore, why were you withholding the information from me?"

"I didn't want you to worry you. We don't know anything yet."

"Oh, yeah? Now you think I'm not going to worry more?" Tuesday raised her eyebrows.

"I've no doubt, Tuesday, but I think this could put McCallister in jail for good. The good thing is, it doesn't have a thing to do with Patty."

"That's true enough, but there's no telling what Jacob will do. If he believes Patty's getting in his way . . ."

"You're stretching it, Tuesday."

"Am I?"

"I think you are. After playing ball with the big boys in prison, McCallister's out for a bigger payoff. And, Tuesday," Cliff said, taking her face between his hands, "bigger time."

"Oh, I guess you're right." Tuesday let out her breath as if she'd been holding it.

"Yeah, now that Ozzie Moats is behind bars and Jess Willis took his place as sheriff, McCallister isn't likely to go about his business unnoticed. Willis is not an Ozzie Moats, and he and his deputies are not going to allow McCallister to break the law, doing as he pleases. They're keeping an eye on McCallister, and he knows it."

"Anyway, I can't wait until she's back home tonight."

"I'm with you on that."

Just then Winter Ann ran up the few steps to the porch.

"Hi, Mommy! Hi, Daddy! When's Patty coming home?"

"She'll be here before dark," Tuesday said, picking up her small daughter and setting her between Cliff and herself on the swing.

"You and Daddy look worried when Patty goes to the mountain," Winter Ann said. "Is it because it's dan-ger-ous?"

Wide-eyed, Winter Ann had drawn out the word she'd heard many times over her short life.

CHAPTER 33

IN HER BEDROOM, ANNABELLE HAD HIDDEN her discoveries, collected from her frightening trip to dark basement. She was looking at TV when she heard Aggie call to her from the hallway. "We have company, so we do. Annabelle, put th' dress an' other stuff away, an' come see."

"Ya thinkin' I'm not very bright. I've already gone and hid 'em."

Aggie had seen the group approaching the house from her bedroom window, and took the time to cross the hall to tell Annabelle. She hadn't bothered to wait for Annabelle's response but instead had hurriedly crossed the hall back into her own room. She opened the French door, which led to a stone walkway that ran between the mansion and the landscape shrubbery to the front door.

"Oh, my gosh!" Isabel cried out at the sight of the old woman emerging at the end of the shrubbery, where the walkway met one of the corner pillars that fronted the mansion. She stepped from behind Mark Allen, no longer scared, but wondering who the woman was.

"I never thought I'd see th' like, so I didn't. How did ya youngins knowed we was here?"

"You were not at your cabin or Annabelle's, so this is the only place I could think to look." Patty said as she left the protection of Orval Frank's back and stepped forward. "Where's Annabelle?"

"In her room, I expect, so I do. I've called to her, an' she'll be here directly. In this place what's too big for a body to live in, ya can't hear anythin' goin' on outdoors, so ya can't."

Aggie couldn't take her eyes off Isabel.

"How'd you know we were coming?" Mark Allen asked.

"I have th' front bedroom. I keep my rockin' chair by th' window, an' I saw ya comin', so I did. I keep watch at my window. I'm one to knowed what's goin' on, so I am."

"Come on in, now. I'll get Annabelle." Aggie led the others inside through the front entrance.

Inside, the group looked around in astonishment at the entryway, marveling at the high ceilings, while Aggie went off to hurry Annabelle along. Annabelle rushed to the front of the house, and unlike the aloof Aggie, Annabelle hugged Patty tight. Then, holding her by the shoulders, she took a good look at the young girl that she had raised from birth. Seeing Isabel over Patty's shoulder, Annabelle gasped. "Who is this, Patty? She could be your sister."

Patty pushed Annabelle back so she could see her face. "That's what I came here for—I want to know. I think she is my sister."

Knowing where the conversation was heading, Aggie backed away, intending to go to the kitchen to sit in her rocking chair. Patty and the others followed.

"Patty, y'are always askin' questions, so ya are. Why don't ya leave well enough alone?"

Over the years, Jess Willis had been the self-chosen one to deal with McCallister's family, so the deputies had never met Aggie or Annabelle. Mark Allen couldn't help but to like the contrary old woman. He leaned against the range—ankles and arms crossed, taking in the reunion between the women, and paid no attention when Aggie's cat appeared. Purring loudly, it wound around Mark Allen's ankles, rubbing its fur against his jeans, first going one way, and then back the other direction. Leading with its nose, it rubbed around and around Mark Allen's ankles.

"Annabelle, Aunt Aggie, did my mother have a baby before I was born?"

"Yeah, she did, so she did. It was a girl. Why ya wantin' to knowed that now?"

"How come no one told me?"

"Are ya kiddin'?" Aggie asked. "Since when's my nephew allowed th' women to tell his business?"

"Really, the two of you could've told me. Anyway, how long before me was she born?"

"How'd I knowed?" Aggie asked. "I don't keep no calendar, so I don't."

"It wasn't very long," Annabelle said. "Why, no sooner than Jeb sold th' baby, Betty was with child again. I said it was too soon, she was too young, an' that's probably why she died. I told Jeb, th' poor girl hadn't th' time to heal from birthin' her first child when she learned she was goin' to have another one."

"Do you know who Pa sold Betty's baby girl to?"

"Ya knowed betta than that, Patty. He never told us anythin' 'bout his business, especially me," Annabelle said. "I don't think he even knowed. Didn't he use that lawyer, I heard 'bout?"

"He knowed I was against his sellin' his own flesh an' blood, so I was. He didn't tell me nothin' 'bout it," Aggie declared.

"Is there anyway I can find out?"

"How'd I knowed?" Annabelle said. "Why ya so bent on findin' out where ya ma's baby went to, anyhow?"

"That was my sister! What did she look like?"

"She looked like a baby, dark hair an' dark complexion. I reckon as a baby ya looked like that too. An' I've always said ya look a spittin' image of ya Pa."

"In what way do we look like Betty?" Patty asked.\

"We?" Aunt Aggie asked.

"Yes, we," Patty said. "I think we're sisters."

"Like th' two of ya, Betty had dark hair an' dark eyes, an' was about your size before she got huge with child."

"Is there anything else?"

"Nope," Annabelle said. "That's it."

"Ma! When you saw Isabel, you said she could be my sister."

"Sure looks like ya, so she does."

"Do the two of you think she may really be my sister?"

"She could be. Ya knowed, your pa sold many of his youngins over th' years," Annabelle said. "And as far as I'm concerned, I have no way of knowin' if she's one of 'em or not, exceptin' she does look enough like ya, an' your pa to be. I'd say th' two of ya favor Betty too."

"There are ways to be sure," Mark Allen offered as he pushed himself off the range. "A DNA test will tell you."

"How do we get a sample from my mother? She's dead."

"I'm pretty sure a sample from your grandmother will do," Orval Frank said. "I mean, you'll need one from yourself and Isabel. You only need a hair or a swab from inside your mouth."

"Really? Isabel, let's have it done first thing when we get home."

"Like, I'm all for it, but whose going to pay for it? It's probably expensive. I don't want to ask my mother—I'm afraid it would hurt her feelings. She's so sensitive about everything. I think she pretends she's my real mother."

"There's another problem you're not going to like, Isabel," Orval Frank said. "If you are McCallister's child, your parents must have gotten you illegally."

"Oh, my gosh!" Isabel cried. "I don't want to cause my parents to get into trouble."

"Don't worry, Isabel. If it's anything like Pa's other dealings, a lawyer and a doctor would have been involved to make it look legal. Really, it will be okay."

Isabel did not look convinced.

"I hate to be the stumbling block," Mark Allen said, "but we need to get a sample from your father, too."

"Oh, sure," Patty said. "He'll step right up and say, 'Do whatever you need!'"

"All we need is a sample of his hair. Can we can get into his room and get one from his hairbrush?" Orval Frank asked.

"We ain't 'lowed in his room, so we ain't."

"That's right," Annabelle joined in. "He keeps it locked."

"That's okay," Mark Allen said. "Where's his room?"

"What'd ya need to knowed that for?," Aggie asked. "Told ya, we ain't 'lowed in it, so I did. An' I told ya, it's locked."

Patty turned to Annabelle. "Please tell us."

"At th' end of th' hall." Annabelle pointed the way. "I'd like to knowed myself who Isabel's father is, but that don't make th' room unlocked."

"Jeb said y'are a traitor, an' he was right, so he was." Aggie trailed behind the group.

Mark Allen took a plastic card from his wallet, and with one hand on the doorknob, he inserted the card into the latch and jimmied it open.

"Hurry up, Mark Allen. Pa could come home anytime!"

CHAPTER 34

"OKAY, WHAT?" BUDDY DEAN ASKED, irritated by McCallister's reluctance to be more open with him.

"All right, all right," McCallister said. "In the meantime I have some shopping for you to do." McCallister handed Howerton a list that had the items that he was to purchase. "I'm on my way back to the mountain and I'll call you when I'm ready to meet you here."

Buddy Dean looked the list over and raised his eyebrows. "What's this?"

"Don't you know when to keep your mouth shut? If you want to work for me, you're going to have to be more trusting." Jacob smiled, unaware that his smile never reached his eyes when he was working a double-cross.

The problem for McCallister was that Buddy Dean *was* aware of it.

"The job will be done by tomorrow noon. I'll be waiting for your call."

Buddy Dean put the list in his pocket and left.

Jacob sat on the sofa waiting for Joe to return. He did not have long to wait. Only a half hour had gone by when Joe's key turned in the door and he walked into the living room.

"Joe, I'm going back to the mountain. I want to be there well before dark. I need the light of day for the errands I have to do, so I'm leaving now. I want you to watch my back. You told me that you wanted to work for me, so now's your chance to prove yourself."

Joe's eyes lit up. He had long wanted to quit his boring night watchman job and work for his pa. "You're going to let me be your bodyguard?"

"That's what watching my back means," McCallister snarled. "I'm leaving for the mansion now. First, I want you to do a little checking on Buddy Dean Howerton. Here's his rap sheet."

Jacob pushed the paper into Joe's hand.

Joe looked at the photo at the top left-hand corner. "I've seen this guy around."

"Where?"

"Hanging around here and on the mountain several times, you know, when I was taking supplies to Ma and Aunt Aggie. You know how it's suspect to see a stranger there, but after the militia you see strangers once in a while. I guess it's not as out of the ordinary as it once was, so I didn't think no more of it."

McCallister did not show his surprise at the information. He did not like what he was hearing either. "Keep an eye on him too, Joe. I have a hunch he's not to be trusted."

McCallister left for the four-hour drive to Winding Ridge.

The door opened and Mark Allen entered the room, with the others close behind. The men were quick to find a hairbrush in the bathroom. Orval Frank took a small plastic bag from his back pocket and put a several dark hairs into it. Mark Allen saw a few cotton swabs in the wastebasket. He wrapped a few of them in his handkerchief. "Might be useful," he said. "Let's get these to Jess Willis. I think we can get him to send this stuff to the lab for the DNA. After all, it's evidence."

"We'll get the doctor in town to take a sample from the two of you and your grandmother," Orval Frank said to the girls.

"It's time we headed for home too," Patty said. "We've been here way too long and it's getting late. Our parents are going to worry if we don't show up."

"Okay," Orval Frank said. "We'll stop at the doctor's office first. Mark Allen and I will help you load your car."

"Thanks," Patty said. "We'll be back in a few days to finish this. Isabel and I talked and we aren't going to finish the second half of summer school. We can cram next fall."

"Let's get out of here before we get caught!" Isabel said, pulling Mark Allen toward the door. Upon leaving the bathroom, the group had to laugh—Aggie and Annabelle were snooping about the room.

"Move it!" Orval Frank took Aggie's arm and led her to the door, with Annabelle and the others following. When everyone was out he relocked the door.

"He'll never know," Mark Allen said as he turned to the women,

"Unless the two of you disturbed something," Orval Frank warned.

"It'll be all right," Mark Allen said.

Tuesday was relieved when Patty—with Isabel in the passenger seat—pulled into the driveway late Sunday evening. She had been uneasy the whole time the girls were gone, just knowing they were on the mountain. Tuesday's own encounter with Jacob McCallister had scarred her for life, and the very mention of Winding Ridge gave her cause to shudder.

"Hi!" Patty kissed Tuesday on the cheek as she held the door for her and Isabel to enter the house. Patty set her luggage aside and placed her doll on the piano. Isabel had left her bags in the car, as she was going home after having dinner with Patty's family.

"How was your trip, girls?" Tuesday asked, ignoring the doll and clearly relieved that Patty and Isabel were home safely. At the sound of Patty's voice, Cliff came into the room.

"Really, it was great," Patty answered while Isabel stayed quiet on the subject. "You won't believe everything that happened. We can tell everyone at the same time at dinner. Is it ready? We're starving."

"I just have to put it on the table. By the way I've invited Cora and Bill over. They're anxious to hear about your trip."

"Guess what?" Winter Ann asked, skipping down the stairs, curls bobbing with every step.

"What?" Patty squatted down and took Winter Ann by the arms.

"Hi, Isabel," Winter Ann said politely, before turning her attention to Patty again. "Linda's coming to play."

"Really? What fun for you two!"

"Oh, I hear Aunt Cora's car," Winter Ann squealed. "Do you think Linda's with her for sure?"

"I'm sure she is. Cora wouldn't go anywhere without her, especially to visit you!" Patty poked Winter Ann in the stomach to make her giggle. "You know Cora never comes here without your little friend."

Mary Lou ran down the stairs. "Hey, Patty, Isabel! Good to see the two of you home. Tuesday and Cliff were worried."

The doorbell rang.

"That must be Cora and Bill." Tuesday hurried from the kitchen.

Tuesday took the time to introduce Isabel to Cora, Bill, and Linda.

"Linda, are you hungry?" Tuesday asked.

"Yeah." Linda smiled at Tuesday. "But we want to play. Can me and Winter Ann go to her room?"

"Oh, no, young lady," Cora admonished. "You are going to eat first. Then you can play, okay? And how many times do I have to tell you, 'May Winter Ann and I play?'"

The two little girls ran to the dining room, giggling, eager to eat and spend the rest of their time playing.

After dinner, the two little ones were in Winter Ann's room, playing board games. Although Linda was four years older than Winter Ann, they got along well and always looked forward to spending time together.

Meanwhile, the others sat around the table listening to Isabel and Patty's account of their trip to the mountain, including meeting Orval Frank and Mark Allen.

"You should have seen Patty," Isabel laughed. "I thought she had taken ill or something when she fainted at the sight of Orval Frank."

"Oh, Patty, I'm overwhelmed!" Tuesday said. "I don't know what to say."

"Really?" Patty smiled. "That's unusual."

"Oh, you're too funny."

"I have an idea," Cora said. "Tuesday and I could help in your research. I think it's something you must do. You'll never be able to come to terms with everything if you don't find out as much as you can."

"Would you?" Patty put her hands together with her fingers to her lips.

"I think it sounds downright dangerous," Bill offered.

"It will be more dangerous if we don't get involved," Cliff said. "We know from past experience that she's going to find her past no matter what the cost."

"Paul Frank paid the price," Patty said. "I'm not going to let him die for nothing."

"You see?" Cliff said. "I told you. I know Patty, and she's not going to rest until she knows all she can. The best thing we can do is help. Otherwise, she and Isabel here will be out there all on their own."

"I guess you're right," Bill said. "But this is the weirdest thing I ever heard."

"You've got that right, but you remember the times Patty's dreams played out just like she said," Cliff said. "Had it not been for Patty and her prognostic dreams during the past few years, I wouldn't be able to swallow this at all. After that experience of watching her dreams become actuality, we can be sure it's the right thing to be with her all the way."

Patty looked at each of the adults. "You're really going to help Isabel and me?"

"We are. And we need a plan," Tuesday said. "The two of you can't go off on your own without the rest of us knowing what's going on."

"I agree," Patty said, nodding. When she saw the doubt on Tuesday's and Cliff's faces, she promised, "Really, we'll work with you!"

There was a collective sigh of relief.

After the kitchen was cleaned up and put back in order, the seven of them, Tuesday, Cliff, Cora, Bill, Patty, Isabel, and Mary Lou, all sat at the table again. The girls told the adults about the DNA testing to confirm Myrtle's declaration that the girls were sisters, and how they got Jacob's DNA for the test.

Tuesday and Cora put themselves in charge of doing research into the Hathorne family, which was also Myrtle Landacre's background. So far as they knew, and according to Myrtle, her mother's maiden name was Hathorne. Her mother had married a Moats, and both families could be traced back to Salem. Ozzie Moats and Myrtle were the only ones in the two families who ever lived in or above the town of Winding Ridge. It was possible that Myrtle knew more, and it was going to be Tuesday and Cora's job to find out.

CHAPTER 35

EARLY THE NEXT WEEK THE GIRLS WERE back at the boardinghouse, and Patty and Isabel were getting prepared for bed. Isabel was unusually quiet. She was finally convinced that the possibility that she and Patty were sisters was real, and although she was more than happy to have a sister, she deeply feared the consequences for her parents.

"Isabel," Patty began, "Orval Frank said he'd check it out for sure, but he thinks that no matter what circumstances your parents adopted you under that they can't get into trouble, because 'the statute of limitations' has run out."

"That's comforting, but why didn't he tell me?"

"He's not sure, and he didn't want to get your hopes up until he checked it out."

"I hate to think that they could have broken the law. Oh, my gosh! It's like I've lived a lie."

"Don't be so melodramatic! You're jumping to conclusions."

"I know, but like it's scary to think that your parents, who taught you to tell the truth no matter what, are liars."

"Come on, Isabel, that's not fair to them. Really, give them the benefit of the doubt. They told you the truth that you were adopted. I can understand that they wanted a child so bad they might have used bad judgment."

"The law wouldn't see it that way." Isabel raised her eyebrows.

"Let's get some sleep. I want to see my, I mean our, grandmother tomorrow. I want to tell her about her daughter having a child before me."

"Now you're jumping to conclusions, but I'm with you. Goodnight."

Since the day the girls had brought the detectives, Aggie, had been struck mute about the whole thing for a change. Now with Aggie having retired to her room with her cats trailing behind her, Annabelle had hurried to her own room to examine the bags from the tunnel and to study the contents more closely.

On the bottom of the first of the bags were the five items she had already sorted through earlier. But now a locket that she hadn't noticed before had fallen onto the bed. *What on earth is this?* Annabelle pried it open and gasped A lock of dark brown hair fluttered to the bed. She looked at the picture inside. She would have sworn that the girl with the old-fashioned hairdo and high-necked dress looked just like Patty and Isabel without their blow-dried hair and makeup. Along with the locket was a piece of blue lace, a broach, and a black velvet ribbon with a clasp on each end. All those things were visible in the photo of the woman.

Opening the second and third bags, Annabelle found similar items. The lockets all contained photos of different women. *What on earth does this mean? It's witchcraft for sure.* Annabelle put the items back in their respective bags and tucked them in her drawer. Next, she held the dress up to her body, tucking it under her chin. The dress was half a dozen sizes too small for her. The tiny waist would never fit Annabelle's matronly figure. She held the dress out so she could see it better and noticed that there was a hood. *My word, that is strange. I've never seen a dress like this.*

She was tired and would discuss the items further with Aggie in the morning.

Annabelle tossed and turned in her warm, cushy bed. She told herself that she missed having Jeb beside her, but in reality, it was the other women she missed. The fact was that it was rare to have him at her side during the night, or any time for that matter. Besides, she was not used to such a cozy bed and the comfort of the air-conditioned room.

The next day found Patty and Isabel heading for Myrtle's cabin for their second visit. They had stopped at the small gas station and purchased coffee. They had also selected breakfast sandwiches from the refrigerator in the fast food section that had been installed during the militia gathering a few years back. The girls heated up the sandwiches in the store's microwave and ate them as they headed up the mountain.

Myrtle was pleased to see the girls again. She was lonely most of the time, but living so remotely was a better existence since Mark Allen had given her a radio, taught her to use it, and kept her supplied with the batteries she needed for it. Like Annabelle, in the days before the mansion and her own TV, she had kept her prized radio turned on all the time, enjoying the news programs and talk shows. And although Annabelle had been to Wheeling, the one time, and to Winding Ridge on rare occasions—Myrtle and she were also alike in that neither of them understood much of the commentary. Myrtle had been off the mountain only for her rare and short trips to Winding Ridge. Neither of them had had any schooling; they were not knowledgeable about many topics.

"Come on in. I'm so glad to see ya again," Myrtle had heard the car outdoors and then the girls, as they stepped on the porch.

Patty hugged her grandmother, and Isabel, not so overwhelmed this time, took a good look around and realized the cabin was not nearly as nice as Aggie's, which really didn't seem all that nice until compared to this one and Annabelle's. Isabel had not been able to understand why everyone thought Aggie's cabin was so cool—until now. Isabel had had no experience with living in a cabin with no water, no electric for light, and no gas for heat; she couldn't, therefore, have a true understanding. Where Aggie's kitchen was equipped with nicely finished, modern cabinets, in both Annabelle's and Myrtle's cabins the cabinets were made from wooden crates and nailed to the log walls. Here at Myrtle's they were partially filled with boxed and canned food, but overflowed with an assortment of tin plates, dented pots and pans, and old yellowed papers and catalogs. An iron bed with a feather tick mattress stood in a corner with a ragged quilt spread across it. She noticed in another corner the ever-present pot-belly stove, with a rocking chair placed in front of it and a wood box beside it. Woodchips lay scattered around the area.

They each took a chair at the table. "I talked to Aunt Aggie, Grandmother. She said that Betty delivered a baby girl a short time before I was born, and the baby was sold! Grandmother, I believe Isabel is that baby."

"I knowed ya do. We talked 'bout it, but this's the first I knowed for sure she had two babies." Myrtle wiped a tear from her face, turned her attention to the pretty girl sitting next to Patty, and once again saw the resemblance. They certainly looked like they could be sisters, and the fact that Betty had two babies seemed to negate her reservations.

"We're going to try to get a DNA test to prove it," Isabel offered, "but it's expensive. I think my stepfather will be able to get it done."

"My stars, girl, I don't have no idea what a DNA test is."

"It's new, so I didn't think you would've heard of it, but the test can determine all sorts of things, one of which is who your parents are. One way is that they get a sample from the people involved, using a swab inside the cheek. The results are enough to identify criminals too! DNA from a suspect can be matched to DNA found at a crime scene that was left behind by the offender."

"I think, now that ya've mentioned it, that I've heard talk on th' radio ''bout it," Myrtle beamed. "Since ya've explained it, I'm goin' to understand more when they talk 'bout it next time."

Patty saw that her grandmother was satisfied by the possibility of having Isabel as a second granddaughter.

To Myrtle's way of thinking at learning of Isabel, the three of them—Patty, Isabel, and Myrtle—had forever been destined to be together, drawn by their history.

Patty got up from her chair and put her arms around the old woman for a second time. "I'm sorry to dump all this on you at one time, but I'm so happy to find I have a sister I couldn't wait to tell you."

"Girl, I'm happy too. I just get tears in my eyes when I think of my girl an' how she cried when her pa took her away from me."

Isabel got up and hugged her too.

"Grandmother, I want to take you to see Annabelle and Aunt Aggie. I have a few more questions for them, and I'm sure you do too."

"My word, I never thought I'd get to go in a car to call on folks. Patty, ya knowed I've never been in a motor vehicle except for a dirty, old, farm truck or tractor in my entire life. Why, I've not been on th' mountain 'bove my own cabin since I was a mere child, runnin' an' frolickin'." Myrtle smiled at the memories the upcoming trip had evoked.

Patty took pleasure in her grandmother's smiling face. "I know this will be a treat for you, Grandmother. I know that, except for pictures in a magazine or in a catalog, you've never seen a modern-day house, let alone one as fabulous as the one Aggie and Annabelle are living in now."

"I just can't thank ya enough, Patty. I've not seen Annabelle or Aggie in a coon's age, an' that's since I was a mere girl." She gave them a rare grin again.

"Really! You'll love it, Grandmother. Seeing something in a magazine—and I know that first-hand—is no way the same as seeing it in person.

The girls helped Myrtle with a wrap, and Patty took her hand and led her to the passenger side of the car. Isabel climbed in and settled into the backseat.

Myrtle could not help but to gush over the leather seats and carpeted floors. "I ain't seen anythin' so clean an' nice."

"You're in for a treat then, Grandmother. You're in for a treat."

Patty slowly turned the car around in the narrow, rutted-out, road and drove down the hill toward Winding Ridge. Myrtle was at once curious about the knobs and gadgets; she asked what this was and what that was until she ran out of knobs to inquire about. The car radio could not pick up a station, so Patty played a CD of country music.

As they passed through the edge of town that led to Winding Ridge Road, which would take them to Route Seven, Myrtle gazed around with great interest. "Ya girls knowed, to my memory, I've never been even this far off th' mountain in my life."

"Oh, my gosh!" Isabel gasped. "Never?"

"Never," Myrtle said, watching—with wonder—the landscape whiz past as they gained speed on Route Seven.

"Isabel, the first time I was off the mountain was just six years ago," Patty said. "You've wondered why going to the mall fascinates me. This is why. I wasn't raised to take anything for granted, not even food. You saw the cabin I was raised in. That's all I knew, and everything that our Grandmother owns is in that cabin we just left. Except for very occasional trips to the town of Winding Ridge, she knows nothing else—just as it was for me."

"Oh, my gosh!" Isabel gushed.

"Yeah, it's only four hours to Wheeling from here. And even closer to Weston and Salem, the towns east and west of the mansion Annabelle and Aunt Aggie are living in with Pa."

"I can't wrap my mind around it all," Isabel sighed. "Like, it's two different worlds."

"Really!" Patty agreed. "I know, and it's hard for me to understand how people can take what they have for granted. Living with my adoptive parents is like night and day to the way I lived my early years—and that's an understatement. The cabin was too cold in the winter. The potbelly and woodburner stoves just were not enough to warm the rooms. In the summer it was too hot, with the woodburner constantly burning wood to cook and heat water. Most always there were babies to feed and bathe. There was never enough to eat. I never knew there were such things as ice cream, cookies, and other good foods like fresh fruit that you don't have to forage for in the thickets."

"But oh, my gosh, Patty. You were so close to the city!"

"Although, I got to see catalogs with pictures of glamorous people wearing the most amazing clothes, I had no idea of large, modern homes or of shopping areas where you can buy anything."

"My word, what's that?" Myrtle gripped the dashboard.

CHAPTER 36

PATTY SUDDENLY BRAKED AND THE CAR stopped with a jolt. "What is it, Grandmother?"

"What's that?" Myrtle pointed to a grove of trees.

"I don't see anything, Grandmother." Patty squinted as she strained to peer into the slice of darkness where decayed limbs hung from dead trees, all mixed in with wild brush. Her pleasure in sharing her new life with her grandmother was overshadowed by the deep-seated fear of her father stalking her around every turn. *Could it be him?*

"There, look!" Myrtle said as she saw a large figure fade into the thicket and disappear.

Patty saw the figure as a dark streak as it swiftly disappeared, and a shudder ran through her body. The hair stood up on the backs of her arms and on the back of her neck.

"This place is being watched," Myrtle said in a low voice, as if she were afraid someone other than the girls would hear her. "Mark my word on that."

As suddenly as the dark figure had come into view, the mansion appeared around the bend like a miniature castle set in a glorious grove of trees, so unlike the dark grove they had just been trying to look into. Myrtle had never seen a house like it. The first thing she saw as they grew nearer was the impressive circular driveway meeting midway at the expansive double doors fashioned from carved oak. The focus of the door was a brass emblem of a five-pointed star gleaming in the sunlight.

Patty parked the car and the women climbed out. Myrtle was obviously relieved to stretch her legs.

"Well, what do you think?" Patty asked her grandmother. Myrtle turned toward the girls, and Patty saw her face.

"Girl, haven't ya dreamed of this place? I have, many times. See that five-pointed star? It's a pentagram, that's the mark of a witch's coven. This is th' Hathorne place."

"Aggie told us, Grandmother, but it didn't mean anything to me at the time. However, it wasn't when I lived on the mountain that I first heard the Hathorne name. It was when I was doing the research on witchcraft at school. Really, at the time, I didn't associate it with the mountain, and I had never heard of Weston or Salem, the towns nearest to here."

Abruptly the huge door opened, revealing two women. In contrast to the size of the door, they looked small and insignificant. A long, seemingly endless foyer extended behind them.

"Patty, who've ya got with ya now?" Annabelle called.

"Hello, Ma, Aunt Aggie." She walked forward, pulling Myrtle by the hand as Isabel followed behind. "Meet my grandmother."

It was obvious Myrtle had never seen inside such a grand mansion. She was looking past Aggie and Annabelle into the grand hallway that was always lighted by the great chandelier, as well as the many sconces that lined the hallway. They were placed just so to display the artwork in the best possible lighting.

"Your grandmother?" Annabelle asked as though she had no clue.

"Shut your mouth, Annabelle! Ya look like a frog waitin' for a fly, so ya do. That's Myrtle Landacre that Patty's hangin' on to," Aggie said, finally getting the old woman's attention.

Myrtle had been put off balance at seeing the dark figure, the pentagram on the door, and such a grand setting, but the excitement of seeing the women she had not seen since childhood put all these things to the back of her mind for the moment.

"This is th' best day of my life," Myrtle gushed. "I've never seen such as this. Ridin' in a car, comin' to this house that's come to life like a picture right out of a magazine. I just can't take it all in."

Just inside the entryway the group stopped, while Myrtle took everything in. The others, particularly Annabelle and Aggie, enjoyed watching Myrtle's reaction to the beautiful mansion. As she looked around, Myrtle gradually came to understand that this was the place of her most frightening dreams, although in her dreams, the images were distorted. She had had no idea that she would become a part of it in her waking hours. Neither had she had any inkling of just how grand the mansion of her nightly slumbers really was.

"Come on, Myrtle. I'll show ya 'round," Annabelle offered, taking Myrtle's hand.

"I want to show her too, so I do." Aggie got between Patty and Isabel. "I want to make sure Annabelle tells her right, so I do."

"Why, ya old woman, I was in th' city long before ya saw this place, an' I'm a little more knowledgeable."

"Ya old hag, ya been listin' to th' radio too long, so ya have. Usin' th' big words I bet ya don't even knowed what they mean." Aggie stuck her stubborn, snuff-stained chin out in defiance.

"Oh, my gosh, Patty! Why're they fighting?" Isabel was not accustomed to adults bickering just for their own amusement.

"Don't pay any attention to them, Isabel. They argue like that all the time. It's a sport for them.

"You three go ahead," Patty suggested, "I want to talk to Isabel about something."

Now Aggie was torn between hearing what Patty had to say and being included in Myrtle's education on modern living. When she hesitated, Patty gave her a nudge and told her to go ahead.

After the women left, Patty and Isabel sat on the sofa in the formal living room to the left of the grand hallway. "I want to go as soon as we can," Patty said. "I don't want to run into Pa if we can help it."

"Do you think he'll harm us?" Fear showed in Isabel's eyes.

"No, or I wouldn't have come here, and I certainly wouldn't have brought you. I just don't want to face him, although I know he can't hurt me any longer. I'm confident I've endured his abuse for the last time. I can tell you one thing: I would have been better off had he sold me like all the others. Really, I can't think of a worse fate than living under the care of my father."

"So that's why you've never really talked about your relationship with your father before, like except to kinda acknowledge you had one that lived on the wrong side of the law."

"For me, what he did to break the law was the least of it. Being abused is always very painful, and I'll never get over it. That was a factor in my keeping a distance between Paul

Frank and me. I'll always feel guilty that he died probably thinking that my reserve was an indication that I wasn't serious about him. I doubt he knew that the fact was I couldn't get beyond the abuse.

"Anyway, let's catch up with Grandmother and the others. I want to see my Grandmother's reaction." The girls found the women still in the kitchen. "You didn't get very far."

"My word, Patty, look at this kitchen. It's so shiny an' clean. Look at what Aggie showed me." She took hold of a shiny, black knob and turned it, smiling in self-importance at the red-hot circle that appeared like magic. "Have ya ever seen anythin' like it?" Myrtle spun around taking in everything at once. "Look at that," she said as she pointed at the refrigerator. "It's cold in there, an' there's no block of ice to keep it cold. Not that I could find, anyway."

Aggie stepped up, predictably ready to display her smugness. "I had one of those in my cabin for th' last couple years. Th' leader of th' militia modernized my place an' made it electric, so he did. Ya should've seen it, Myrtle."

Myrtle barely heard Aggie's boasting about her own precious cabin. In this event, Myrtle was seeing the modern side of life firsthand. She walked around touching the different surfaces, the counters, tables, and walls.

Not to be ignored, Aggie opened a cabinet door and, getting Myrtle's attention, told her it was for storage of food.

"Why don't it spoil?" Myrtle gasped.

Annabelle and Aggie looked stumped, so Patty decided to save them the embarrassment of having to tell Myrtle that they didn't know.

"Grandmother, the packaged food has added preservatives and is sealed from the air, and can be stored for a very long time."

Patty took out a box of cereal and showed Myrtle the interior wrap of wax paper filled with wheat flakes. Next, Patty found a box that had not been opened yet and showed Myrtle how the box was sealed. Then she opened it to show her how tight the seal was.

Remembering her first experience with prepared food, Patty ignored her intuition, of just a minute earlier, to get out of there, and invited Myrtle to sit at the table. She asked Annabelle and Aggie, who she knew wanted to show off, to fix them all lunch and not to forget the ice cream.

"Oh, my gosh, Patty, you just said we needed to go as soon as we can, that you don't want to run into your pa. And for sure, I don't!"

"I know, Isabel, but I can't resist watching Grandmother having lunch with Ma and Aunt Aggie, using foods right out of the refrigerator."

"Patty, I can't believe you are going to chance a meeting with your father, after all he's done to you. Are you crazy? We don't know who it was we saw in the wooded area."

Myrtle ignored the exchange with her granddaughters, watching with fascination as Aggie and Annabelle scurried around the kitchen preparing lunch, Aggie, who rarely helped in the kitchen—as she expected to be waited on—had no qualms about helping this time.

Myrtle had never, in her wildest dreams, fantasized about such a place, where all the food you needed was at your fingertips. The women pulled jars and packaged meats from the refrigerator and boxes from the cabinets above their heads.

In all her life, the first step in preparing any meal had been to place firewood in the belly of the woodburner, topping it with wood scraps, and to commence building a fire hot enough for cooking. Following that, she'd had to go outdoors to the cellar house to gather the flour or cornmeal to mix the bread, cold-packed fruit or vegetables, potatoes, or fresh kills that had been preserved in the cellar house. Cooking time was always hours of various chores, no matter what she decided to prepare.

Watching the woman was the most fascinating thing Myrtle had ever experienced in her life. Plates filled with various sandwiches, fruits, and fresh vegetables, with a side of ranch dressing for dipping, were placed in the center of the kitchen table. Annabelle and Aggie preferred the coziness they had created in the kitchen—by circling the stove, oven, and the end of the small kitchen table with their rocking chairs—to the overly formal dining room.

Finally, Annabelle placed a plate, knife, fork, spoon, and napkin at each place setting. "Help ya' self!" Annabelle beamed and took her place at the table.

"My word, are ya done fixin' th' food already?" Myrtle quickly snatched a sandwich from the heaping plate and took a huge bite from it.

"Oh, this is good," she said through a mouthful of ham and cheese. "I don't think I've tasted better!" She wiped the dripping mayonnaise from her mouth with the corner of her feedsack dress. "Who'd ever dreamed that ya could fix a meal in no time a'tall?"

"Just wait till ya taste th' ice cream," Aggie said with a knowing look on her face. "Ya'll think ya've died an' gone to heaven, so ya will."

Isabel sat quietly listening to the conversation, nervous for the three of them to get out of there, thinking of how she had experienced reverse culture shock. She fully understood the feelings coursing through Myrtle's heart and mind.

"Not to change the subject," Patty said, "but we saw someone lurking in the trees as we drove toward the house. It appeared to be a man. He was in dark clothes and in the deep shadows of the trees. Who do you think it was? Ma, Aunt Aggie . . . ?"

"I don't knowed so I don't," Aggie declared, not wanting to tell Patty or the others anything that might affect her nephew.

"There's been visitors at odd hours," Annabelle said in all innocence and with no intention of saying anything that would get Jeb in trouble. "I knowed one is called Buddy Dean an' th' other one I can't remember how it goes 'cause it's a strange name. He has a strange way of talkin', too."

"Ya always have to run ya mouth, so ya do." Aggie was furious. She had heard enough talk between the men to know there was trouble brewing for her nephew. As a distraction, she quickly offered to continue showing the mansion.

"I'm too old to take in all this at one time." Myrtle, bewildered by the wondrous surroundings, had not caught the implications of Annabelle's statement only holding to her concern about her man. Myrtle had marked the sighting of a man in the wooded area down to stories in times past of witchcraft in the area. In the height of the era, there had been stories abounding of strangers lurking in the wood and dale from time to time, as she recalled.

"We'll take our time, Grandmother. I know firsthand how unsettling these differences in lifestyles can be," Patty cut in, knowing she would have to get Annabelle alone to find out more. The visitors Aggie had talked about must be the explanation for the dark figure lurking out of sight. She realized if he were on the up-and-up he would have been traveling on the road like anyone else.

"Patty, ain't ya afraid your pa'll come back while y'are here?" Annabelle asked. With a worried expression, she continuted, "I am."

CHAPTER

37

BACK AT MYRTLE'S CABIN, PATTY AND ISABEL hugged their grandmother, who was exhausted and overwhelmed by the trip to see Aggie and Annabelle. The girls assured the old woman that they would be back soon. As they drove off the mountain, the sheriff's Jeep moved slowly up. Seeing Patty's car, Mark Allen pulled off into the ditch so it could easily pass by.

Just opposite the Jeep, Patty stopped. "Hi, guys," she called out. "Are we still on for dinner"

"It's Fran's place again," Mark Allen said.

"Great!" Patty replied. She continued, "We just learned that Pa's been having visitors. Annabelle got in trouble with Aunt Aggie for letting it slip, but the information may be important to you."

"Did she say who the visitors were?" Mark Allen asked.

"She remembered one was Buddy Dean, and she said the other one was foreign. She couldn't remember how to pronounce his name."

"I think that's what we've been waiting for." Mark Allen nodded to Orval Frank.

"Thanks for the information, girls," Orval Frank said. "I mean, we'll need to talk to Johnny Michael as soon as possible.

"We'll pick you up at five," Mark Allen told the girls.

Isabel smiled. Buddy had his nose against the back window, wagging his tail for all he was worth.

"Buddy gets keyed up when he sees the two of you." Mark grinned.

"I can see that!" Isabel said. "See you soon."

With a wave of her hand, Patty put her car in drive and continued down the rutted-out road, heading for home, as the guys continued upward on their surveillance of the mountain.

"Patty, do you think the figure we saw in woods was one of those Hathornes, or someone going to see your father?"

"Any one of them!"

"Oh, my gosh! It could be a witch."

"Really, Isabel, I don't believe in witches."

"Like, what have we been talking about all this time then?"

"A sixth sense. Witchcraft is just superstition, a myth."

"That makes sense, but so many believe in witches."

"I know, and it bothers me a lot because I'm not a witch. My grandmother is not a witch, even though for years people have enjoyed calling her 'the witch that lives beside the forest.' I want to talk to Grandmother about the figure when she's calmed down from the excitement of the visit to the mansion. Really, it's like how much more can happen on the mountain? Sometimes I think I have no control of how my life is going."

"I can see that. I feel that way myself."

"Isabel, I'm anxious to hear from Tuesday and Cora, and learn how the research into the Hathorne family's history is going. Maybe there's some kind of connection."

"Oh, my gosh, Patty! Who's that?" Isabel pointed to the right. The driver of a gigantic black truck, in his endeavor to cut them off, had tromped his brakes, ramming the truck into a skid. As the vehicle came to an abrupt halt, the air filled with a thick cloud of road dust.

At the same time Isabel shouted, Patty saw him and thought her heart was going to stop, it was pounding so hard. Her father's truck had suddenly appeared from the logging trail that ran to the tunnel entrance where the militia had gathered from all over the USA two years earlier. *What's he doing hanging around here? He never had any use for the men who used the tunnel.*

Jacob McCallister swung from his truck. With his menacing look, he looked larger than life. "So finally we meet again—head to head." He grabbed the door handle and jerked it open, grabbing Patty's arm at the same time.

Isabel was sobbing in terror, feeling useless as she watched Patty go down when she was violently jerked from the car. Isabel recognized who the huge man was—how much Patty resembled him!—and knew the threat he posed.

"No . . . ," Patty shrieked as she hit the hard-packed dirt road.

CHAPTER

38

IN VIEW OF THE INFORMATION ANNABELLE had given to Patty and Isabel, McCallister had been linked to Buddy Dean Howerton and Abu-Musab, Al-Zarquwi's right-hand man, in the ongoing investigation conducted by Johnny Michael. Late on Friday afternoon Cliff Moran received word from Homeland Security that McCallister had officially been tied in with the attack on the World Trade Center on 9/11.

The story was that Buddy Dean Howerton—who had been under Homeland Security's surveillance—had been spotted working with Abu-Musab, who worked directly under Al-Zarquwi. The latter two had already been under investigation by Homeland Security and connected with 9/11; subsequently Buddy Dean Howerton's actions were considered questionable. Now, after being connected with McCallister and Al Qaeda, he also was linked to 9/11 and officially a suspect.

The report sent a red flag up for Cliff Moran, simply because in their quest for information Patty and Isabel could get in McCallister's path and spook him. Not having any love for family ties, McCallister would not buy the story that the girls were looking for long-lost relatives. Like any guilty man, he would see their nosing around as somehow in connection to his unlawful business. Cliff had no trouble believing McCallister capable of treason. After all, he had been capable of selling his own children for profit. Which crime was more contemptible?

Feeling a chill of dread, Moran called his friend Johnny Michael at Homeland Security. Johnny Michael was Mark Allen's older brother and Paul Frank and Orval Frank's nephew. Cliff had gotten to know Johnny Michael when he had come to Wheeling and joined the police academy, before going to work for Homeland Security.

"Hello?" Johnny Michael answered his cell phone on the first ring.

"Hey, Johnny Michael. Cliff here."

"Hey, Cliff. What's up?"

"I need your help," Cliff said "About the investigation into Buddy Dean Howerton and Jacob McCallister?"

"Anything I can do," Johnny Michael said. "As far as I'm concerned he's directly responsible for my cousin Paul Frank Ruble getting killed, and like you, I won't be satisfied until that bastard's behind bars for good."

"I've got to tell you, I'm more worried with Patty and her new friend, Isabel, on the mountain looking for Patty's family," Cliff moaned. "I wasn't that concerned at first, because I didn't know about McCallister's connection to Abu-Musab and Buddy Dean Howerton. That tells me he's up to something big. How much can you speed up your investigation?"

"Done," Johnny Michael said. "I talked to Tuesday the other day. Didn't she tell you?"

"Yes, but there's more. How about meeting me for coffee?"

"I'm not in town," Johnny Michael said. "Like I said, I talked to Tuesday, and what she had to say worried me. I'm on Winding Ridge scouting around the mountain. I can't ignore the bad vibes I've been getting, telling me to check on the girls. So far everything's okay. I'm ready to head back to town. I should be there in a few hours. Name the place, and I'll call you when I get there."

"How about my house?"

"Good enough. See you soon."

CHAPTER 39

RANDY MCCOY AND JIM JONES, WHO WAS commonly called JJ, were covering the area between the mansion and Winding Ridge, on the lookout for Buddy Dean Howerton and Abu-Musab. They had enough information on Howerton to take him in for questioning. Currently they were on Route Seven heading toward the road that wound its way up to the little town. So far they had not been able to spot Howerton or Abu-Musab, but were confident that Howerton would, in time, lead them to him. They also believed that Abu-Musab would eventually show up at McAllister's mansion.

"What're you going to do if you run into Patty?" JJ asked.

"Nothing. I've heard that she's interested in Paul Frank's cousin, Orval Frank."

"That's good. I know Mary Lou was worried about hurting Patty's feelings."

"No sweat," Randy said. "I'd like to see her, though. You know we've been good friends since we met. I think I knew all along that she didn't feel the same way about me as she did about Paul Frank.

"Look! Who's that? I haven't seen that truck since we've been surveying the area," Randy remarked.

"No idea," JJ responded. "We don't have a description of the vehicle those guys drive. The man in the truck was too much in shadow to be recognizable."

"I'm going to follow," Randy said, looking for a place to turn. "We've nothing better to do."

"It could be Howerton, Abu, or maybe it's McCallister himself. Moran said he moved the women and their belongings to the mansion. Sure don't look like a local!"

"How far's the mansion from here?"

"About twenty minutes, half hour. Depends on how fast you drive," Randy said.

"The guy could be there by now if that's where he's heading. Anyway, it's been fifteen minutes since we started looking for a place to turn."

"Damn!" Randy said. "I don't want to lose him."

Johnny Michael drove around the next sharp curve just in time to see McCallister dragging Patty by the arm from her car. He skidded to a stop, but not before ramming McCallister's prized truck, and jumped from his own, his gun aimed at McCallister's head.

The girl in the car screamed, having no idea who or what this new threat was.

Thwarted by Johnny Michael's untimely appearance, McCallister scampered back to his truck. The motor was still idling. He spun the wheels as he headed down the mountain, in a cloud of dust of his own making, and he sped toward the mansion.

Having fallen to the dirt where her father had thrown her on the side of the road, Patty grabbed and held onto Johnny Michael's extended hand as he helped her to her feet. "I'm going after him," Johnny Michael said. "Where are you going to be later?"

"You're Mark Allen's brother, aren't you?"

"None other," Johnny Michael grinned.

"We're to meet the deputies at Fran's place for dinner."

"Okay, I'll catch you there later." Johnny Michael crossed to his truck and wasted no time going after McCallister.

The five young people sat in a booth in the back of Fran's restaurant finishing their dinner. So far, the girls had brought Johnny Michael, Mark Allen, and Orval Frank up to date on the attack by Patty's father and the research Tuesday and Cora had done on the Hathorne family.

"Patty's attacked by her father right on the heels of the sheriff's conversation with Moran," Mark Allen said, "Willis was really on the ball when he asked Orval Frank and me to keep an extra close eye on the two of you. Now there is no doubt that McCallister's a major threat to the two of you."

"Really?" Patty said. "What an understatement."

"Yeah," Mark Allen said. "We knew your pa has been seen on the mountain, even before today, and my brother here can attest that he's being investigated by Homeland Security regarding the 9/11 attack on the World Trade Center."

"His connection to Al Qaeda has been confirmed," Johnny Michael said. "Annabelle's information on Howerton and Abu-Musab has been of great value."

"Oh, my gosh! Patty, this is getting worse and worse by the day."

"Don't be so dramatic, Isabel. Really, we got through his attempt to grab us."

"Us?" Isabel grimaced. "I think he's after you."

"Wait until I tell him that you're my sister—his daughter," Patty said, trying to lighten the mood.

"This is serious. I mean, he'll still be after you," Orval Frank said. "He's not going to let his run-in with Johnny Michael stop him. It only confirms that the last thing he wants is for the two of you to be nosing around in his business."

"That's right," Mark Allen chimed in. "I'd bet you that in his eyes each time he's gotten in trouble, Patty, you've been right in the middle."

Patty sat with tears welling in her eyes. *Pa can threaten all he wants; I won't allow him to scare me away!*

Johnny Michael motioned for the waitress and paid the bill. "Cliff and Tuesday are waiting to meet with me back in Wheeling, and I need to get going to get there at a decent hour. You guys take care of the girls and keep me posted."

"What's wrong, Patty?" Isabel asked after Johnny Michael left.

Patty put her head in her hands and moaned. "I'm spooked! Was my father so determined to take me under his thumb once again—or is he determined to get rid of me like all his other children? And, I'm thinking about what happened to Paul Frank because of me and my problems with Pa." She looked up, stricken. "I can't get the three of you, and Johnny Michael, involved in my problems."

"Like it's not our problem too?" Isabel asked. She patted Patty's hands, which were clasped on the table, surprisingly close to Orval Frank's. "Even if I sometimes complain, I have something in this! Besides, I want to find out who I am, who my parents are. We've gone too far to stop."

"Okay," Mark Allen said. "We're all in agreement. We're all in this together, as long as Orval Frank and I can keep an eye on the two of you. Like my brother witnessed, your father is not done with you. Until we put a stop to it, you never will be safe."

Everyone nodded solemnly.

"Okay," Patty said. "My pa is not hindering me in my search. I want to go to the mansion again and search the place from top to bottom. All we got from sneaking into Pa's room was DNA for the paternity test."

"That's too risky," Orval Frank said. "We know he's on the mountain and must have gone back to the mansion after his attack on you."

"I'd say not," Mark Allen said. "He's not going to take a chance on being cornered there."

"My bet is he's gone back to Wheeling to lay low for now," Orval Frank guessed.

"McCallister's not dumb by a long shot," Mark Allen said. "He's gone to wherever he goes when the going gets tough. Look, over the years, how he just slips out of sight for years at a stretch."

"It'll be all right. He's not going to buck us if he can help it."

"Okay," Patty said. "Let's go. My goal is to learn more about this witchcraft stuff and about my and Isabel's family." Patty took Isabel's hand in hers. "Pa would never think we'd have any interest in the mansion."

"He'd never even consider that the two of you would be investigating the witchcraft of the past or that the mansion is connected with it, for that matter," Orval Frank said.

"We probably have to go into the basement or attic to find anything the Hathornes may have left there those years ago."

"Oh, my gosh!" Isabel said. "We have to find out—for sure—where Patty's father is before we go there again."

"You're damn straight," Mark Allen said. "We can't take a chance on a second confrontation between the two of you and McCallister."

"How are you going to find him?" Patty asked. "Like you guys said, he has the ability to hide for as long as he needs to."

"We'll track him from where he attacked you," Mark Allen said, determined. "If you remember, Cliff Moran found him and put his ass in prison a few years back."

"He knows the sheriff's Jeep and will spot you," Patty reminded him.

"I have a four-wheel-drive Honda," Orval Frank said. "I'm sure McCallister wouldn't recognize it."

"Okay, let's get on it," Mark Allen said. "There's no time like the present. We need to start at the place you ran across his path, ending at the mansion."

"And, I mean, that's only a start."

"We're going with you." Patty stood up.

"It's too dangerous," Orval Frank said.

"It'll be all right," Mark Allen said. "We said we'd keep an eye on the girls, and we can't do that if we leave them behind. They go with us."

"Okay," Orval Frank said. "I can see your point. Let's go and get my car."

On the way to the house Patty and Isabel were more than a little scared, but were determined to see this through to the end. Patty prayed that her father had not returned to his mansion. She was—to this day—embarrassed by what he did to her when she was just a child, but was too proud to show it or talk about it. Now, after his most recent attack on her, she had a new understanding of the cruelty he would and could inflict on not only his own children—herself included—but anyone who got in his way.

It did not take much time to get Orval Frank's car and make the drive to the place where they had crossed paths with Patty's father and on to the mansion. As the foursome neared the property, the first thing they noticed was that McCallister's truck was not there.

"Thank heavens," Isabel breathed. "I don't ever want to meet face to face with your father, Patty, not ever again. So, oh my gosh, what am I hanging around here for?"

If she only knew how much I was so not ready either, Patty thought. Then, aloud, she asked, "Are we going to let Annabelle and Aunt Aggie know what we're up to?"

"Not right away," Orval Frank said. "We'll play it by ear, and don't mention the confrontation with your father either!"

They banged on the door, using the brilliant brass knocker, and could hear it echo a thudding reverberation inside. Soon, Annabelle, with Aggie peering over her shoulder, opened the door.

"Patty, what on earth are ya doin' here bringin' them deputies with ya again?"

"I know you don't like the law coming around, Ma, but we didn't cause you any trouble being here before, and we aren't going to now."

"Hah, ya don't knowed what y'are talkin' about. Take them boys and get outta here before Jeb comes back, an' thinks I'm runnin' my mouth too much again like when th' detectives took me to Wheelin'. Anyway, he ain't breakin' th' law an' I don't want trouble brewin'."

Annabelle was fearful because she knew she shouldn't have mentioned the name of Jeb's visitor and described the other one to the deputies, the first time they came around, but she always had trouble keeping things to herself. Ever since that day, she'd been edgy about it all.

"Ma, you wouldn't know one way or the other about what Pa's doing," Patty said, matter-of-factly.

"Let 'em in, ya old woman, an' see what they're wantin'. Ya knowed better than to let yar kinfolk stand outdoors waitin' to get in, so ya do. If'n ya'd keep your mouth shut like I do, ya'd not have anythin' to worry about, so ya wouldn't."

"Ma, we need to know where Pa is and how often he comes and goes." Patty insisted.

"Ya knowed perfectly well your pa never tells us what he's up to or where he's goin'," Annabelle huffed.

"I know, Ma, but you must know something. You have to notice his routine."

"Don't knowed it."

"Aunt Aggie?"

"He tells me stuff, so he does, but I don't knowed where he's gone to now."

"We're going to look around," Orval Frank said. "And we don't want to do that if you expect him back soon. Will you warn us if you hear or see him returning?"

"I suppose I can," Annabelle replied. "I just don't want no trouble, an' if he'd catch ya all here, there'd be hell to pay for all of us."

"Aggie?" Orval Frank looked at the older woman.

"Are ya just helpin' Isabel here to find who she is? 'Cause if it's trouble for Jeb, I ain't havin' nothin' to do with it, so I ain't."

Since finding information to help Isabel and Patty verify that they were actually sisters was part of the plan, the group nodded in unison. "Yeah, that's it," Orval Frank confirmed.

"I can see anyone comin' or goin' from my window, so I can. I'll sit in my room an' watch, if'n one of ya come in an' let me knowed what's goin' on. If ya don't, I might feel like stoppin' before ya all are done lookin'."

"It's a deal." Mark Allen shook Aggie's hand, getting a rare, snuff-filled, snaggle-toothed smile out of her.

Aggie headed for her room, and Annabelle followed the group as they headed for the basement. “I’m plagued,” she mumbled. “He ain’t goin’ to like this if’n he finds out.”

“Then don’t tell him,” Patty said.

“I’ve not gone ’round th’ bend in my head just yet,” Annabelle said, aggravated. “I’d never vex Jeb that-a-way. It’s enough he gets cross when I stand up for myself.”

With Mark Allen in the lead, they started down the narrow stairs that led to the depths of the dark basement.

Annabelle who was bringing up the rear, moved to the side where she could steady herself by holding to the banister. The bright light from the kitchen filtered past her into the basement. In the feeble light, the group got an impression of how deep the basement lay below ground.

The door closed behind them with a final click, shutting off the bright light from the kitchen, leaving them in total darkness.

CHAPTER 40

IT WAS COMPLETELY DARK, AND FOR A SECOND the five of them were speechless. Then Patty gasped, breaking the silence. She reached out and grabbed Orval Frank's arm.

"I don't like this," Isabel murmured, gripping Mark Allen's hand. He was keeping his cool by deliberate self-control, which he had been trained to do by his years in law enforcement.

"It'll be okay," Mark Allen said. "There's only a basement at the foot of these steps."

"But, Ma, who closed the door?" Patty was fighting panic.

"I did," Annabelle declared a little too loudly for someone not wanting to be discovered on the stairs. "Ya don't want no one to follow us, do ya? That scare should be a lesson! Your pa could come back anytime, so ya'd better be quick."

"I thought he *had* come back," Patty said, relieved it was only her ma who had closed the door. *If Johnny Michael hadn't happened upon us, what would Pa have done?*

"It'll be all right," Mark Allen comforted Patty.

Orval Frank laughed in relief to know they were not being locked in the darkness behind the kitchen door. "It's as dark as it gets, Patty. There're no windows in this basement."

In her smug, all-knowing manner, Annabelle turned the switch that lit the stair steps. "I was feelin' 'round for th' switch, I didn't knowed ya'd panic."

With their way lighted, the group continued cautiously. When they reached the bottom and gathered around the foot of the stairs, Annabelle pulled a string and a second light glimmered dimly. She pointed out the trunks and told them about the items she had found in them.

"That's proof that there really was witchcraft and the Hathorne family was involved," Isabel said.

"Really! Involved?' Patty turned toward Isabel. "They were not really witches, but some were responsible for fueling the witchcraft stories going on in this area. I think a few of them—like grandmother—had developed their sixth sense, and others were practicing witchcraft, and it was used against all of them."

"Oh, my gosh! You know what I mean. Like, this just proves it."

"Proves what?" Orval Frank asked.

"Witchcraft," Isabel said.

"Isabel," Patty said. "I don't believe that there is such a thing as witchcraft where people can put a hex on someone or whatever. According to the Bible, we're not to deal in the practice of sorcery or astrology."

"My mother would agree with you," Mark Allen said.

"Can we take some of these boxes and trunks upstairs and take a good look in them?" Orval Frank asked Annabelle.

"No! My word, if Jeb comes home an' finds I've allowed ya all in th' basement an' lookin' through everythin', he'd lock me down here for my remainin' lifetime."

"She's right," Patty said. "Maybe we can take whatever we can carry and hide it in the trunk of the car. Then we can take our time looking at the contents in our room at the boardinghouse."

"Aggie's watching to make sure the coast is clear," Mark Allen said. "It'll be all right."

"'Spose ya can do it, then," Annabelle said. "I can't imagine Jeb wantin' anythin' what's in them. Just don't want him to drive up an' catch ya loadin' th' stuff. Or even ya all bein' here, for that matter."

"We'll take our chances," Mark Allen said, picking up a trunk and hefting it up onto his shoulder. "And there's no way the law is going to step aside and allow McCallister to lock you in this dungeon."

The four started up the stairs, each of them carrying a box or trunk that they could handle.

At the same time, Aggie had her TV on as she kept watch on the front of the mansion, where anyone would have to pass to get to the house. The TV newswoman said something that caught her attention: *terrorist*.

This just in, new information on the bombing in the UK first reported to you by CNN this morning. A spokesman for Al Qaeda, Al-Zarquwi, says his group of terrorists are responsible for that attack. He wants the men and women of his nation who are being held as prisoners for war crimes to be released by the end of this week. Otherwise, he will attack again, and this time in an even more heavily populated district. We've also learned that the attack resulted in three of his top men being killed in the bombing. Keep tuned to CNN for new information as we get it. The security code level in the United States has been raised to code red . . . . .

Just as the report ended, Aggie heard the others in the kitchen. She knew she that should not leave her post, that it could be a risk they could not afford, but she hurried to the kitchen to tell the others about the report anyway.

"Aunt Aggie, you need to keep watch! We can talk about that later. It's getting late and I'm afraid Pa will return anytime."

Too late, they heard the front door slam.

At the same time Aggie did, Tuesday and Cliff heard the latest bombing news as they were discussing McCallister and his attempt to abduct Patty, with Johnny Michael. He assured them she was fine and in the protection of the two deputies.

"That news report doesn't sound good!" Johnny Michael said.

"No, it doesn't," Cliff said. "Sounds like Al Qaeda is stepping up its terrorist activities.

"I've recently learned that Abu-Musab works for Al-Zarquwi, and that Abu-Musab is not Al-Zarquwi's closest confidant and right arm, meaning the man is an expendable plant. I've learned just recently that Abu was McCallister's connection to Al Qaeda. That's why I made the trip to the mountain."

"Can you find out if McCallister was in on the bombing?" Cliff asked.

"I'm on it."

"Whatever McCallister was up to will most likely be slowed down with this latest," Cliff said.

"I'd say it's connected," Johnny Michael said.

"You may be right. Anyway, Tuesday and I are going to the mountain first thing tomorrow. We'll make it look like a surprise visit to Annabelle and Aggie, like we promised the girls we'd do. Mary Lou can take care of Winter Ann, with Cora looking in on them."

"I still don't know what you hope to accomplish, going there," Johnny Michael wondered.

"I have to make sure Patty and Isabel are safe," Cliff said.

"Not only that, you know Cora and Tuesday are doing research on Patty's ancestors and on the witchcraft that seems to be connected to them. The information they have come up with concerns me. Because of the ability Patty has to dream things that come true, it bears looking into."

"Before I came back from there, I talked to Mark Allen, and he and Orval Frank are helping the girls find out what they can. The idea behind extending their help like I said, is of course to make sure they don't run into any unexpected trouble. They're as safe with them as they would be under the protection of anyone I can think of."

"Knowing Jacob is still bent on getting at Patty scares the life out of me," Tuesday said.

To lighten the mood, Cliff asked, "Did you know that Patty fainted when she met Orval Frank, because he looks just like Paul Frank?"

Johnny Michael laughed at the thought of Orval Frank causing a female to faint. "No, I didn't hear that, but I know that the two look uncannily alike for cousins. It never occurred to me that she'd mistake him for Paul Frank."

"The girls are getting close to the two deputies," Tuesday said.

"It was obvious even to me," Johnny Michael said.

Tuesday smiled, knowing it was good for Patty to meet someone who would help her get over Paul Frank's death.

"Never thought I'd admit it about my brother," Johnny grinned, "but he and my uncle are as good as any two men you can find to watch out for the girls. Especially in today's world of extremes."

"That's good to hear," Tuesday smiled. "And it solves the problem of Patty getting hurt when she learns that Randy McCoy is seeing Mary Lou."

"I asked McCoy to tell Patty," Johnny Michael said. "You know, just in case it's a problem."

At the slam of the door, Patty and Isabel—weak-kneed with fear—clung to the handrail, while the two men quickly moved into the corridor and saw that it was Joe who had slammed the door.

"Hi, Joe!" Mark Allen said in greeting. "What're you doing here?"

Joe looked around like he was checking to see if he had walked into the wrong house. "This is my Pa's house. What're *you* doing here?"

"Joe!" Patty ran to her brother and flung her arms around his neck. "How are you doing? You sound like a city slicker."

He raised his eyebrows as he held her shoulders, pushing her back so he could see her. "Your face! I never thought it'd look so great, Patty. You were pretty anyway, but now you're beautiful."

"Joe, don't exaggerate. I'll never be beautiful, but thanks to lots of pain and surgery, I'm not a freak to laugh at and tease anymore."

Mark Allen and Orval Frank looked at each other, at a loss as to the dialogue between Joe and Patty. "We'll ask later," Mark Allen said as he crossed his arms, leaned into the wall, crossed one foot over the other, and continued listening to the conversation.

"Who's this with you?" Joe pointed to Isabel. "She looks enough like you to be your sister."

"She probably is, Joe. Yours, too."

"I wouldn't be surprised, and I'd love to spend more time catching up with your life now, Patty, but you guys better get out of here. Pa's on his way home." Joe nodded to the deputies. "I don't want any trouble. Pa hasn't done anything against the law."

Knowing of the loyalty Joe had toward his father, and not ready to tell about his father's attack on the girls, Mark Allen and Orval Frank nodded their agreement.

"We're helping Patty and Isabel investigate Patty's family and how—and if—Isabel is related," Orval Frank said in explanation of their being there.

"We're not here about your father," Mark Allen said. He pushed himself away from the wall and stood up straight, an inch taller than Joe.

"Don't get interested," Joe ordered, showing he was not intimidated by Mark Allen. Confident that Patty would not be involved in anything to do with their father, he believed they were being truthful about her search for family members. He'd heard from his Aunt Aggie about what Patty was trying to do, as well.

"We'll just get these things to the car," Patty said. "Okay?"

"For you, anything" Joe answered. "Just don't tell Pa I seen you all here. Go now, and be quick about it."

"We'll see you again." Patty started for the door. "Come on, you guys."

"I told you all you'd better hurry. Pa's on his way." Joe was getting nervous about their being caught in the mansion. He had no doubt his pa would hold him accountable. "I can't be responsible for what he'll do if he sees you taking stuff from his house."

"Here, before ya go." Annabelle handed Patty one of the bags she had hidden in her room. She wanted Patty to see the locket.

"Thanks! We'll see you soon." Patty hugged the woman she had always known as a mother and followed the others out.

Annabelle called after them, "Now don't ya forget, tell Sara I'm wantin' to see her. I'm wantin' to knowed all ya can tell me 'bout her an' Kelly Sue. Maybe ya can take me to see 'em, 'cause maybe it'd be too dangerous to take a chance on ya bringin' her here, an' her father seein' her an' tryin' to make her stay."

Patty called back, "We've seen Sara, Ma, and she and Kelly Sue are happy and look very well. Jess is a good husband for her. You don't have to worry about them. Sara and Kelly Sue are well taken care of and are happy. I'll see what I can do about your seeing them."

Half an hour behind Joe, Jacob McCallister *was* on Route Seven, heading home. Knowing that he could not be seen since the failed attempt to get Patty, he paid close attention to the occupants of each and every car coming the other way. Passing the slow ones going in the same direction he was, he was startled to get a glimpse of Cliff Moran and Tuesday in one of the cars he went around.

"What the . . . . . ?"

CHAPTER

"CLIFF, DID YOU SEE WHO JUST PASSED us?"

"I did. It was McCallister, going over the speed limit too."

"That's the least of his disregard of the law!" She threw a punch at Cliff's shoulder.

"You can say that again." Cliff increased his speed to keep McCallister in sight, just to see if he was heading for Winding Ridge or to the mansion.

"Should we follow him?"

"No, unless he's going the same place we're heading. He doesn't know what we're doing here. I'm sure he saw us too. I don't want a confrontation without help, and for sure, I don't want to you put in jeopardy, Tuesday."

"I want to be involved.,Anyway, he knows we're coming for him because of his attack on the girls. You don't think he'll go after them again to use for hostages to keep us away?"

"Don't worry! Patty and Isabel have a lot of protection. Anyway, we can't have him arrested on the basis of him pulling his own daughter from her car. He can't be thrown into prison for that. It would become a useless mess of court battles over parental abuse."

"You're right. We need to find out what he's up to. I'm betting that it will be enough to put him away forever; a day marking our freedom from his constant threat to our family."

At the intersection, McCallister kept going toward Weston, and Cliff turned left and drove up the winding road. When they reached the cobblestone road, the little coal mining settlement was revealed on each side of the street that ran the length of the town. "What a lost-in-time little world," Tuesday observed, not for the first time in her life.

"It sure hasn't' changed, has it?" Cliff agreed. "It is truly a world all of its own."

"A time warp! That's it, and I think Patty is caught in it, Cliff."

Tuesday seemed about to say more on the subject, but suddenly said instead, "Look! In front of The Company Store, there's Sara and—I'd guess that's her daughter—Kelly Sue."

They pulled over to where Sara and Kelly Sue were standing.

"Hi, Sara!" Tuesday stepped from the car. "I'm surprised to see you in town, especially looking so good."

"Thanks, Tuesday. I guess you're the last person I thought I'd see again in my lifetime. You too, Cliff!"

Tuesday looked at Cliff, showing her surprise. Sara not only looked great, she sounded a little more educated. Turning back to Sara, she said, "We didn't really expect to see you here either!"

"I live in town now." Sara smiled and showed Tuesday and Cliff her wedding ring. "I'm married to Jess Willis."

"Oh, we knew that. Jess told Cliff. It's just that seeing you looking so happy and so well-groomed, away from that horrible cabin, is still a surprise."

"Seeing is believing." Cliff winked.

"Jess hired a tutor for me, and I'm studying with her two nights a week while he looks after Kelly Sue," Sara said, looking pleased with her new life. "And as you can see, Jess taught me to drive. I have use of the car since the sheriff's department has two vehicles now."

"You can't know how happy I am for you!"

Tuesday acted on her impulse to hug Sara. They had not gotten to know each other as she and Patty had, but Tuesday had been witness to Sara's miserable plight living on the mountain with a father who cared little about her and used her, instead, for his financial gain.

Jess had seen the group from the window at his desk. After giving Tuesday and Cliff time with Sara, he hurried out to greet them. "You should've called and told me you were coming and we'd've had you over for dinner tonight."

"Sara here has her hands full taking care of a child and going to school," Cliff said. "But thanks for thinking of us. Anyway, we're anxious to find Patty and Isabel and learn how they're doing."

"As far as I know, they're doin' okay, givin' that McCallister has shown he's not done with his fixation on you, Winter Ann, and Patty ," Jess answered.

"Jess, McCallister passed us, going the same way, as we were back a ways on Route Seven, and I know he saw us," Tuesday said.

"My deputies have seen him coming and going for a while now. He's living in the same mansion that he apparently bought to take you and Winter Ann to before he got sent up. The boys told me he's got Aggie and Annabelle there too."

Jess saw Orval Frank's car moving toward them.

"There they are now," Jess waved in the direction of the car.

"Oh, the girls are with him." Tuesday wrapped her arm around Cliff's waist and squeezed. "They must have crossed paths with Jacob," she said worriedly.

The car stopped at the curb and the four got out almost simultaneously, two from each side of the car.

"Dad! Mother!" Patty ran to her parents. "Is something wrong?" she asked after she hugged both of them. As Patty stood with her parents, Orval Frank, Mark Allen, and Isabel hung back, giving them time together.

"Oh, no," Tuesday said. "We wanted to come and share Cora's and my research with you. We're sure it could help now."

"Really, the two of you being here wouldn't have a thing to do with the confrontation Isabel and I had with Pa now would it?"

"I do have to admit that Cliff was a bit worried after talking to Johnny Michael," Tuesday admitted. She withheld from Patty that the bones found in Aggie's cellar house matched McCallister's DNA, linking him and his aunt to the likely murder of his parents, since no one had ever known what had become of them.

In spite of her concern about Patty and Isabel's safety, Tuesday noticed that the four young people paired up after they climbed from the car. She was convinced, more than ever, that there was romance in the air. It was pretty clear that being concerned about Mary Lou and Randy McCoy spending time together was pointless.

Randy and Patty had met during the investigation into her father's crimes, and Paul Frank's murder threw the two of them together a great deal. To Tuesday's relief, seeing Patty's happy smile and quick glances at Orval Frank, it came home to her that the attraction between Randy and Patty had been a simple friendship that had spun out of the investigation. They had each tried to sort out the ramifications of the murder of someone as close to them as Paul Frank had been, and obviously that had been the only bond for them.

Although they had been told of the likeness, Tuesday and Cliff were so startled when they noticed the man who was the embodiment of Paul Frank Ruble that they were unable to completely focus on Patty.

Looking over Patty's head, Tuesday stared at Orval Frank, and she and Cliff now understood why Patty had fainted at the mere sight of him.

Patty realized that her parents were having an experience similar to hers as they saw Orval Frank for the first time. Patty motioned to the others to come closer, "Orval Frank, Mark Allen, these are my parents, Tuesday and Cliff Moran, and my sister Sara."

"Yeah, we know Sara," Orval Frank said. "Nice to meet you!" He reached out his hand to Cliff and Tuesday, and Mark Allen followed suit.

"We've been taking care of the girls," Mark Allen said, smiling, "mainly by keeping them out of trouble of their own making."

Isabel gave him a swipe with her fist.

"You mentioned research," Patty reminded Tuesday.

"Yes, Cora and I started with what you had done in school. As you already know, the Hathorne family settled in the area hundreds of years ago. They built the mansion, and over time, as the family grew and formed ranks against those who accused them of witchcraft, the place became sort of a hotel for the extended family. Over the years, many were burned at the stake, after being charged with witchcraft by the townspeople. It seemed that it was only the women who developed their sixth sense. In attempting to warn others of accidents, deaths, and the like, they put themselves in harm's way, when all they wanted to do was help."

"Just like me, my mother, and my grandmother," Patty said. "I realize now that there are no witches—only people who don't understand and people who want to profit by using the term witch. It's sad how many women died for nothing!"

"That's right, Patty. They—you have the same abilities, and like Annabelle and Aunt Aggie and the others, the people were afraid of them. They thought the women in the family were witches and could put spells on them. There are documented cases where, when there was a tragic happening, the family was blamed, particularly if there had been a warning from a female from the Hathorne family."

"I too was made to feel like I was abnormal or peculiar."

"That's not a good way to feel growing up, but at least you, your mother, and grandmother were not threatened by death or harmed. In our reading, we learned that people are increasingly more accepting of the people who exhibit those capabilities. There have been many studies conducted—and some are going on now—to get an understanding of why some have it and others don't."

"I know," Mark Allen said. "But many people think it's a lot of bull. My mother had dreams of things that happened. Like when her brother was killed in the coal mines. Two weeks before it happened, while Johnny Michael and I were riding our horses, she was napping, and half asleep on the couch she had a dream—she said it was like an entity came to her. Inside her mind, she saw a dark figure point down. She followed the direction of the dark finger and saw two men. The figure put the words death and brother in her head. It scared her. She thought something was going to happen to me and my brother, Johnny Michael, but it turned out to be her brother, Harry. He was killed two weeks later in a coal mine. He must have been one of the two men she saw as the entity spoke to her and pointed to a dark place. He was on a roof-bolting machine, pretty safe for the operator, seeing as the bolting machine had a covering to protect the miner's head. When his boss came around to instruct Harry, who was a new miner, of a better method for roof bolting, Harry climbed off the machine. The boss got on and began working the controls, and the roof fell, killing Uncle Harry."

"Wow!" Patty said, "I can see that she had no way to make a distinction. She must've thought of you and Johnny Michael because you are brothers. Not her brother."

"That's what happened. There were many other dreams, but where we lived it was different. People just thought it was interesting, not like in this town that seems stuck in time."

"I think the main thing," Patty said, "is that Salem is a gathering pool for people who are of a kind. It's common for like beings to want to be with those who are like themselves. Misguided, they believed they were witches, and therefore, so did the town."

"That's right," Tuesday said. "In the news articles we clipped, Salem was originally called Little Salem because the people migrated there from Salem of old. By building the mansion well outside the town proper, higher on the mountain, they could track who came around. The settlers who had built homes and established businesses in the low-lying area, which soon became known as Little Salem, were able to provide employment for others who fit into their practice of witchcraft. But as the town grew, others settled there, and over time they did not understand the citizens who were thought to have special abilities. The old timers experienced the same fear and resentment at the hands of the new establishment that the early settlers, who had left Salem of old, had wanted to get away from."

"The first lesson I learned when I moved to Wheeling was that it's different off the mountain, because whether or not they believe it," Patty said, "people are aware that others do believe, and of the research going on. They accept it, and it's not seen like it was when the Hathornes were being persecuted."

Coming back at present matters, Patty asked, "What do you want to do first?" "Eat lunch," Tuesday said.

"Sounds good to me," Cliff said. "But we just saw McCallister and it looked like he could be heading for the mansion."

"Johnny Michael's arranged to put a tail on him," Mark Allen said. "Jim Jones and Randy McCoy are on the mountain, and tailing McCallister is now their priority."

"Let's make our plans at lunch," Orval Frank said.

"Afterwards, why don't you women go and talk to Myrtle?" Mark Allen suggested. "If she has a mind to, she could add a great deal to what you found out. Orval Frank and I will put the crates in your room."

"Okay." Patty gave him her key. "Are the two of you going to meet us at Fran's place before we go to Grandmother's?"

"Yes, and maybe you can tell me what Joe meant about the change in your face." Orval Frank said as he cocked an eyebrow.

"Maybe," Patty grinned.

Joe did not like it, but his father wanted him to stay in the cabin where he had lived most of his young life, reckoning that it would not raise any suspicions on the part of Al Qaeda or the law, as it would if he moved into the mansion with his father. Besides, with his father out of the picture, Joe could get his old friends to help watch his father's back.

Joe had managed to leave the mansion before his father returned. He wanted to get settled in. Although he knew his father wanted him to stay in his own cabin, Joe chose to go to Aggie's more modern one. He had no desire to go back to the primitive life he had known growing up. Aggie's cabin was not up to the level of the house in Wheeling, but it was, by far, superior to his place of birth.

Joe did not run into another person as he made his way to the mountain cabin, and without incident he carried his supplies in and put them away. He sure was going to miss having a TV to watch, but Aggie had left her radio, and that was better than no connection at all to the outside world.

After spending an hour at the cabin, putting his things away and fixing a sandwich for lunch, Joe left Aggie's cabin to make a check around the town. He also wanted to drive to the mansion and report to his father and learn if there were any unusual activities he may have to deal with.

"Let's go!" Cliff took Tuesday's arm and led the way to Fran's Place.

After Mark Allen and Orval Frank had carried the crates to the girls' room at the boardinghouse, they headed to Fran's place, where everyone had settled around the table beside the large picture window. There was a great view of the road that snaked up the mountain. Mark Allen noticed a truck slowly making its way down the mountain toward the cobblestone road that began at the foot of the mountain and leveled out toward the heart of Winding Ridge. The road continued through the town for a mile and led to a cliff that made a shear drop off to Route Seven. Route Seven wound its way to Weston and Salem to the north and I-79 to the south. As the truck drew nearer, Mark Allen realized that it was Joe at the wheel.

"That's Joe McCallister. Something's going down! First we see his father taking the women to the mansion, and later Joe shows up at the mansion in Salem. Now he's coming off the mountain. I bet he's coming from the tunnel. What do you make of that?"

"Since Jacob McCallister's connected to Al Qaeda in some way, Joe's right in it with him is my guess."

"I can't imagine what McCallister's connection could be. He was against the militia, and to me it's the same thing." Jess said. "But we need to find out, and pronto."

"We'll get to that later," Cliff said. "Right now, I want to fill you in. According to Johnny Michael, McCallister has been seen with Buddy Dean Howerton, and Howerton is connected to Al-Zarquwi. Homeland Security is looking into it."

"Have any of you seen anyone suspicious around the town?" Patty asked. "I remember Melba said that there was unusual activity at the boardinghouse, and that reminds me of the militia days."

"There has been," Jess said, "and we've been taking notice of the comings and goings. I can't get Melba to require more information from her guests. She says:, 'It ain't none of my business, an' it ain't none of your'n.'"

"I've gotten that answer from her myself," Cliff laughed.

"My gut says if there are people coming and going and they are not showing their faces around town, they may be using the tunnel for their activities," Orval Frank said. "They have to eat, and they would be seen in the restaurant and The Company Store."

"I haven't seen no one unusual in the store," Sara said.

"Don't you remember?" Cliff said. "The militia had stocked enough food and supplies to keep them fed and clothed, to be self-sufficient enough to live in the tunnel for years, maybe."

"You're right," Orval Frank replied. "The thing that compelled the militia to choose the tunnel for their operations was the fact that they could travel underground, exiting and entering at the town of their choice, north or south of here for countless miles."

"Has anyone stood watch at the entrance to the tunnel or checked it out?" Cliff asked.

"No, we haven't had a reason to watch the place," Orval Frank said.

"Let's do it," Mark Allen said. "If there's something going on, it won't take long to find out."

"Okay," Jess said. "A twenty-four hour watch. I'll make a schedule."

"With JJ and Randy there are enough of us to put two men on at a time," Mark Allen offered."

"Of course, it goes without saying that we need to keep this among the eight of us," Jess worried.

The schedule was arranged, and Mark Allen and Cliff were on first watch, with Orval Frank and Jess next. They finished their meal, and Cliff and Mark Allen headed for the tunnel in Orval Frank's car so they would not stand out as much. Orval Frank, Jess, and Sara accompanied the women to the boardinghouse, where Tuesday registered for a room for herself and Cliff. Orval Frank and Jess headed for home then to get a few hours sleep before they were to relieve Cliff and Mark Allen from their watch.

Because it was so well camouflaged, Cliff would not have remembered the way to the tunnel's entrance without the help of someone who knew it. He commented on the fact that it seemed to be even more disguised than he remembered, and Mark Allen agreed. Still he was able, even in the dark, to find the entrance to the manmade cavern left by the militia. He backtracked enough to park the car out of sight of anyone heading for the cavern.

At the entrance, and to their surprise, the door was not locked. The lock hung open, useless for keeping intruders out.

"Let's have a look," Cliff said. "We'll leave the door open so we can see head-lights—if anyone comes around."

After they stepped inside, they left the door ajar and turned on their head-lamps, revealing a fully operational headquarters.

"Look around, Cliff," Mark Allen said. "I remember there was an opening into the main tunnel right about here." He walked to the place where Al-Zarquwi's men had sealed off the opening that was a means of access to the length of the tunnel.

"Maybe someone wanted to keep the gangs or occasional adventurer from coming to and from this part of the tunnel, but I bet there's a hidden way—for whoever is using this place—to get into the tunnel and disappear to wherever. The freedom of being able to come and go off the mountain would be the major factor in making this the ideal, number one place for their undertaking."

"Who in the world did all this work right under our noses?" Mark Allen asked in wonder. "I was here after the militia was disbanded, and I don't remember all the apparatus, computers, desks, and lab stations."

"They didn't bring all this through the tunnel," Cliff said. "It took trucks to transport all this. Let's get out of here right now and keep watch. I'm pretty sure there are those who can't afford to be seen coming from time to time via the tunnel. We don't want to be caught inside and ruin the advantage of surprise on our part."

Outside, turning off their head-lamps, the two got comfortable in a spot where each of them could see if anyone came toward the cavern from any direction. Hours later, at the agreed-upon time, a pair of headlights moved up the mountain. It was time for Jess and Orval Frank to take their watch.

After Jess parked his vehicle out of sight, he Orval Frank, Cliff, and Mark Allen walked to the entrance once again, having a little trouble this time finding it in the darkness. They talked for a while about the hi-tech equipment that had been installed inside the cavern, and it was agreed that they had to call Johnny Michael at once so he could inform the FBI, CIA, and Homeland Security.

"Jess, listen!" Orval Frank whispered urgently. There was a truck moving slowly up the mountain road.

"Let's get out of sight. Hurry!" Jess ordered.

The truck turned onto the road that had been cut, over the years, by the traffic coming and going from the tunnel to the mountain road. When it stopped at the entrance, a man jumped from each side of the cab.

"Man, I hate doing these deliveries in the middle of nowhere where it's so dark that you can't see your hand in front of your face," said the man who had been riding shotgun.

"Quit complaining and open the back. I'll open the door, and we can get unloaded in no time." The man found his way to the opening to the cavern, with the help of the truck's headlights that he had left on and shining directly on the entrance. "Habib, you know something? The lock is open. You know anything about that?"

"Nope, I don't," Habib said. "I can't say if it's always locked or not. Don't really know."

For an hour the men unloaded the truck, talking as they worked and taking a smoke break midway through.

"Habib, you know there's talk that Al-Zarquwi and two of his closest men were killed in the bombing in the UK, and the one saying he's the spokesman for Al-Zarquwi is actually responsible for the attack."

"That doesn't surprise me, since Al-Zarquwi is totally committed to making an attack here in the good old US of A."

"Does it ever bother you, Habib, that Abu and the two of us were brought here as young boys to grow up just to do this one simple job for our countrymen?"

"I guess, on some level, but I don't live near Washington like you, and my family is safe."

"Your family may be safe, but what about us, Habib? We will be killed."

"Diab, it's an honor to die for Allah. We will have many virgins in heaven."

"Sometimes I wonder . . . ."

"You can die just for saying that, and I assure you it won't be an honor. You will surely die in vain! Look at McCallister, working for Al Qaeda, taking orders from Abu. Just like us, he's helping kill his own countrymen. He's doing it for the money! There's going to be no virgins for him."

The men had finished their work and drove the truck back the way they had come. Orval Frank and Jess were stunned.

"I can't believe that McCallister's actually working with the terrorist movement," Jess said. "He was against the militia, and like I've already said, I can't see much difference."

"We have good information to suspect him, but we still need to check those men out before we conclude that McCallister is actually involved in this plot," Orval Frank said. "It's for sure he wasn't involved with the assembly of the militia, a few years ago—he was in jail."

"It's the money." Jess hooked his thumbs through his pant loops with an upward hitch. "The man has more than proved to me he'll do anythin' for money."

"There's no need to stay here now," Orval Frank said. "We need to get word to Johnny Michael to get a tail on that truck. I recorded the license, company name on the truck, and the phone number to be called if the driver is observed breaking any driving safety laws. Who would've thought they'd care about that?"

The women were in their rooms, and McCallister was getting weary of waiting for Abu-Musab. The man had always been as on time as the wake-up call of the rooster in the mornings. Everything the man asked for was crated up in the garage and set to be picked up—in return for final payment from Abu-Musab's hand to McCallister's. Having such a great amount of cash, he would be done with Abu-Musab and the Al Qaeda ties that came with the man.

Annabelle came up the hall wanting to start the evening meal. "A body can't do her chores around here, bein' sent to th' bedroom to twiddle her thumbs."

Disgusted with the wait forced on him by Abu, McCallister allowed the women back into the kitchen to do their work. "Annabelle, I get your point. You don't need to go on and on. I'm going to my room. Let me know if you need me."

"What was that about?" Annabelle asked. "Don't think I've ever heard 'im say call 'im if'n we needed 'im."

"Somethin's wrong, so it is. He's lookin' worried. Remember what we heard him talking 'bout to th' stranger that night ya caught me listenin' at th' end of th' hallway?"

"I don't want to think 'bout it," Annabelle said.

"Y'are goin' to have to, so y'are," Aggie insisted.

"Ya old nib nose, what ya thinkin' we're goin' to do? Especially when we don't even knowed, if th' truth be told, what's really goin' on."

Aggie took on a worried look. She had not thought of that.

The group met at Fran's for breakfast the next morning. Johnny Michael had notified Homeland Security, and agents had found and tailed the truck used by Habib and Diab. Each of them was followed to his home and from there taken in for questioning.

"There's nothing we can do on that now, and I don't want to lose focus on my reason for being here," Patty said.

CHAPTER 42

TUESDAY, CLIFF, PATTY, ISABEL, MARK ALLEN, and Orval Frank were in the girls' room looking through the crates they had brought from the mansion. They were filled mostly with robes and odd items, but there were pieces of parchment with a dozen names from the Hawthorn family Tuesday and Cora had all ready uncovered, but mostly with not-so-legible writing on them.

"There's nothing here—except to verify what Cora and I have already found—to aid in helping you find your family," Tuesday said. "Let's go and talk to Myrtle now."

"Wait!"

Patty rummaged about and found the bag Annabelle had given to her as they were leaving. She dumped the contents on the bed. An odd assortment of items tumbled out. A gold locket was the first item Patty was curious about. She opened it. Inside were a lock of brown hair and a photo of a young woman. Patty looked at the others in the room and held out the locket to Tuesday.

Tuesday gasped, "This girl could be either Patty or Isabel!"

On the bed was a piece of graying lace. The cut of the lace looked like the same lace in the photo. There were a broach and a black velvet ribbon with a clasp on each end. All those things were also visible in the photo of the woman.

"Look, Patty," Tuesday said. "The contents in the locket are mentioned on the parchment. I can't make sense of most of the words though."

"I want to take all this, especially the locket with the picture of the girl, to show my grandmother," Patty said.

Tuesday began putting the items back in the bag. "Maybe Myrtle will understand what all this is about."

"While you're at Myrtle's," Orval Frank said, "Mark Allen and I are going to the office and talk to Jess Willis about the delivery to the cavern."

"I'd go with you," Cliff said, "but I don't want to leave the women on their own right now."

It was getting late in the day when Buddy Dean Howerton showed up at the mansion, looking for McCallister. Jacob had seen him drive up the circular driveway and had gone to the door before the women, who were working in the kitchen, could get to the front entrance when Buddy Dean knocked.

McCallister was in a foul mood at being stood up by Abu, and he greeted Buddy Dean in anger.

"Don't growl at me," Buddy Dean said. "I came to give you news."

"Whatever could you have to interest me?"

The women had scurried from the kitchen to see what was going on, and Buddy Dean nodded toward them. McCallister took notice and sent them back to the kitchen.

"Let's go to the den," Jacob said.

Buddy Dean had not been in McCallister's den and was not surprised that it was as grand as the rest of the mansion.

"What is it, Howerton?"

"Al-Zarquwi is dead and that leaves Abu-Musab powerless."

Surprise showed on Jacob's face. "How the hell do you know anything about them, and why the hell do you think I care?" He was visibly troubled.

"That means no more briefcases full of money! You think I didn't know about the payoff? I'm not a stooge!" Buddy Dean said. "I know you were working with him. Al-Zarquwi was killed in the bombing in the UK. It's official."

"So I was right," Jacob said. "You were playing us against each other."

"Actually, no," Buddy Dean said. "I just wanted part of the pie."

McCallister sat behind his desk, indicating for Buddy Dean to be seated across from him. "Today was the day I was to get my final payoff."

"You're lucky he didn't get here," Buddy Dean said. "I think Homeland Security is on to you."

"How could they be? I haven't done anything."

"You collected at least one payment I know of," Howerton smirked. "And I want half of it."

McCallister leaned back in his chair, "Just what makes you think I'd give you anything? Anyway, you can make any amount of money you want. You told me yourself you could fool anyone with your expertly made twenties."

"I want half, McCallister. If you want me to keep my mouth shut, I want half. I know he gave you thirty thousand up front."

"No."

Buddy Dean stood. “You don’t want the trouble I could make for you. I know more than you realize. I know you killed your parents. Homeland Security has DNA from old bones found in your aunt’s cellar house, and it matches yours. Need I say more?”

“Get out!” Jacob demanded. “And you’re not welcome back. Not ever!”

Howerton walked to the door. As he opened it, he said, “You haven’t heard the end of me.”

After Howerton left, Jacob sat at his desk sorting through his options. He was fairly sure he could not be tied to Al Qaeda, but what about his parents? First, he would make plans to take back the purchases he had made on behalf of Abu-Musab. That would get him an additional grand or two. Too bad Howerton had shown his hand; taking the purchases back would have been a perfect job for him. But Jacob could have Joe do it in piecework.

McCallister pored himself a glass of scotch, swallowed it in one gulp, and threw the glass against the paneled wall, leaving the scattered glass for the women to pick up.

I will not allow myself, or my aunt, to be associated with the death of my parents.

CHAPTER

AT MYRTLE'S CABIN, SHE, TUESDAY, CLIFF, Patty, and Isabel sat around the table, looking at the items from the bag that Annabelle had given to Patty. Myrtle knew what the items stood for and explained them to the others.

They were used by those who did not have the gift of dreams but wanted to make others believe they could cast a spell on them if crossed. These people were simply imposters, claiming they were capable of doing witchcraft to settle the score when they perceived someone had done them wrong. Many people had seen these odd items when confronted with the supernatural or paranormal: lace from the victim's clothing or a broach from her jewel box, a black velvet ribbon, a feather from a crow, and most common, bat wings used in fortune telling.

"That means that there were people posing as witches living in the mansion with the Hathornes," Patty said.

"Oh, my gosh!" Isabel said.

"I would say that's the case, and I believe a few of them were like you, Patty, and others decided that all of them were witches because of the imposters who claimed fortune-telling ability," explained Cliff. "The two of you may be descendants of the original Hathornes. The photo in this locket could be of either one of you." He looked at Isabel and Patty. "It sure looks like the two of you are the offspring of that family."

"I think y'are right," Myrtle said. "I think there was too much made of witchcraft, an' most of it was those who wanted to frighten others. I don't even believe it is witchcraft. It's a gift of dreams is all. Just like my granddaughters say it is."

"I agree one hundred percent," Tuesday said. "I think all this stuff should be thrown out, except for the locket and pictures."

"Patty," Cliff said, "other than the DNA we're waiting for, one way to find out for sure if you and Isabel are sisters is to find out who your father sold Betty's first child to. I don't think you are going to find that out here on the mountain."

"How could we do it then?"

"I know where to find the lawyer and doctor that your father dealt with. It's worth a try," Cliff said. "They must have records somewhere.

"Isabel, would you be willing for me to talk to your mother? If she would tell us the people's names we could make short work of this."

Isabel had known from the moment she had stood in Annabelle's cabin that she would have to confront her parents. She did not want to face it. To hurt her parents was the last thing she wanted to do. "Oh, my gosh! I can't."

"You must, Isabel," Tuesday said. "You can't go through life not knowing for sure. Your parents will understand if you handle it properly. I would venture to guess it will be a relief for them. When people do something that they know is not on the up and up, they never feel right until it's made right. If you have the true loving relationship I believe you have, you'll all come out for the better."

"I'll do it," Isabel said. "Like, I've always known by my dreams that I had something lacking in my life."

"Grandmother," Patty said, "Isabel and I want to get you into a comfortable apartment in the city, where you'll be warm in the winter and cool in the summer. We want you to get to know the others in our family."

"I've thought 'bout it since ya showed up th' first time, an' I'm wantin' to go, but I want th' choice of comin' back if'n I'm homesick."

"Deal!" Patty and Isabel hugged their grandmother.

CHAPTER 44

"I DON'T LIKE IT, SO I DON'T. TUESDAY AND Cliff should've told Winter Ann who her father is."

"It's none of your business," Annabelle said. "They'll tell her when they want to, if they want to."

"Ain't right, so it ain't. Just look at what's happenin' now. Patty an' that girl with her's lookin' to find out who her father is. That little girl oughta knowed who she is. Everyone oughta knowed who their father is." With her forefinger, Aggie scooped her snuff into her spittoon. Then she picked up the cat that was rubbing around her legs and set it in her lap.

"One day, I'm goin' to tell the girls all about their pa an' th' troubles we had, why he'd done what he did, so I am."

"Your goin' to start trouble, Aggie. Ya don't knowed when to keep ya mouth shut."

"I'm leaving for a while," Jacob said, startling the women, who had not heard him enter the kitchen. "I think you can take care of everything without me here. Joe will come around and check on you, but you have enough food to keep you for a very long time."

"Ya runin' from th' law again, so ya are."

"Ya said ya wasn't in trouble!" Annabelle said.

"Don't get involved in my business, I told the two of you I'm going on a business trip. I expect you to believe it and that's what you tell others."

CHAPTER 45

THIS IS IT, AND LIKE I TOLD YOU, I'M NOT ALL bad. That's why I'm running, so my Aunt Aggie will not be implicated in the murder of my mother and father. I know that my DNA was matched with that of bones found in Aunt Aggie's cellar and I'm suspected of their murder. I'm not taking any chances, I'm going to drive until I find a place that feels like home. A place I've never been. I can hide from the law. I've been successful before and I will be successful now. My mistake—as always—was in coming back to my home and my aunt. I'll have to give it all up, though I guess I've always known that someday, someone would tie me to the deaths of my parents.

I'll not stay around and let them put me away again, but I will sorely miss all I've built up. Nevertheless I'm still a young, handsome man, and I can do it again.

The world opens for me as I travel to my new unknown.

EPILOG

Aggie and Annabelle were down hearted and happy at the same time. Happy that Jeb had not gotten the chance to make the huge mistake that he was heading for. Sad that he was gone and there was no way they could know when he would return—maybe he would not.

In keeping with their nosy nature, the two women discussed at length: Patty, Isabel, and Winter Ann, getting into harsh disagreements about Aggie's plan to disclose to Winter Ann who her father really was.

"How're ya goin' to get her to th' mountain? Ya have to be face to face with her to tell her anythin', ya can't go to her. She's too young to come to you," Annabelle smugly crossed her arms.

"You're a foolish old woman," Aggie spit in her spittoon. "Winter's growin' up, so she is. I can wait. I been waitin' all my life. Mark my word, she'll come, and Patty'll bring her." Aggie looked Annabelle directly in the eye. "What ya don't knowed is I got bait, so I do. I had a hunch," Aggie tapped her finger to her temple, "and went to the cellar when ya was sleepin'"

"What is it ya found? Can't be that important."

"All I'm goin' to tell ya is, what I found will be of great concern to the three half sisters. It's a piece of the puzzle that'll bring out a connection they'd never find without me, so they wouldn't."

Patty and Isabel left the mountain with much to do in preparation for college. Both girls had made arrangements to keep in touch with Orval Frank and Mark Allen. The girls were happy to learn that each of the men owned property in Wheeling and lived at Winding Ridge temporarily, as they were dedicated to putting McCallister behind bars—where he belonged.

The final novel in the series will tie the story together, answering the many questions readers may have about what happened to children McCallister sold. What happened to Daisy after she ran from Jacob and the mountain cabin; and Sara and Jess. Also, find out how Tuesday, Cliff, and Patty are freed from the evil shadow Jacob McCallister cast over their lives.

Coming in 2012

Cabin Vi – From Aggie's Rocking Chair

Novels by: CJ Henderson

The Cabin – Misery on the Mountain
Cabin II – Return to Winding Ridge
Cabin III – The Unlawful Assembly at Winding Ridge
Cabin IV – In Jacob's Shadow
Cabin V – I am Jacob

Coming soon:
Cabin VI – From Aggie's Rocking Chair

Check out CJ's website:
www.thecabinseries.com

Email: cj@windingridge.net

Made in the USA
Lexington, KY
07 February 2012